SHADOW

B.L. MOONEY AND LAURA EMORY

Cover design by Sarah Hansen from Okay Creations

Photography
Front cover: Lauren Perry of Perrywinkle Photography
Back cover: Christie Q Photography

Models
Front cover: Lyman Winn
Back cover: Asianmanbun and Madison Lee

Edited by Paige Maroney Smith

Interior Formatting by Stacey Blake of Champagne Formats

ISBN: 978-0-9907551-2-8

DEDICATION

Dedicated to friends who have each others' backs and can read each others' minds.

CHAPTER 1

Brynn

"**S**PECIAL AGENT BENNETT." I HOLD out my hand to the first FBI agent I find and regret it the moment he takes it. It may be the fact that it's my first day and meeting my new team at the crime scene is a little unsettling, but dead bodies don't wait for paperwork.

"Well, well, well. What do we have here?" He holds on a little longer than he should as he looks me over. "I'd say we hit the jackpot this time."

He's attractive, but apparently that's the only thing going for him. I look him over just as he did to me and arch my eyebrow as if I'm not impressed—which I'm not. He's got the body I'd go for, but the personality of a snake. It takes more than muscles and a pretty face to get my attention.

His dark hair, with eyes to match, is his best feature, except his eyes are a little too beautiful. They're the kind of eyes that cut right through you if you look at them too long. I'm sure there's a nice smile in there somewhere, but the smirk he's got on his face now just proves he thinks higher of himself than he should.

I take my hand back and wipe it on my slacks. Everything about him seems slimy, and I'll remember not to touch him again.

"I'm looking for Special Agent Williams." *Please, God, tell me this isn't him.*

The move to wipe his slime feeling from my hand must be new to him. He gives a curt nod in the direction of a couple of other FBI agents and walks away.

I take a deep breath and hope the rest of the team isn't as friendly as the asshole I just met. I wish I had gotten his name. I clear my throat as I approach to try to get their attention.

The first guy to turn around looks as if he's taking his job seriously, and he's actually looking at the details of the crime scene. When he smiles, it's because he seems genuinely happy to meet me and not because my tits will give him something to look at besides dead bodies all day. He hasn't looked down once.

His longer than average caramel-colored hair is wavy and inviting. I want to run my fingers through it. Too bad he's my new partner. I'd rather get to know him on a more personal level.

"Special Agent Brynn Bennett?" He holds his hand out and tips his head. His hand is warm, his smile is inviting, and he makes me feel like an important member of the team.

"Yes." I squeeze his hand to prove I'm not just a pretty

face, and he smiles brighter. "I'm looking for Special Agent Hunter Williams."

"You've found him." This may not be a bad assignment after all. "It's nice to finally meet you. I wish it were under better circumstances, though. We'll get you all settled later, but for now, do you feel like jumping in?"

"Of course." I let go of his hand, embarrassed that I held it for so long. "I've handled crime scenes before, so I'm comfortable to hit the ground running."

"Great. Let me get you up to speed. There isn't much info, so it won't take long. Emily Churchill was found by some early morning walkers. As you can see, the medical examiner is with her now."

I look at the body he points to and notice her striking long black hair. It seems the killer took the time to brush it after he carried her out here. It's too perfect for someone to just lay her down and leave.

"Preliminary information is that she's twenty-two. We're still working on employment status, but she lives with a musician. It's unclear if they're just roommates or if they're romantically involved."

He smiles and looks at me. "Lady's choice—body or witnesses?" He points to the group being held back by the local police.

There is no hesitation in my answer. "Body."

The surprised look on his face doesn't last long before it's replaced by a grin. "You're not like other girls, are you?"

"No, I'm not like other *women,*" I say, challenging his term of girls.

Instead of responding to the challenge like most men I

3

know in this field, he just smiles. "I think I'm going to like you."

The asshole from earlier comes behind him and leans in as if to whisper, but he says it loud enough for all to hear. "Be careful, Williams. This one will eat you for breakfast."

I tilt my head and know I shouldn't play the game, but this jerk just makes it too easy. "It seems you still underestimate me, and I don't even know your name."

"Special Agent Scott Porter at your service." He extends his hand again, but I don't take it this time.

I look him up and down again and take a step forward. "You may be more of a snack for me, but Williams here is more the main course. I haven't run into breakfast yet."

Seven months later

Pounding my sneakers on the pavement as the sun rises is where I find my peace. I can collect my thoughts without the monotony of reporters and deputies asking a slew of questions. Running has always been therapeutic to me. I developed a passion when I was younger. When your life revolves around surviving and fighting, you learn that speed and endurance are the first steps in Survival 101.

Stopping only to tighten the band on my long dark ponytail, I check the surrounding area out of habit—the second step in Survival 101. I've stopped short just fifty yards from my beachside condo's balcony. I've spent the past seven months waking up with this view, and it still takes my breath away.

The Pacific Ocean is a beautiful sight no matter how many times I look at it.

When you have a childhood like mine, you take the time to notice beauty. As I've learned, and the many victims I've fought to get justice for, life isn't always beautiful. Sometimes it can be full of ugliness and evil.

My father tried his best to teach me how to live and defend myself from the evils of the world. I hope I'm living up to his expectations of me, but I haven't truly been tested yet. Evil will come for me one day, just as it tried to once before, but I hid. I've been taught to fight since then. I've been taught that hiding is no longer an option. I must fight as I've been trained to do. Fight for my life. Fight to avenge.

The buzzing on my arm snaps me out of what is my daily nightmare. "Bennett! Have you finished the report on the Lynch case?" Special Agent in Charge James Matthews' bark is worse than his bite. However, I never intend to test that theory.

"Yes, last night. I plan on dropping it off when I get to the bureau."

"You won't be coming in for a while. Seems our dear, sweet Shadow has left us another victim. You and Williams need to get on it. I'm afraid the media has already caught wind, so there'll be a shitstorm of reporters there already. It's a pretty public location. Local PD has it taped off."

"Where?" I pick up the pace as I head to the shower.

"East and 33rd, a garden in the park on the north side next to the Old Mill River walking path. Trust me, you can't miss it."

"Okay, I'll get Williams to pick me up on the way. We'll

5

be twenty or twenty-five minutes, tops." I take two seconds to text my partner, Hunter Williams, before stepping into the shower.

Hunter isn't only my partner, but a good friend, as well. He knows about my past and the case I really long to solve, but he's coming over to go to the latest crime scene for the case I need to be working on.

The Shadow is a case my partner and I have been tied to since I started with this team. We've investigated several murders we believe to be connected to him, but it's still too early to be certain.

The cases were passed on to us because they lack sufficient evidence or any leads at all. Once it becomes a repetitive crime, the FBI takes over. The Shadow knows this and tends to taunt us.

Our serial killer definitely has a type. His victims are always beautiful women, in their twenties, and he virtually leaves them unscathed. The ligature marks around the neck where he strangles them and two small bruises on the back of the shoulders are all that tie these victims together.

He leaves them in plain sight—haunting and taunting us like a sick game. The women look peaceful, almost like Sleeping Beauty or Snow White, as if they're merely resting. How and where he meets them is a mystery. Family and friends know of no one new in the victims' lives, and yet the victims know him well enough to have sex with him before they're killed.

We haven't had a single lead other than the fact they all died the same way—strangled and usually right after the throes of passion. They're always missing some kind of jewelry, so we know he's keeping trophies. After he gains their trust and seduces them, he lays them to rest in his own form of poetic justice.

I hop out of the shower just as I hear my front door buzz. I grab my towel and my Glock 22 out of habit. "Come in!"

"Brynn, you really shouldn't leave your front door unlocked while you shower."

"Oh, please. I knew you'd be here any minute." I peek down the hall at my partner and friend of the last seven months. "Plus, I had my Glock 22 within reach. Make yourself at home. There's a fresh pot on the counter and fruit in the fridge. It'll just take me a second to change."

It's the same ritual every morning. I don't need to give him permission to fix himself something. He was most likely already pouring his coffee when I offered it.

"Don't forget the files on the Lynch case or SAC Matthews will be pissed."

"Yeah, yeah. I got it."

SAC Matthews has been like a father to me since my transfer. I was recruited by the FBI while I was in college at the ripe age of twenty-two. It only seemed fitting to recruit the daughter of a former agent—especially one who didn't have any family left, but still had a fight in her heart.

I spent my early training years at Quantico and the FBI Academy. In my spare time, I searched for anything that could lead me to the asshole who murdered my mother and tore my family apart. Unfortunately, everything leads me to dead ends and sealed files.

I made some waves and helped solve a few big cases, so I was transferred to Southern California and became a special agent over violent crimes in Los Angeles. I was born in Southern California, so it only seemed fitting that I found my way back.

SAC Matthews welcomed me with open arms. Hunter has been my favorite partner to work with so far. He's sweet and easygoing—one of the last true gentlemen. I can't say the same about people at the Academy. The men there only saw curves and full lips and figured I was only in the program to screw my way through it. Becoming top of the class without fucking a single one of them proved them wrong, but didn't help them become gentlemen. I feel sorry for any female who had the misfortune to end up as their partners.

My father had always taught me to use my looks toward my advantage. I resembled my mother so much, which tore at my father's heart. Every time he looked at me, he was reminded the love of his life was ripped away from him.

Shea Bennett was extremely beautiful and one of the sweetest people out there. She passed down her heart-shaped face, big green eyes, long dark hair, and full lips to me. I also had to thank genetics for my tiny but curvy stature. She was an exotic beauty. I loved sitting on the counter and watching her primp herself. She didn't need to do much, but I think she loved that time with me just as much, so she played it out a little longer than she needed.

She would always smile and say, "Brynnie, beauty is only skin deep. People will love you, not for the way you look, but for the way you treat them. First and foremost, always have a kind heart and a smile on your face."

I always smile at the memory, but it leaves me sad a little. It's been twenty years since her murder, but I've never stopped missing her.

I shake myself from my gloom and finish getting ready. There's a job that needs to be done and a partner waiting for me in the kitchen. I turn the corner and see Hunter leaning against the counter, reading today's newspaper.

My heart flutters for half a second as my breath catches. I usually have control of myself when I look at him—something I learned to take care of early in our partnership—but today as I see his broad shoulders rest against the cabinet and watch his blue eyes scan the front page, I can't help myself and allow his beauty to wash over me. I need it to prepare myself for the ugliness I'm about to discover.

He takes his hand and runs it through his caramel wavy hair as he glances up and grazes over my appearance. "Morning, pretty lady."

"It's too early to start with the flattery, don't you think?" I wink and smile. My cheeks flush when he holds his stare a little too long. I shouldn't have let myself stare at him this morning. I would be oblivious to all of this right now.

"What do you call this look? Special Agent Chic?"

I look down at slacks and buttoned blouse with a sharp blazer and accessories. I always dress like this. There's nothing wrong with being tailored and trendy, even if we are investigating dead bodies. If you look good, you feel good. And I love to feel good.

Plus, being a special agent limits the dating pool in the criminal justice area. I usually meet Mr. Narcissist, Mr. Serial Killer, Mr. Sociopath, and let's not forget, Mr. Asshole. A single lady in my line of work needs to be ready to meet Mr. Right at all times.

Hunter grips my upper arms. "I'm serious, Brynn. I need you to start locking your door. Be careful. You're a beautiful young lady who lives alone. Gun or no gun, it makes me nervous to think that you could get hurt. Especially in our line of work, we've both seen way too many dead bodies to brush this kind of thing off."

The fact he's concerned about me sets my heart fluttering for different reasons. It's good to know there are people who care and I'm not always as alone as I feel.

He squeezes my arms before letting go and heading back to his coffee. "If you're worried about me waiting outside while you get all beautiful in here, you could always give me a key."

I throw my head back and laugh. There's the punch line I was waiting for. We do care for each other, and we would each be devastated if anything happened to the other, but we aren't serious that often. Our friendship is based on fun and being goofy. We see too much seriousness in our jobs.

"No way. I may not have had big brothers growing up, but I know how your minds operate. The second you know I'm on a date, you'll just let yourself in."

"Someone has to protect you."

I ignore his comment regarding my need for protection. "Besides, maybe I leave my door unlocked while I shower because I want a little excitement in my life." I wink. Harmless flirting has always been part of my game.

He gets serious again. "Wanting to have a little excitement and having a death wish are completely different things. You need to be smart. If not for yourself, then do it for your family."

I hate where this conversation is turning. I put my hands on the counter and hang my head. "I don't have a family. My family is dead."

I can feel him stand behind me, supporting me, but not touching me. "We're your family. Do it for me. Do it for the SAC." He finally puts his arms around my waist and his chin on my shoulder. "I wouldn't be a good partner if I didn't try to help you. All these dead bodies of twenty-something, beautiful women make me too nervous."

I hug his arms to let him know I heard him, but I need to get this back to light and fun if I'm going to make it through the day.

"Okay, boss man. I'll try harder with keeping myself pro-tected." I slap his arms to get him to let go. "Let's get going. This case isn't going to solve itself." I turn with a smirk. "Now, are you driving, or am I?" He never lets me drive.

It's usually a somber feeling in the car when we're go-ing to investigate a dead body, but after the conversation this morning, it's even more so. There's a rule when you become partners with someone. If you want to stay alive, you stay out of each other's beds no matter how strong the attraction is. Hunter will always hold a piece of my heart, but I think that happens when you become willing to take a bullet for your friend.

He isn't easily shaken. His smile is infectious, and he al-ways has a good attitude, even around the yellow tape. So the conversation this morning threw me a little. I didn't know he'd be so bothered by my unlocked door. I look out the window and smile. He still isn't getting a key, though.

CHAPTER 2

Brynn

W E PULL UP TO THE Old Mill River Park and head down the jogging path. The scene is already littered with reporters and bystanders. Of course, there are no witnesses; our killer is too discreet. If anyone did see anything, it probably looked normal, and they didn't realize what they'd seen.

Hunter heads over to interview the joggers who found the body on their route this morning while I check the surrounding area for clues.

Nothing.

He's a perfectionist as always. The Shadow leaves nothing behind. He's compulsive about his setup. One day something will happen and we'll catch something about who he is, but right now, he's too clean and meticulous.

I turn to the nearest LAPD. "Has anything been tampered with or removed?"

"It's kind of hard to tell, but I don't think so. She just looks as if she settled in for a nap and never woke up. When we got here, there were no suspicious individuals lurking and nothing suspicious was reported overnight. A couple of joggers on their morning run stumbled upon the body, but they didn't go near it."

I look over at the body. "What do you know about the victim?"

"The victim has been identified as Victoria Reynolds, twenty-three, recent graduate of USC. Her parents are headed in for questioning as we speak. They last had contact with her four days ago."

"Four days? Did they report her missing?"

"Not that I'm aware of. They said she was a good girl with no known boyfriends. They don't know of any sort of conflict or altercations with anyone. She did have a roommate, but it's been reported that she went to Santa Barbara with a boyfriend for the weekend."

"Thank you, Officer. I'm going to keep looking around a little bit."

I glance at my surroundings. I close my eyes and visualize the killer's placement. How could a man carry a grown woman across a very popular park, down a path, and lay her perfectly in a garden without a single witness? She was thin, but even at 135 pounds, he would need to be fit to make it quick and quiet work.

No matter how many times I go over it in my mind, I still can't find the motive. Until we figure out the why, we'll never find the who.

There will be more victims.

Hunter and I head back to the bureau to report our findings to SAC Matthews and to turn in the damn Lynch reports. I close my eyes and exhale when our resident asshole makes an appearance.

Special Agent Scott Porter is as cocky as they come. He's full of himself and full of shit. He gets the job done, but it's a classless and choppy job that I'm surprised stands up in court sometimes. I'm happy to not have been partnered with him. He's someone I wouldn't take a bullet for. In all reality, he probably would deserve it.

He's attractive on the outside, but a complete waste of space on the inside. He's only good for two things: playing the bad cop role and being a great fuck. I can see him filling the bad cop role, but he's never filled anything else for me. If all I want is a cheap night of quick and easy orgasms, I can handle that myself.

It doesn't stop him from trying, though. He comes up really close behind me, careful not to touch, and whispers into my ear, "I think these are my favorite pants. Just look at that ass."

Hunter turns and shoves him back. "Shut the fuck up, Porter."

"Fuck you, Williams. If you're too stupid to see what you have attached to you, then I'm more than happy to step up and be the man Bennett needs." He looks at my top buttons and holds his gaze a little too long.

I tilt my head and bring my hands up to my chin. "Thanks so much for thinking of my needs," I say in a fake, sweet voice. I stand up straight. "But I think I'll pass. There's nothing you have that I want." I look at his crotch. "Well, maybe for target practice."

The daily ritual is getting old, but this is the unplanned lesson I learned in the Academy, and I can handle it. Guys like him are a dime a dozen. They're more a nuisance and a headache than anything else and aren't worth any real time, so I don't give it to him.

We head to SAC Matthews' office and walk inside since the door is already cracked open. He's pacing the room and rubbing his hands along his jawline. This doesn't look good.

He brushes past his mahogany desk to close the door, but leaves the blinds open. At least we aren't in trouble . . . yet. "Did you guys find anything? Was there any evidence this time? He will eventually mess up, and we need to be on top of our game when he does."

SAC Matthews is flustered. He must be getting heat from upstairs to track down this killer, and fast. It makes me want to do a better job, to make him proud. He's like a father figure to me now, and I hate to disappoint him.

I toss the Lynch reports he's been after me about onto his desk like some kind of consolation prize. "No on the evidence, but here are your reports."

"Thanks, Bennett. You guys have a busy day ahead of you. Go do your interviews. I want you talking to family, friends, neighbors, ex-boyfriends, and even talk to the mailman. I want this asshole found now!"

We leave his office with a nod. I'm concentrated on where

to start and miss when Porter steps into my way. His hand comes up to steady me when we collide, but brushes against my breast in the process. I grab his wrist and twist, pulling him close to me.

I get in his face to show he doesn't intimidate me, and that I'll take no shit from him. "Do that again, and I'll rip your fucking arms off and beat you with them."

"You like it rough and dirty, huh? I can take care of you if Hunter doesn't know how to handle that mouth of yours."

I press up on his arm until he gives a slight wince. "Back off." I let go and leave him shaking out his arm.

Hunter glares at him the entire time. He knows I can handle myself, but what he wouldn't give to knock Porter on his ass. Hunter has about thirty pounds of muscle and at least five inches of height on Porter. He was also a Navy Seal, while Porter played college baseball on a scholarship. It really would be no match, and Hunter knows this.

I pull Hunter's attention back to me. "Let's go. We've got bigger assholes than him to deal with."

Going through the victim's things is always weird for me. It reminds me of the police going through our things the night my mother was murdered. I hid in the closet, so there wasn't much I could tell them. At six years old, I didn't pay attention to every noise or detail the evening my life changed. After my father's training, I can't help but notice everything now.

They said it was an intruder—a home robbery gone wrong. The killer didn't plan on my mother fighting back. They said he didn't know she was the wife of an FBI agent, but my father knew differently. The only thing the killer didn't know was that my father had been called away on unexpected business. He was the real target. The local cops hadn't a clue what was going on.

I do. And I will catch the bastard who killed my mother.

"Finding anything?" Hunter startles me out of my thoughts and narrows his eyes at me. "Everything okay? Are you still thinking about that douche, Porter? I'll lay him out for you if you want."

I shake my head. "No. You're better to me as my partner than out of a job. He isn't worth it. I lost my cool when he copped a cheap feel, but there's nothing cheap about me, and he'll learn that soon enough." I wink and turn back to the victim's bedroom.

"I'm not seeing anything in here that's out of place." I walk over to the vanity. "She got ready in a hurry, but we all do."

"You call it a hurry? It takes forever!"

"Shut up and listen. She didn't really put anything away. I think it was a spur-of-the-moment date. Her roommate was gone, and she didn't have anything else to do."

He looks around. "Nothing in here sticks out to me. It just looks like a girl's bedroom."

"That's because you're a dude, but yeah, nothing sticks out to me, either." I smack his chest as I walk out. "Let's go wait for the mailman."

CHAPTER 3

SHADOW

LONG LEGS . . . I CAN'T WAIT to have those wrapped around my waist later. This one has been an easy target. Cliché to say, it will be like taking candy from a baby. I can see the way she is eye fucking me from across the bar and can practically smell the arousal coming off her.

The best way to go unnoticed by those around you is to sit alone. Keep your head down. Don't talk to anyone. Don't cause a scene. Tip well and only order one drink. Don't stay at the bar for longer than twenty minutes, then move to a table farther away by the bathrooms. Women always head to the bathroom when they go to bars.

Dress impeccably and wear your nice watch and no wedding ring. Make eye contact and smile at your victim, but avoid them the rest of the night. They will come to you. They always do.

This particular redhead, Sheridan, has been on my radar for the past few weeks. I've followed her home a few times. Her apartment is within walking distance from the bar. In this middle class area, they will just chalk her disappearance up to local neighborhood crime.

She's a frequent drinker. I usually don't like to kill women who are always drunk, but I have a soft place in my heart for fiery red hair, big boobs, and cock-sucking lips.

God, I love thick, pouty lips.

Her curves are sexy. I'll have fun with this one. Sheridan is just a pawn in my game. She can be sacrificed while I set the game in play to take down the queen. Sheridan won't be missed. From what I can tell from checking out her apartment, she really isn't close with her family. Her roommate is a nurse and is taking on extra shifts to help pay for her boyfriend's coke problem. These women really should make my job harder. At least carry pepper spray . . . or don't invite a complete stranger upstairs to your apartment for sex. That might preserve your life a little better.

Red gets up from the bar and excuses herself. She is headed to the restroom. Bingo. Her friends are too dickmatized by the wannabe Fall Out Boy cover band that is playing, they don't even look this direction.

"Hey, want to buy me a drink?" she practically moans into my ear.

"No, sweet cheeks, you've already had one too many."

Hook . . . line . . . and sinker.

"You want to get out of here? I don't live very far. We can grab a drink back at my place, and you won't have to sit here alone . . . looking all sexy."

"I really shouldn't, but you are gorgeous. How about you head outside and text your friends? Tell them you don't feel well and you are calling it an early night. I'll cover their bill and mine and be out in a few minutes."

Another way to stay low-key is to always pay in cash. It not only impresses my victims to see a fat billfold, but it also leaves a cold paper trail. I flash a few bills at the bartender, but I don't pay for her friends' tab. She'll never know. She'll be dead.

Five minutes is all it takes. Her friends get the text and discard it. I leave without her by my side, no commotion. Just a fucking phantom who is going to have some ginger tonight.

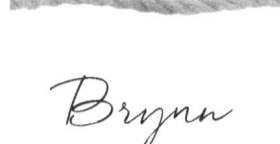

Brynn

"Bennett, we have another one. She's twenty-five, red hair, and about five-foot-ten." SAC Matthews sounds defeated. The victims keep turning up, but the clues don't.

"What else do we know?" There's no point in making him feel better. I feel just as shitty as he does, but the work isn't going to get done if we sit around feeling sorry about it.

"Sheridan is a fashion consultant at a trendy little boutique. She was last seen with friends at X Bar in West Hollywood. She left early because she said she wasn't feeling well, but there's no evidence she made it home. Porter and Lopez are at her apartment checking it out with forensics. I need you and Williams to head to the scene and see what you can find."

"We're on our way." I look at Hunter, and he knows. He didn't need to hear the conversation to figure out there was another victim.

"Where to?" He starts the car.

Twenty minutes later, we're walking into another sea of press, bystanders, and police. If anything, trying to get through the wall of people is the most exhausting part of this job. Questions are hurled at you, even though you won't answer. I don't even bother replying with, "No comment," anymore. They continue asking.

"He was a little sloppy with this one." Officer Ryan walks up as we approach the scene. I've worked with him before and am happy to see him here. He's an officer who gets it. This job is more than a paycheck to him, and he really wants to make a difference in this city. He wants to make it safer for his wife and the baby they have on the way.

"Did he leave anything behind?" I look around, but can't see anything myself.

"No, but if it's the same guy, he wouldn't have."

I look at him. "Same guy? Do you have doubts on that?"

"There are copycats all the time. Not much is a secret with this guy when it comes to the media. They see what we see."

We all look down at the victim who's about to be taken by the medical examiner. She still has the same thin bruising around her neck the others did and is laid out as if she's sleeping. He's right; the media and whoever watches the news reports probably know just as much as we do.

Dr. Leachman, the medical examiner, comes over to report his initial findings. "I believe the neck injuries are consistent with the other victims, but I won't know for sure until I get her back to the morgue. I'll keep you posted."

I turn to Hunter. "The usual?"

"Yeah, I'll take the people. You take the surroundings. I still want to head to her apartment afterwards. I don't trust Porter to not fuck it up."

Porter walks out for a smoke break as we arrive at the apartment. "Have you changed your mind and want to switch partners?"

Hunter answers before I can. "Nope, I trust that cigarette you're smoking more than I trust you."

"Come on, guys." I'm tired and don't want to listen to them bicker all day. "A woman is dead. Let's show some respect and get past this bullshit long enough to solve this case."

"I'd love to respect you all night."

I walk over and rip the cigarette out of his mouth. "Just do your damn job and quit trying to fuck with me. It isn't going to happen, that I can promise you."

I feel his gaze searing into my back when I walk away. I need to learn to just keep walking and not give him any reaction. That's what he wants. It's what he gets off on. I need to remember that and stop giving it to him.

I walk into the apartment and stop fast, causing Hunter to walk into me from behind. "Look at this place!"

"I would, but you're standing in my way." Hunter pushes me inside and stops short himself with a smirk. "How in the hell are we supposed to see if anything was tampered with in here?"

He walks over to the pile of clothes on the couch and looks back to me shaking his head. This is not how our Shadow usually likes his victims. The only thing out of place at the last victim's house was makeup that wasn't put away. Everything else was spotless.

We'd come to the conclusion early in the investigation that he is a perfectionist. His victims are always taken care of with utmost care. Even though the medical examiner is confident there has been consensual intercourse each time, you'd think the victims are innocent virgins by the way they're displayed.

I look at Hunter to say something and notice he's completely lost in thought. I walk up and bump him with my shoulder. "What's going on in there? Anything I need to know about?"

"I just don't get it. Who is this guy, and why do women trust him?" He turns quickly and grabs my neck. "If I came at you and tried to strangle you, you'd rip my hands off."

Holding his hands, I can feel his fury. "I'm not most women. They probably didn't even see it coming."

He lets go and nods. "You're right. They trust him, but how can you sleep with someone you don't know?"

I scoff. "Are you kidding? People have one-night stands all the time!"

"Yeah, but their friends know they hooked up with them. Their friends know *something* about the person they go home with. No one knows anything!"

"Sometimes people are desperate and lower their inhibitions. When you're looking for Prince Charming and someone like this guy comes along who looks normal, you tend to ignore that little voice of caution in the back of your mind."

Porter walks back inside from his smoke break. "Oh, yeah? Sounds like you're talking from experience. Care to elaborate?"

I look at Hunter and motion with my head that we're out. I've had enough of Porter, and it's time to start ignoring him.

"So, you're saying you're not the kiss-and-tell type." Porter's smirk is enough to set me off, but I need to keep my cool. It will bother him more if I ignore him.

"Come on, Hunter. We've got people to interview."

Porter stands taller and narrows his eyes. "I'm headed over to X Bar. I know the owners. They'll talk to me."

Hunter waits for Porter to leave before he starts laughing. "I like this game now. We stop talking, and he goes and finds someone else to play with."

I smile and shrug.

CHAPTER 4

Brynn

AFTER INTERVIEWING THE VICTIM'S PARENTS, we drive back in silence. My mind is racing, but I can't find the words. Meeting with loved ones is always the hardest part. They're dealing with the worst news they'll ever receive and being asked to remember the smallest detail when all they want to do is be left alone to grieve.

I remember that feeling too well and hate putting anyone through it.

"Do you remember much about your mother?" Hunter cringes at his abrupt questioning. "Sorry, I mean, because you were so young at the time."

I look out the window. "I remember her every day. I think I'll always wish I could remember more."

"How can you handle this job and not let your personal

experiences get in the way?" He reaches over to squeeze my knee. "I'm sorry if that sounds like I doubt you. I don't. I'm just not sure I could do it."

I cover his hand with mine and look at him. "I know you don't doubt me." I let go of his hand and look back out the window. "My mother and I were two peas in a pod. My father was always so busy working that it was just us two for the most part."

"He was away working when your mother was murdered, right?"

"Yeah. Part of me feels like I could've done more. Maybe I shouldn't have hidden. Maybe I should've run to the neighbors or something. I know I couldn't have taken him on then, but there had to have been more options than just hiding. I'll get my chance one day to make it right. It won't bring my mother back, but at least I'll get some peace."

"Why do you think he's coming after you twenty years later?"

I shrug one shoulder. "It's just a feeling I can't explain."

"It's your old man, is what it is. I think he got paranoid after your mother died and didn't want to lose you. I think he taught you all he did so you would be protected, unlike your mother. I don't think he intended for you to join the FBI."

I turn in the seat and face him. "I was supposed to be dead that night. He has an unfinished job, and he will finish it. We know this. We interview people all the time who keep trying to kill the same person because it's an unfinished job. Don't give me this paranoid bullshit, and don't tell me what my father would've wanted me to do."

He glances my way a couple of times. I rarely go off on

him. He's the one who balances me and keeps me sane, so my sudden defense of my feelings must have startled him.

"Brynn, I didn't mean to imply—"

"I know, Hunter. I'm sorry. It's hard to talk about it. I miss her so much. I know it sounds crazy, but even if he isn't coming after me, don't you think it's better if I'm prepared for him on the off chance he does?"

He nods as he pulls into the bureau. "But leaving your door unlocked while you take a shower isn't being prepared."

"I already had a father, Hunter. I don't need a new one." I turn and open the door, but before I can get out, he takes my arm.

"What do you need, Brynn?" He waits until I look at him to continue. "If you don't need a father, what kind of man do you need?"

The air in the car is getting a little thick. It's getting harder to breathe the longer we look at each other. His eyes tell me he'll be any man I need him to be, but I'm not sure I want him to be that man for me. He's my best friend and my partner. Adding anything will just complicate things, and my life is complicated enough.

Before either of us can speak, Special Agent Lopez slams his hands down onto the hood of the car. Hunter's eyes immediately change to kill mode, and it breaks whatever spell we seem to be under. I start laughing as I get out of the car.

Special Agent Lopez hides behind me as if he's frightened. We all know Hunter won't do anything no matter how much he loves his gray Cadillac CTS. He does check for damage, though.

"Damn it, Lopez! Do you know how much a stunt like

that could cost in repairs?"

"If anyone needs a drink, Williams, it's you! Come out with us and loosen up for once."

Hunter narrows his eyes at Lopez. "For once?"

I turn and smack Lopez on the back of the head. "He's just messing with you, but come on. Let's go out." I want to go home, but I think a couple of drinks are in order first.

"Nah, you guys go ahead. I've got plans."

I tilt my head. "You're going on a date?"

"I wouldn't call this a date. Jamie and I still need to deal with some of the wedding stuff."

Hunter was supposed to be married just two months ago, but it was called off hours before the wedding. He still won't tell me what happened or who called it off. He'll only say it was for the best.

If I were to lay bets, my money would be on Hunter calling it off. He shook off my condolences and almost acted guilty whenever I brought it up. It could've been embarrassment, so I'm not really sure. He's an easygoing guy, but no one should be that at ease if they're dumped by their fiancée.

Lopez puts his arm around my shoulders. "I'll make sure she gets home safe and sound."

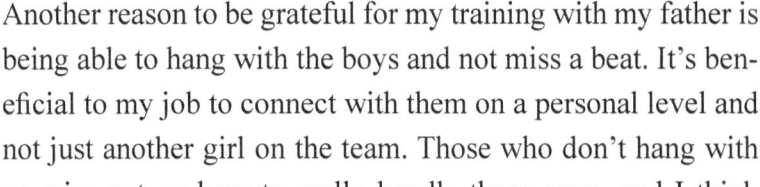

Another reason to be grateful for my training with my father is being able to hang with the boys and not miss a beat. It's beneficial to my job to connect with them on a personal level and not just another girl on the team. Those who don't hang with us miss out on how to really handle these guys, and I think they respect me a little better when I can keep up with them off the field, too.

I run my fingers through my long dark waves. Just because I can keep up with the boys doesn't mean I need to look or act like one. I'm a woman first and foremost, even if they forget it sometimes.

I down my first rum and Diet Coke and check my surroundings. We may be out for a night of fun, but Survival 101 never takes a night off.

The trendy little bar we're at is already at maximum capacity. Each table is filled with groups of men who are most likely accountants or attorneys. They order rounds in between their competition to talk over one another.

The women who are clearly here to find their next sugar daddy are what I find most entertaining. They try to dress sophisticated, but really just look trashy. They'd catch real men with more buttons buttoned, better posture, and actual conversation. Instead, their breasts are popping out, their butts are sticking out, and their fake laughs are annoying.

Then there's our rowdy table. I wonder who chose this little bar. It isn't the usual scene for us. We're more comfortable with pretzels and peanuts lining the floor and regular people just having a good time. Someone's trying to up our game, but I doubt we come back here.

While I'm here, I'm getting another drink. "Anyone need anything?"

Lopez smiles. "Just more nights like this!" He raises his beer, and the table erupts in agreement and cheers.

I shake my head as I head to the bar. The woman next to me is alone, but looking around. I give my order and look her over. She doesn't look like the others. She's probably just looking for a stress reliever for the night. I look around, because that sounds good to me, and I lock eyes with Porter on my other side. I didn't hear him come up.

"So, that's the reason you won't go out with me."

I tilt my head. "Are the voices talking to you again? They have pills for that." I thank the bartender and take my drink, but Porter stops me from leaving.

He looks to the woman behind me and leans in. "If she's your type, I say go for it." He looks at me, but doesn't back up. "Just let me watch."

"She is really pretty, but she's missing a vital part." I look at his crotch and lick my lips. "But then again, so are you."

He takes my drink, puts it on the bar, and stands even closer to pin me in as he presses his erection into my hip. "I'm not missing anything. I'm *well* equipped to handle this job."

I slide my hands up his torso and find his nipples. I run my thumbs over them as I look up into his eyes. He's amused, thinking I'm finally caving to his harassment. I pinch and twist—hard.

"I meant a heart, asshole. You're missing a heart."

His hands go to his chest as he cusses through his pain. He's trying to be quiet about it to not draw attention, but my table has all eyes on us, making sure I can hold my own. I'll always hold my own.

I grab my drink and turn into a solid suit, spilling my drink everywhere. "Motherfucker!"

A strong hand takes the now empty glass from my hand and sets it onto the bar. "Another for the lady, but put it on my tab."

I look up, but I take my time. He isn't one of the lanky guys who throws a suit on to look professional. He's filling the suit as if it's a second skin. I'm afraid to look all the way up and ruin the moment. To my surprise, it only gets better. Beautiful brown eyes, deep dimples, and a cocky smirk that says he knows he's got my attention await me.

"My apologies for spilling your drink, but I wanted to introduce myself before you returned to your table."

"Oh? Do you and your colleagues over there have insurance you think I need, or maybe you all think I have a great aunt who's ready to kick the bucket and you want to make sure I get my share of the estate."

"No. Nothing like that." He smiles and looks me over again. "I just wanted to say I like you."

"Wow." I didn't expect that answer. "You're not subtle at all, are you?"

"Subtle?" He reaches behind me, leaning in a little too close, but I don't back up. He hands me my new drink. "No, I don't think I'm familiar with that word."

"What makes you think I'm not with someone at my table?"

He glances behind me and smiles. "Somehow, I don't think—even as ungentlemanly as he seems—that he's the type to hit on someone in front of their significant other."

I look behind me and see Porter all over the woman whom I was looking at earlier. It looks as if she'll get her wish for a stress reliever tonight. I shake my head and turn back to him. "You're right. He isn't a gentleman."

"Am I right about my other assumption?" He flashes a wicked smile.

I lean onto the bar for support. I haven't had a reaction like this to a smile like that in a long time. "What other assumption?"

"That we'll be having dinner together tomorrow night."

I smile. "I don't even know your name."

"Benjamin Drake." He holds out his hand.

"Brynn Bennett." I slip my hand into his, and before my name is out of my mouth, I imagine that hand roaming my body.

"It's a pleasure to meet you, Brynn Bennett."

My gaze is directed to his lips at his choice of words. I'd like there to be pleasure and lots of it. His lips are my sole focus as I forget where I am and who can be watching. I finally look back up to his eyes, and there's a spark looking back at me. I'd love nothing more than to lean forward and see where that spark would take us, but my training is nagging at me that I don't know who he is.

For once, I don't care.

He takes his phone out of his pocket with his free hand, but never breaks eye contact. I need to get myself back under control. I clear my throat and place my drink back onto the bar. I take his phone to add my contact info and call myself to get his number.

"If you think you can handle me," I say as I slip his phone back into his pocket, "then call me. We can talk about dinner." I turn, grab my drink, and walk away.

CHAPTER 5

Brynn

I T WAS A RESTLESS NIGHT. I couldn't get the image of Ben's body out of my mind. The way he filled the suit, his beautiful eyes, and the lips I wanted to take for a ride were all keeping me awake and frustrated. I'm not sure how I'm going to talk to him today with those thoughts running through my mind.

I reach up and grab the showerhead to try to relieve some of the tension that keeps building, but my bathroom door bursts open. Reaching on the shelf behind the conditioner, I grab my Glock 42 and pull the curtain back with my finger on the trigger, ready to shoot.

"What the fuck, Hunter?" I lower my gun and flick the safety back on. "I could've killed you!"

I look back at him, thinking maybe I did shoot because he

isn't saying anything, and I realize . . . I'm completely naked. I close the shower curtain and silently curse myself. I should've known he'd try to do something like this.

He doesn't say anything, but I can hear his boots walking out. I look up to the ceiling and exhale. This is going to get awkward. I smile when I realize just how awkward it might have been. I do need to start locking my doors when the showerhead may be a possibility.

I have to hurry, but it's hard to go out there when I know he's going to be thinking about me nude. I look at myself in the mirror. He would want to think about me, right? I'd think about him if I caught him with nothing on. I tilt my head as I think about it.

Maybe he never wanted to see me naked, and it's going to be awkward like when family members walk in on each other. I shake my head and grab my jacket. Family members don't look. He was definitely looking.

He's sitting at the table with the paper and coffee as I turn the corner. He usually just stands and leans against the counter. I wonder if he wants to talk about it. I don't want to talk about it. I grab a cup and pour some coffee for myself.

I don't look at him when I ask, but I have to know. "Is it going to be weird now?"

"Yep."

I look at him. "You've seen women before, right? This wasn't a first time thing for you, was it?"

"I've seen women before." He takes a sip of coffee. "Just no one that beautiful."

I smile and look down in my coffee. "It still doesn't get you off the hook for coming into my bathroom." I finish the cup and set it into the sink. "Come on. We need to get going."

"We can't." He peeks at me over the paper. It's the first time he's tried to make eye contact since I came out. "The owner of the bar won't be there for a little while yet. I'd rather finish the paper than sit in the parking lot and wait."

"The parking lot?" I shake my head. "We've got to hit the surrounding businesses. Come on." He won't move, and I put my hands on my hips. "What's so interesting in there anyway?"

"I'm reading the obituaries."

I snatch the paper out of his hands and startle him. "We have enough dead bodies to deal with."

He looks down to his crotch and back up to me. "I need a minute, okay? I've done everything I can think of to get rid of this thing, but you're beautiful."

I don't think I've ever seen him embarrassed, but it just got more awkward. I'm flattered and impressed that he's still holding an erection after seeing me in the shower, but we have things to do. I do the only thing I can think of to help him.

I sit at the table next to him. "How did things go with Jamie last night?"

"She thinks I've made a mistake."

"So, you were the one to call it off. What happened?" I lean on the table, letting him know I'm willing to listen.

"I could live without her. You shouldn't feel that way. A wife is someone you should not be able to live without. She's someone to cherish and love with everything you have, and I just didn't."

"Did you at one time?"

"I think I thought I did, but I don't know anymore." He

runs his hands through his hair, and as he leans forward to rest on his elbows, I want to run my fingers through his hair to comfort him, but I don't. "I just feel really bad for hurting her. I know she loved me like that. She was at the point where she couldn't live without me, but now she has to."

I reach out and grab his hand. I hate to see my friend hurting because he hurt someone else. I know this will eat him up for the rest of his life.

"It may hurt like hell now, but if you didn't love her, you did her a favor. What kind of life do you think you would've had if you went through with it?"

"I know." He squeezes my hand. "You're right."

"Of course, I'm right. I'm usually right." I wink and stand up. "So, are you ready to go yet, or do you and your pecker need a few more minutes?"

Just as I thought. Talking about the ex deflates them every damn time.

I walk around the empty bar and try to imagine what her night was like. The table they were sitting at isn't hidden in the corner. It's out where the action is. I look to the dance floor and wonder if she met someone there. I look back to the bar and wonder if someone spiked her drink and that's why she didn't feel well.

Her friends said they didn't see her talking with anyone, but the bar is massive. She could've bumped into someone and started a conversation without any of them knowing. I walk up to the bar and listen to the answers the owner, Mike Daniels, gives Hunter.

"Just as I told Scott, there wasn't anything suspicious going on that night. We didn't have any major fights to break up, and no one got out of control drunk. It was a calm night, and I'm shocked one of our patrons was murdered after leaving here."

I believe him, but I'm not sure that's the whole story. "Were you here?"

"No, but my employees don't lie to me."

"Any surveillance video you'd care to share?"

"I already gave it to Scott."

Hunter and I look at each other. We haven't heard about that yet. I'll be sure to rip Porter a new one if he fucked up and didn't take it straight to evidence. He could cost us this whole case with something as stupid as that.

"When will the employees who were working that night be in? I'd like to talk to them myself." I glance at my phone as it buzzes and smile when I see the text from Ben.

Stuck in a meeting and all I can think about is dinner with you.

"They'll be in this afternoon. I've called a meeting. I think we need to up our security. I don't want the bad publicity of something like this again."

Hunter narrows his eyes at me and looks back to the owner. "We'll be back. I know they've told their stories before, but we need to hear them, too."

"No problem. I told Scott the bar is open to you guys. We want this asshole caught just as much."

Hunter and I walk out with an appointment to come back.

My phone buzzes again since I haven't responded yet, and I smile again.

> **Where are you? I need help escaping this meeting. My brain is going to seize up.**

I smile and stop walking to text back.

> **We can't have that. What good would you be to me then?**

I take two steps and run into Hunter. "Damn! Why did you stop?"

"Why did you stop?" He doesn't look happy with me.

I look at my phone and back to him. "You're right. Sorry. I'll focus." I put my phone into my back pocket.

"Who was that?"

"Just a friend." I walk to his car and leave him standing there. "Let's see that video and why we weren't told about it."

It's taking me too long to decide what to wear. Ben is going to be here at any moment, and I need to get dressed. I'm sure he'd love to see me in nothing but my unmentionables, but that's going to have to wait.

I look at the two outfits I've narrowed it down to and have no clue which to choose. If I choose the shorter skirt, it may send the wrong signal. I tilt my head a little. The signal would be right, but it's too soon. I go with the dress. It still shows my legs off a little, but it doesn't invite trouble. I glance at the skirt again.

Huffing my frustration, I start to put the dress on. I need

to be on my best behavior. If all he wanted was a quick lay, he wouldn't have asked me to dinner. My nerves are out of control for this. I wonder if I have time to kick back a drink before he gets here.

I turn to the sound of someone knocking on my front door. "Damn." I put my second earring in as I walk to the door, take a deep breath, and place my hand on my belly. I'm so nervous. I exhale as I open the door and see Ben's beautiful smile light up as soon as he looks at me.

"Wow. You look amazing." It isn't said as some cheap compliment. He really means it. His eyes sparkle as he takes me in again, and his smile is stretched across his face. I wonder what his reaction would've been to the short skirt.

"Thank you. You look very handsome."

He tips his head in thanks. "Do you need a few minutes?"

"Oh, just let me get my handbag. I'll be right back."

I rush back to the bedroom and pick up the handbag I laid out. I check the side pocket to make sure my Glock 42 is right where it should be and then tuck the handbag under my arm.

"Ready when you are." I walk back out and smile. He really knows how to wear a suit.

"After you." He waves his arm toward the door.

We walk into a very busy five-star restaurant that I've never even been to the parking lot of before, and he's seated within minutes. I look around to the enormous line of people waiting and almost feel bad for going in ahead of them.

I hear him order our wine, but don't pay attention because

I'm still trying to take it all in. I'm so glad I went with the dress. A short skirt would've looked trashy in this scene.

"Would you like to go somewhere else?"

I look at Ben and shake my head. "I'm sorry. No, I've just never . . . it's really pretty in here." I can't tell him I've never been to a place this fancy. It'll turn him off before we even get started.

"There are a lot of people who've never been here before. It's okay if you haven't."

I look back at the door we came through and see yet another couple turned away. "So, how long have you had reservations for tonight? It looks to be a hard place to get into."

"I didn't have reservations." He picks up the menu as if it was no big deal to walk in and be seated immediately.

"Who are you?"

He looks over his menu at me, and I can tell by the crinkles next to his eyes that he's smiling. "Who are you, Ms. Bennett?"

I smile back. "I guess you'll just have to wait and see, Mr. Drake."

"I'm looking forward to it."

His smile heats me up again, but the waiter comes back to take our order and saves me further embarrassment. Once he's finished and walks away, I notice Ben's face has turned a little hard. He doesn't seem to be as carefree as he was moments before. I reach out and touch his hand. "Is there something wrong?"

He smiles and takes my hand in his. "No. I just didn't like the looks he was giving. You may need to show your license to drink the wine I ordered."

I shouldn't laugh, but I can't help it. I did notice the age difference when he approached me at the bar, but it doesn't bother me. "We'll be fine."

"I feel as if maybe I should've brought my cane. Do you think they'll give me a senior citizen discount?"

"I think you're about thirty years early for that discount. Your age doesn't bother me, so don't let them bother you."

"You don't even know what my age is."

"I'm twenty-six. Is that too young for you?"

"I'm thirty-eight. Is that too old for you?"

"You're lucky. Thirty-nine is my hard limit. I can date you for a year." I point to him. "But nothing beyond that."

The sound of his laugh relaxes me a little. I didn't think he was too old, but if he's going to continue to have a problem with the age difference, I'll have second thoughts whether I continue to date him or not. I don't want to have to reassure him that it isn't an issue.

I decide to change the subject and forget our ages for a while. "I have it narrowed down to attorney or accountant, but I'm leaning toward attorney."

"Going back to school?"

"I may be young, but not that young. I'm happy with my career path, thank you. I was talking about you."

"What career path are you on, exactly?"

I shake my head. "You're not getting out of this. Now, I think you're an attorney, but I don't usually get along with them, so I'm hesitant to settle on that. However, you're much too stylish and confident to be an accountant."

"Why is it only those two things?"

"I have my reasons."

"Does it have anything to do with *your* career path?"

"You could definitely say I've been trained to look at all angles and form an opinion using the process of elimination."

"And you're eliminating an accountant because I'm stylish and confident?"

"Also, you keep answering a question with a question—another sign of an attorney." I raise my eyebrow and challenge him to deny it and smile when he doesn't. "So, what kind of law do you practice?"

"Would you care to take a guess at that?"

I tap my finger on my chin and look him over. "I'm not sure you'd be happy with just mundane paperwork, but you're too rested for constant court appearances. You also don't take just anyone because not just anyone can afford you."

"I agree with that so far."

"Beyond that, you're going to have to give me a hint because there are too many possibilities."

Just then, the servers come out to bring us our first plates. I'm not sure how to classify this dinner. The places I usually go to have appetizers, but here it seems to be courses. I think I'm going to explode before the night is over. I tell myself at each plate I'll only eat a couple of bites, but it's all so good that I can't help myself. If I had pants on, I'd unbutton them.

He leans forward, places his elbows on the table, and puts his fingertips together in front of his face. "What are you looking for in a man?"

I give him a sideways glance.

He doesn't let me answer. "Let me clarify my question. I feel I've kind of tipped my hand with you and have already proven I'm wealthy and powerful. We wouldn't be sitting at this table if I weren't."

I nod. "That's true."

"So, what do you look for in a man?"

"I think the better question is what I find attractive. He has to be kind. Manners are still important, even though most people don't have them. He doesn't have to be wealthy or powerful, but he does have to have a job and be confident. It also doesn't hurt if he can fill out a suit."

He tips his head back and laughs. "I think that's my favorite answer yet."

"Yet? Do you plan on asking more women what they look for in a man?"

He smiles and takes a sip of his wine.

"Okay, then. How about you?" I raise my eyebrow. "What do you find attractive in a woman?"

"Most importantly, she needs to be a lady. After that, I feel pretty much the same as you."

"They need to fill out a suit?" I wink.

He leans forward and looks at my breasts, but doesn't linger. "Why do you think I approached you last night?"

I smile and finish my glass of wine. He starts to signal for the waiter, but I put my hand on his. "I think I've had enough. If you'd like me to still be a lady, I'm at my limit."

He smiles and nods. "I should probably see you home. It is getting rather late."

I sigh but agree. He signals for the check, and I look around once more. It's been a magnificent night, but tomorrow morning is going to come way too soon. I need to be on top of my game for the Shadow case. I didn't think about it once tonight, and when I do now, I frown.

"Is something wrong?"

I look at Ben and the concern he has in his eyes is refreshing. Hunter is the only other man who really shows concern for me. "I'm just sad to see the night ending. It went by way too fast."

He takes my hand in his and stands. "There will be other nights. That, I can assure you." He bends down and kisses my hand before pulling me out of my chair. I'd like to tell him I'm going to hold him to that, but I smile instead.

The night air is chilly as we walk out of the restaurant. He notices when I shiver and wraps his big arm around me. "I'll never understand how women will go without a coat so not to mess up their outfit."

"I have plenty of jackets that would look amazing with this dress, thank you. I just didn't know it would be this chilly tonight."

He walks us to the car with his arm around me the entire time, keeping me warm and safe. I can get used to this. I wrap my arm around his waist and snuggle in. I wish we parked farther away.

We get to the car, and as I turn to the passenger side door, he turns me to him and holds my face. My knees are ready to give out before his lips ever touch mine. His arms slide around me and hold me up as I fall into his kiss. I feel the cold of the car behind me when he presses me against it, but I don't mind. The heat from his body warms me.

He places his forehead against mine and sounds as if he's in as much agony as I am. "I almost want to take you home with me, but I don't want to rush this."

I grab the lapels of his jacket and pull him closer still. "I almost want to let you, but I don't want to rush it, either."

He kisses me again, but it's more controlled this time. "I hope you don't think of me rude if I only walk you up to your front step. I don't trust myself to get close to your door."

I smile and wrap my arms around him. "It's probably for the best, but for the life of me, I can't figure out why."

He smiles against my neck as he backs us up to open the door, and I rest my chin on his shoulder, holding him tightly. I'm not ready to let go. It's been a perfect fairy-tale night until I look across the street and lock eyes with Porter.

He's pissed and scowls before kicking his motorcycle to life and taking off. I'm going to hear shit for this tomorrow. I hang on to Ben just a little longer.

CHAPTER 6

Brynn

I DIDN'T GET MUCH SLEEP last night. The date with Ben was on a constant loop. I probably could've fallen asleep and spent the night dreaming about him, but smiling at each thing I remembered kept me awake. I really like him.

He stayed true to his word and wouldn't go up to the door, but he did stay and watch until I waved from my window. That causes me to smile again. I've got to watch that or Hunter will be all over me.

I look at my watch. Hunter should've been here by now. I hurry to finish getting ready. He probably just didn't want to walk in on me again like yesterday.

"I'm ready." I turn the corner to an empty kitchen. Looking around, it appears he hasn't come in yet. I look at my watch again. My cell phone on the table buzzes, and I go to get it.

I'm still looking around as if he's just hiding from me, but the phone shows a text from Hunter.

I'm waiting outside.

I scoff and look out the window, scoffing again when I see him. At least he didn't honk. I rush around gathering my things and groan my frustration when he does honk. "I'm going to fucking honk you when I get out there!"

I get into the car and look at him, refusing to buckle up until he talks to me. I know he won't move until I'm buckled. If he's going to have a shitty attitude, I'll drive myself. "What's the deal?"

"There is no deal. You were taking too long, as usual."

He may be right about that, but he's never said anything before. I yank the seatbelt and snap it into place, crossing my arms when I'm finished, but he doesn't move. "Well, fucking go already if you're in such a hurry!"

"Did your date suck or something?"

The calmness he greets me with infuriates me even more. I take the seatbelt off and try to open the door, but it locks when he starts backing up.

He slams on the brake, and I brace myself on the dashboard. "What the hell is wrong with you?"

I turn and unleash my fury on him. "What the hell is wrong with *you?* You don't come up, you send a text message, and let's not forget about the honking! If you don't want me to ride with you anymore, just say it!"

The unexpected eruption of laughter frustrates me more. He's laughing at me. He's the idiot in the car honking for someone who had no idea he was even here, but he's laughing at me. I unlock the door and start to get out, but his hand is on my elbow, holding me back before I make it.

"Wait." To his credit, he is trying to stop, but he's still chuckling.

I sit back and cross my arms again. This is not a very good start to the day.

"Come on. Buckle up so we can go."

"Not until you tell me what your problem is and why you're laughing. Nothing about this morning is very funny to me."

He reaches over to grab my seatbelt and stops when his face is inches from mine. He looks into my eyes for a moment, and I want to reach out and stroke his face, but I don't. He looks so tired. The dark circles are usually only there when we've stayed up all night working a case, so it's out of place today.

I take a moment to look the rest of his face over and realize he didn't shave today. I do reach out and touch him. My touch startles him, and he finishes buckling my seatbelt and gets back to his side of the car.

"I didn't want to hear about your date." He looks around for traffic and backs out.

It probably is hard for him to hear about dating since he just broke off a long engagement, but I had no plans to discuss that with him anyway. I do consider him my best friend, but talking about a guy you're currently crushing on to a guy you used to crush on is a little awkward.

"I didn't really plan on telling you about it."

He gives me a sideways glance. "Why not? I talked to you about Jamie all the time."

"She was your fiancée. This was just a date. It's different."

"I suppose. Did you at least have a good time, and did he treat you right?"

I smile for the first time since getting into his car. "Yeah."

He looks back and forth between his window and the windshield, looking everywhere but my direction. "I hope you at least used protection."

I hit his arm. "I'm not that kind of date, asshole. What was so funny back there?"

"It just struck me funny that our first fight was over me honking for you." He starts laughing again, but not as hard. "Who knew you had such an aversion to the horn?" He beeps it again. It's going to be a long day.

"What do you mean by blank?" I'm struggling to not reach through the phone and strangle the tech guy on the other end.

He speaks slowly at first as if I'm having a hard time understanding simple English. "It's a brand new disc. Nothing has ever been written on it. You can tell just by looking at it."

I look at Hunter and shake my head when I hang up. "The surveillance footage is non-existent."

"What?"

"They finally got around to looking at the disc that Porter brought in from X Bar, and it's fucking blank. Actually, it's worse than blank. It's a brand new disc. Nothing has ever been recorded on it."

"I'm going to kill him." Hunter stands and looks around.

"He isn't here." Rubbing my temples, I take a few deep

breaths. "Let's just go back to the bar and see if they have a backup."

"We're chasing our tails here!" The entire room stops and looks at Hunter as he sits down with a huff. "I'm calling the owner. I'm not driving out there for nothing."

"Come on. It's better if we go in person so we can see his reaction to the disc being blank. We'll be able to read him better if he gave a blank disc or if Porter fucked up again. Then after that, I'll let you buy me lunch. It'll make up for this morning." I wink as I walk by.

Trying to get Hunter to talk when he's mad is not an easy task. It doesn't matter what subject I try to bring up. Unless it's something else he's equally pissed about, he won't talk. He just gives grunts, scoffs, or head movements to relay his point.

By the time we get to the bar, he's in full-on anger mode, and he storms into the bar. "Where is he?"

The guy behind the bar steps back. "Who?"

"Mike Daniels."

It looks as if the guy is about to piss himself as he points to the back. "His office."

All I can do is follow and try to run interference if it gets too heated between the men. There shouldn't be this much hostility going in to ask for something. You'll never get what you came for that way, but it's too late to reel it back. Hunter is unstoppable today.

He slams the office door open without knocking and startles Mike. "Where the fuck is the video?"

"I gave it to Scott."

"Don't play me for stupid. Where is it?"

Mike swallows. He's hiding something. "As I said before,

I gave it to Scott. You'll have to ask him." He puts his head down and goes back to work.

Hunter walks around the desk and pulls him out of the chair by his shirt and makes them eye level. I'm sure Mike's feet are dangling a few inches off the floor. It's officially gotten out of hand now.

"Mike." I try to direct his attention to me. "The disc was never even used. You gave us a false disc. Where's the disc from that night? We really want to find this guy, and that could help us."

He looks back to Hunter and shakes his head. Taking a deep breath, I walk over and touch Hunter's arm. "Put him down so he'll talk." Hunter lowers Mike but snarls at him before he lets him go.

Mike reaches for a desk drawer, but I stop him. "I'll open that." You never know when someone will pull a gun. There are a few discs and a set of keys. "Are any of these the disc?"

"No." He grabs the keys and heads for the file cabinet but turns when I clear my throat. "Fuck off, lady." His eyes get wide as Hunter takes a step forward. "Here. Top drawer. It's marked."

I take the keys, open the cabinet drawer, and see the discs just as he said. "Now, why did you hide them?" I throw his keys back to him.

"If it turns out that someone from my bar killed someone, people will stop coming."

I nod my understanding but give him a warning to not hide anything from law enforcement again.

Hunter and I settle in with bags of greasy takeout food to watch the video. It's a requirement when watching surveillance videos. Most of the time videos like this are just like watching silent movies except they're very boring.

He's concentrating on the video and fast-forwarding to the time our victim and her friends arrive. I decide to take the time to see what's truly bothering him. "So, that was some interview tactic to get the disc."

"Got the job done, didn't it?"

"Well, it was a little risky. He could've shut down completely."

"He didn't, so do you have anything else you want to bust my balls about?"

"Just your attitude, but I really don't even care anymore."

He hits *Pause* on the video and puts his head in his hands. "I have the weight of the entire world on my shoulders, and there's not a damn thing I can do to shrug it off. Jamie is taking this a lot harder than I thought, we can't catch a break with this fucking guy, and you're dating."

"What does my dating have to do with weighing you down?"

"Guys don't like their girlfriends to have guy friends." He looks at me with such pain it breaks me. "I'm going to lose you."

I place my hand on his arm. "No, you're not. If he's going to be jealous of a friendship I had before him, then he isn't the guy for me."

"You say that now." He picks up the remote.

There's no point in arguing with him, so I change the subject. "I feel it myself with this case, but what's going on with

Jamie?"

"She keeps begging me to come back, saying I made a mistake and we can get back to where we were."

"Do you think you made a mistake?"

There's no hesitation in his answer. "No."

"All breakups suck, but if you feel you didn't make a mistake, maybe you should just stop talking to her. You're too nice of a guy and don't want to see anyone hurt. I get that, but if it's just prolonging her ability to heal, then you need to be the one to let her go. Tell her why you don't think it's a mistake."

"I did."

"What did you tell her? Maybe she thinks it's something she can fix."

He pins me with his stare and is silent for a few moments before he answers. "I'm not in love with *her.*"

I'm not sure why that makes me uncomfortable, but I reach for my soda and take a drink. I focus back on the still frame and almost choke as the liquid goes down the wrong pipe. Hunter starts hitting my back. All I can do is point to the screen where Porter is front and center. He was at the bar the night our victim was killed and didn't tell anyone.

I grab Hunter's back pocket as he gets up, but I'm still coughing too much to say anything. "Don't."

"Don't go? Are you crazy? He has a lot of explaining to do!"

I nod, but still hang on to his back pocket. I shouldn't notice how tone his ass is, but I can't help it. It's literally at my fingertips. I tug to get him to sit down.

"He will shut down." I cough a few more times and clear my throat. "We need to be smart about this. Yes, he should've told us, but I don't believe someone on the team is the killer, do you?"

He finally sits down and picks up the remote to start the video again. "You're right."

I smile and nudge him. "What was that?" I put my hands in the air and do a little victory dance in my seat. "I'm right. Hunter said I'm right."

It's good to see a little smile peek out no matter how much he's trying not to. He can't resist my victory dances.

CHAPTER 7

Brynn

BEN CALLED AT THE SAME time my eyes were ready to cross from staring at the video to see if I was free for dinner again. I left Hunter with the video and made him promise to keep Porter in the dark about what we know. I'm not sure Porter is capable of killing anyone, but I'm not willing to tip my hand yet, either.

I probably should still be staring at the video with Hunter, but he told me to go and have a great time. If tonight is anything like last night, I will.

I'm still puzzled as to why Ben told me to wear jeans. We obviously aren't going anywhere fancy like the last time. It's kind of disappointing, but I'm relieved at the same time. Maybe I'll be able to relax more instead of being in constant awe.

The mirror has become my best friend, but nothing changes. It's still the same tight jeans and blue T-shirt it was when I checked my appearance ten minutes ago. Deep breaths help me feel calm when I'm faced with something unsettling at work, but I just feel as if I'm going to pass out here.

I take one last look to make sure my makeup is perfect and everything is in place as I hear the knock on the door. I nod to myself in the mirror. "You've got this."

Shaking my head at my pathetic pep talk, I head for the door, but I don't expect what I see once I open it. Ben is standing there with a couple of bags in his hands, but it's the outfit that has me speechless. He's wearing jeans and a T-shirt, too. I can't decide if he looks better casual or in a suit. They both make me want to rip his clothes off.

He clears his throat on my second trip down his body. "May I come in?"

Embarrassed I got caught looking at him so closely, I put my fingers to my forehead. "I'm sorry." I look at him again and tilt my head. "I thought we were going out."

"That was the original plan." He shrugs and adjusts the bags. "Then I wondered why go out when all I could think about was taking you home."

I look down his body that's filling my doorway and back up to those lips I couldn't get out of my mind the first night I met him. I probably would spend the entire evening trying to get him to take me home. I back up. "Please, come in."

"I hope you like takeout."

I shut the door behind him. "Yes, of course. I don't cook a lot for myself."

I walk over to the table where he set the bags, but before I'm able to look in them, he grabs me by the waist, pulls me close, and kisses me. Who needs dinner?

He kisses my neck and works his way up to my ear to whisper, "I brought dinner. You supply dessert."

I'm breathless and can't find my voice, but manage to whisper back, "Let's see this dinner first."

His eyebrows rise slightly, and even though he isn't fully smiling, I can tell he's amused by the crinkles next to his eyes. "You doubt my . . . dinner?"

How I find my voice is a mystery to me, but I do. "I'm a *prove it* kind of girl."

His smile tells me he has no doubt proving it whenever I want. I want it now.

I lean in to kiss him, but he backs away. "We need to eat and talk." He lets me go, and I look up to the ceiling. He's right. I know he's right. I just don't like it.

We fix our plates, and I decide to sit across the table from him. He raises his eyebrows in question and looks from the chair I've chosen to me a few times.

I sit and scoot in. "I think it's safer over here. If I'm supplying dessert, I want to get my dinner's worth."

"Oh, you will." Ben smiles. "So, what is it you do, exactly?"

I've been dreading this question. As soon as the men I've dated find out I work for the FBI, they leave. I don't think they can handle having a girlfriend with a more macho job than them. I was able to stray him away from my job by getting him to talk about his work as an attorney last night, but I don't think it will work tonight. Would it be too forward to ask to wait until after sex to tell him?

"Um, well." I sigh. "It's kind of hard to explain."

"I've figured it was something you didn't want to talk about."

"You did?"

"I'm an attorney. I can tell when people are avoiding my questions. You did a nice job, though. I do have to give you credit for redirecting everything back toward me. I'd almost think you were an attorney yourself, but I've never heard of you."

The food on my plate is suddenly very interesting. However, I'm not interested in eating it. I just keep pushing it around. "I'm an agent."

He continues to eat. "That could mean a lot of things, but I understand you're hesitant. It's fine. You can tell me when you're ready."

I look up to see if he's being sincere or if he's pissed I'm not as forthcoming as he was. He takes another bite and looks at me, grinning. Once he finishes the bite in his mouth, he points to his plate. "I'm finishing my dinner, so I get dessert." He points to my plate. "You may not qualify for dessert."

I smile as most of my worry melts away. "Qualify?"

"Yes." He puts his fork down and rubs his face. "Okay, that sounded different in my head."

I decide to just get it over with and tell him. I don't need more cute moments like this to dwell over when he leaves. "FBI."

He looks around and back to me. "I'm sorry, what?"

My food is really interesting again. I can't look at him. "I'm an FBI agent."

"You're with cybercrimes or white collar financial crimes, right?"

I glance at him, but don't say anything. He picks his fork back up and takes a huge bite. It's a bigger bite than he normally has, so I assume it's to keep him from speaking.

I sit in agony waiting for him to say something, but he just keeps eating. Only when I'm about to let him off the hook and complain that the dinner isn't settling well, he finally speaks.

"It's a bit dangerous, don't you think?" He places his elbows on the table with his fingertips together in front of his face. The relaxed guy who walked through my door is now the tense businessman I still like but isn't as fun. "What if you wanted a family one day? Would you quit?"

I almost say my father was an FBI agent, but then realize that isn't a good example since one of his cases got my mother killed. I just stay silent. I wish I had waited until after sex, but I don't even want that now. I just want Ben to leave so I can get over this failed relationship, too.

I scoff at myself since it's only the second date and I really have no reason to consider it a relationship other than the fact I really like him and don't want him to leave. I just really wanted sex. It isn't every day a man like him approaches me—a gentleman with a solid build and gorgeous features. The possibilities of what his lips could do to my clit would've been fun to play out. Now, I'm just back to the showerhead as my only option.

He takes my scoff to be about his reaction and starts defending himself. "Let's think about this. What would your reaction be if I told you when I went to work every day that there's a possibility I may not come home? I'm not being unfair about this."

I have my plate in my hands and am halfway to the kitchen sink before it clicks with me what he is saying. "You're afraid for my safety?" I can't turn to look at him because I'm too afraid of his answer.

"Yes." He sounds dejected. Almost as if he is afraid to tell me what he is feeling for fear I might run just as I fear he'll run from me.

I turn and walk back, but set my plate onto the table and forget about it. I'm only interested in Ben. I take his hands out of his lap, wrap them around me, and sit. "I promise I'll be safe."

"There are very dangerous people out there."

"You don't have to tell me that. I'm capable of handling them and myself."

He shakes his head slowly. "I don't believe you." He looks at my still full plate and back to me. "You need to finish your dinner." I smile and stand to go finish my dinner, but he tugs on my hand. "Sit closer."

I pull my plate over to the chair next to him. "So, you're not put off by my job? Most men are."

"No, I'm put off by the creeps you're chasing." He inhales as if he's cleansing his thoughts and exhales with a smile. "Let's talk about family. What do your parents do?"

"Oh, well, my mom was a stay-at-home mom, and my dad was an FBI Agent."

"So that's where it comes from." He looks down and then back up to me. "You said *was* . . . for both of them."

"They both died." For the second time, I've lost my appetite. "My mother died when I was very young, so there isn't much I can say there." It is my standard response. Maybe one day I'll be able to tell him, but I really want dessert, and the way the night is going, it doesn't look good.

"What about your father?"

"He had a heart attack he couldn't recover from." I wipe a tear away, thinking about the struggle he went through.

He reaches over and holds my hand. "I'm sorry."

"I wish he had seen me become an agent. I lost him before I finished college." I force another bite because I want this date to get back on track and get off the negative train.

"My father died, as well. I was just eighteen and in need of such direction as I tried to become a man."

I reach out and hold his hand. "You are a magnificent man."

He smiles and squeezes my hand. "It took me many years to live up to the expectations of my father. I've finally figured it out, and now everything is falling into place rather perfectly. I couldn't ask for a better life than the life I have now."

"What about your mother?"

"I don't know who my mother is. She left us when I was very young."

"I'm sorry. That must have been hard."

"It was, but my father made sure I knew who I was without her influence." He lifts my fingers to his lips. "Let's talk about something else."

I push my plate forward and smile at him. "Let's talk about dessert."

Looking at my plate, he tilts his head a little. "I guess I can be happy with that, but this is the only pass. I've seen you clean your plate before, and you will do it from now on."

I'm about to counter with the fact I'm an adult and can eat or not eat whatever I please when he pulls me to my feet and walks me backward toward the kitchen. He really wants dessert, and I have no idea what I have.

"Um, I'm not sure there's really much in here."

He looks in the freezer and then looks at me. "You don't even have ice cream." He looks back to the near empty freezer. "Every woman I've ever known has had ice cream."

"I'm not every woman." I stand taller when he looks at me and closes the freezer door.

"You're definitely right about that."

His mouth is on mine before I even blink, and dessert is forgotten. I try to tug him to the bedroom, but he directs us to the sofa instead. As long as he keeps kissing me, I don't care where we are.

We lie down, and the weight of his body on top of me is perfect. I put one foot on the floor to open up more for his hips. I need to feel him. "I want you."

Our hips move in rhythm, and what I can feel he has to offer is amazing, but this isn't enough. I need our clothes off. I tug his shirt off, and he allows it, but he stops my hands from unbuttoning his jeans.

"It's too soon. We'll get there, but not tonight." He continues to kiss my neck.

"Ben, I can't go through another sleepless night because you worked me up too much." My hands can't stop feeling his back. I love touching him.

He props himself up on his arm a little higher and looks at my chest. His thumb comes up and rubs over my nipple that is straining to be released. My body needs him to take that hand and move it a little lower.

As if he read my mind, he looks into my eyes and starts

his trail down my body with just the slightest touch from his fingertips. "I'll help you sleep tonight, but I won't make love to you yet. There are things that cannot be rushed, and I will not rush that."

I nod, agreeing to whatever he's willing to give me and close my eyes as he slides his hand into my waistband. My breathing starts to pick up and becomes shallow as his finger makes its way to my clit. The slightest touch makes me shiver.

He sounds amused, but his voice is deeper. I'm getting to him, too. "You're really in need, aren't you?"

"Yes, please."

He lowers his mouth to my ear and whispers, "Please, what?"

"Make me come."

Those three words spark something in him, and it's now his mission to do just that. Sitting up on his knees, he pulls my jeans down to gain better access, but keeps my underwear on. He's determined to not have sex. I don't have time to think about it as he moves my underwear to the side and plunges two fingers into me while circling his thumb around my clit.

I arch my back. "Oh, yes. Please, don't stop."

He's on his side next to me again and starts whispering into my ear, "I like it when you beg."

I feel his erection pressed into my hip, so I reach out to help him as much he's helping me, but he takes my hand and holds it above my head.

"This is about you."

He links his free hand in mine and keeps it above my head while his other hand starts to pick up the pace. I close my eyes and part my lips with a moan. "Oh."

I clench my walls around his fingers, trying to help the emptiness I feel, but it isn't enough. He curls his fingers up, hitting that place I need touched so desperately and I rock my hips to his rhythm.

I moan. "Yes, just like that." My eyes squeeze tight as he picks up speed and adds pressure. My hand grips his harder as I feel my legs start to shake. "I'm so close. Please, don't stop."

"I wouldn't miss this for the world."

As if he'd been holding back the entire time, he amps it up even more, causing me to cry out. "Oh, God!"

My entire body shakes as the first wave hits, but he keeps going. I don't even need to beg anymore. The waves come faster as he sets up each one and tips me over the edge again and again. I'm a sweaty, exhausted mess by the time he's satisfied that he's given me enough.

He carries me to my bed, but doesn't get in with me, only leaning over to kiss my forehead. "Sleep tight, my sweet, sweet Brynn."

CHAPTER 8

Brynn

"**W**HO ARE WE MEETING WITH today?" Hunter hates to revisit witnesses from older cases, but we need to keep going. They may remember something their grief has kept hidden from them, or they may have found something after the death.

"Travis Clayton. He's the roommate who had been at band practice the night Emily Churchill was killed."

"Oh, yeah." Hunter looks at me with mischief in his eyes. "Think he's written that song yet?" He mocks the statement Travis made the night we talked to him with his fist held up in the air. "I will write a song for this. It will be a bestseller in my heart."

I slap his fist down. "It was a very devastating time for him. Don't poke fun."

"Buzz killer."

Things have been pretty back to normal since that day Hunter almost had his meltdown. He's stopped talking to Jamie, and I haven't flaunted my relationship with Ben in front of him much. There will come a time where he'll be able to hear me talk about him, but I need to respect his need to heal first. He may not have been in love with Jamie, but he still loves her. He never would've asked her to marry him if he didn't.

I tilt my head and wonder if he'll ever double date with Ben and me. I shake my head free of that thought and adjust myself in the seat.

Hunter looks over at me and narrows his eyes before looking back to the road. "Do you need to pee or something?"

"No, it's nothing. I'm just getting comfortable."

"Get it a little rough last night?"

I look out the window and shake my head. "That's really none of your business. Maybe if you asked like a friend instead of an asshole, I'd talk to you about what's going on."

His chest rises with a deep breath before he sighs. "I'm sorry. What's going on?"

"Nothing."

"I said I was sorry. I'll cool it on the teasing. What's going on?"

"Nothing." I look at him. "That's the problem. We make out, but he doesn't want to have sex. I'm not looking for a relationship and want to get to the sex already, but he says it's too soon."

His eyes are battling to look at me and pay attention to the road. "Maybe he has some performance issues."

"No, he can perform. Trust me. He just doesn't want to."

"If you know he can perform, then he wants to. No guy gets hard and doesn't want sex. What's he say about it?"

This conversation is awkward, but he is my best friend. I turn in the seat to face him a little more. "He says he wants to wait and that I need to be patient, but *patience* is not what I need."

"How far do you go?"

"Oh, come on. I'm not telling you that." I face forward again.

"What's the big deal? You said you make out. Is it to first base, second, or what?"

I've never gotten the baseball reference to sex. I'm a little confused when the bases switch. "Let's just say you've seen more of me than he has."

You'd think he just won the lottery with the smile on his face. "I can live with that."

"Well, since you have actually seen me naked . . ." I can't finish my thought, but I need to. I need to know what I'm dealing with here. "I mean, I'm attractive, right?"

He barely slows down as he turns into the first available parking lot and slams the car into park. "Are you kidding me?" He turns to me and looks me over. "Where's Brynn? I'm not used to this self-doubt, and if that's what he's bringing out in you, I have to say I don't like it."

"I don't have one-night stands often, but that's all I was really looking for with him. I still just want him for the sex, but he doesn't seem interested in it."

"Let's get one thing straight. You are beautiful and desirable. Don't you ever doubt that again." He grips the steering wheel and puts his forehead on his hands. "He likes you." He sits up and looks at me. "Jamie and I waited for a while. Probably too long, if you want me to be honest."

"You did?"

"It got hot and heavy early, but we wanted to be more connected, I guess, before we connected, if that makes sense."

"Not really."

"You're not like other women. Sure, you want a guy you can have fun with, go out to dinner, and definitely have sex with, but you're not looking for a husband."

"I've never looked for a husband."

"That's my point. Either you're not at that point in your life that you want one, or you'll never get married. I haven't figured out which one it is yet."

I cross my arms. I don't like how this conversation is going.

"Don't be upset. There is no wrong answer here. You've just been too independent for far too long to think about leaning on someone else."

"I don't need anyone."

"*You* may not, but most people do. Even guys need to be with someone, and I think Ben's trying to be with you. He's trying to get you to want him for him, not just for sex. The question is if you *want* to want him—or anyone for that matter—or do you just want the sex?"

I look out the window. His explanation for why Ben wants to wait makes sense, and I understand the question, but I don't know how to answer it.

We pull up to the address on file for Travis and look around. It's a pretty quiet neighborhood, but you can never be too sure of who's living next door.

Travis answers the door without hesitation. "Hey, did you guys find something?"

"Not yet."

"Oh." I hate seeing the disappointment on their face when they think we're here to bring good news. "Well, could you come in? I've got pancakes on the stove."

Hunter turns to me and raises his eyebrows. I mouth the word, "No." I swear he'd eat everything if I'd let him.

"Sorry it's a pit in here. I had a party last night."

We follow him to the kitchen, and while it isn't exactly clean, I wouldn't say it's a pit.

"Nah, it's okay. You should see Bennett's place." Hunter flashes a smile at me as he walks into the kitchen.

"We don't care about the party mess, Travis. We want to know if you remember anything else. The shock and grief after those first few weeks can take a toll on the memory."

He flips the pancakes out of the pan and adds more batter. "No, I don't remember anything." He hangs his head. "That's not true. I remember a lot of things. I remember Emily was better at this than I am, and she used to make the best hangover pancakes ever."

I stand at the sink to get closer and speak softer. I'm not here to depress him. I'm here to help catch the killer. "I bet she'd be pretty proud of those pancakes. Did you two have parties a lot?"

"Not usually. She didn't like my friends." He picks the spatula back up and checks the skillet.

Hunter starts poking around the kitchen. "Why not? Did anyone bother her?"

I can see it in Travis' eyes—the moment he shuts down. "We're only here to help."

I barely finish my sentence when Hunter grabs my arm and pulls me back. It isn't fast enough, though. Travis picks the skillet up and swings it my way. I raise my other hand to block it, and the bottom of the skillet connects with my palm.

Both the pan and I drop to the floor as Travis takes off running and Hunter follows. "You'd better run pretty fast because if I get a hold of you, I'm going to set your balls on fire!"

I hold my hand to my chest, careful not to touch anything and stand to turn the stove off. My hand hurts like a mother, but I need to call for backup and follow them to help Hunter.

I use my fingers only on my injured hand to hold the phone to my ear while my good hand takes control of my gun. I ease outside and look around. Hunter has Travis secure and handcuffed, sitting on the ground. I lower my gun.

Hunter takes my phone and turns me around. "Go inside and run cold water on that."

I nod and head inside and grab a chair to sit on at the kitchen sink. It takes only minutes to hear the sirens coming a few blocks away. I'm not going to cry. Anyone would have the right to cry over this pain, but I'm not going to do it. I'll cry when I get home, in private where no one can see the weakness.

Hunter comes inside and looks at my hand. "I'm so sorry I didn't pull you faster. I was afraid of hurting you."

"I didn't even see him."

"Because you were too worried about how he was feeling. You've got to stop doing that."

"You've got to stop worrying about hurting me and pull my ass out of the way!"

It wasn't fair to say that. I could've and would've been hurt much more if he hadn't, but telling me what I did wrong isn't going over too well with me. It just makes me want to cry even more than I already do.

"I'm sorry, Hunter."

"It's okay. The paramedics are on their way inside. Let them look at it and then we'll get you out of here."

"Why did he even do it? We didn't suspect him of anything."

"You didn't, but I was getting close to his stash." He walks over and dumps a box of needles and small packages onto the counter. "It must have been some party."

I put my head on my arm as the paramedics come inside.

I'm startled awake by the knocking on my door. I start rubbing the sleep out of my eyes and cringe with pain. "Damn it!"

Ben is on the other side of the door when I open it. His smile fades and turns to a frown when he looks at me. "Is something wrong?"

I lift my hand and go back over to the sofa. I'm so tired. I want to spend time with him, but I'd really like to sleep, too.

"Are you going to tell me what happened?"

I want to play it off as if it isn't a big deal because I know he'll get angry. It is a big deal, but I'm fine and too tired to fight. "I was questioning someone, and he tried to hit me with a frying pan."

"Are you injured besides your hand?"

"No, I have some minor burns and a sprained wrist, but other than that, I'm good." I yawn. "Sorry."

"Maybe you should be in bed."

"I'm not sick. I just took something for the pain, and now I'm sleepy." I blink.

"That's it." He bends down and picks me up. "Off to bed. I'm not even going to ask if you ate anything. You'd probably just fall asleep in the middle of it."

The door swings open, and Ben turns around with me still in his arms. The room keeps spinning, even though he stopped. "Oh, that isn't good."

"Hey, there." Porter is standing just inside the door. He shuts it with his foot and walks across the room with his hand extended. "You must be the boyfriend. It's nice to finally meet you."

"I'd shake your hand, but I'd have to put her down, and if I put her down, I'd have to kick your ass for walking into her home without knocking."

Porter backs up with his hands in the air in mock surrender. "Just checking on my teammate. Calm yourself."

"The fact that you expect me to be calm when you just enter her home without knocking is ridiculous. I think you need to go."

Porter takes a step forward. "Well, the only thing true in any of that statement is that this is her home, Gramps. I'll leave when she tells me to."

"Gramps?" Ben starts toward Porter until I put my hand on his chest.

"Porter, just go. Thanks for checking on me, but I'm tired, and I just need to sleep."

"I'll go, but you have my number if you need anything." He snarls at Ben once more before leaving.

Ben walks me to my bedroom, and I'm halfway asleep before he gets me there. "Does he do that often?"

I shake my head. "Not usually, but it was nice he wanted to check on me."

"It would've been nicer if he had knocked first."

He tries to stand, but I won't let him go. "Stay with me."

He hasn't slept over yet, and I can't wait to wake up in his arms. "Since sex won't be a factor tonight, I'll stay. I just want to lock up first."

I nod and drift to sleep before he leaves the room.

CHAPTER 9

Brynn

I WAKE UP TO SOMEONE kissing my neck. "If this is a dream, I'm not waking up."

Ben smiles against my neck and continues his kisses. "I need to go to work. Don't wake up."

Rolling onto my back, I wrap my arms around him. "I wish you could stay here all day. I like feeling you behind me."

"You take it easy today, and I'll bring dinner by tonight." He kisses my neck again and starts to stand, but I still cling to him.

"It's just my hand that hurts. The rest of me is perfectly fine to do whatever I want."

"I bet it is, but I want both of your hands on me when that happens." He pulls my arms off him and kisses my good palm. "Go back to sleep. I'll see you tonight."

I sit up and groan. "I really need to get working, too."

He turns just as he reaches the door. "You're not going in today."

"No, I've been instructed to take a couple of days off, but Hunter is bringing paperwork here that we can go over. I have a lot of work to do on this case."

"Hunter's going to be here with you all day? Alone?" He takes a step toward me.

"He's my best friend and partner. We're solving this case. You have nothing to worry about."

He looks at his watch. "It still doesn't mean I have to like it."

I get out of bed and walk over to him, wrapping my arms around his waist. "How many women do you work with?"

"They aren't at my home. It's completely different."

"You're right. Point taken, but you have nothing to worry about with Hunter." We both look toward the door when we hear knocking. "See, you'll get to meet him now and be satisfied that there's nothing going on. Plus, he just broke off an engagement two months ago that's still a little raw for him."

Ben narrows his eyes as if he doesn't believe me and walks to the front door. I stay back, hopeful but nervous. I need them to get along. These are the two most important people in my life right now, and this needs to go well.

"Hey, why's the door—" Hunter stops in mid-sentence when he realizes it isn't me who answers the door. "Is Brynn here?"

"She's sleeping." Ben isn't giving him an ounce of space to come inside. His solid frame is blocking the door to keep Hunter out.

"I'm not sleeping, Ben. Let him in."

Hunter and Ben glare at each other as Hunter walks past him. I look to the ceiling and shake my head while I walk over between them.

"That's enough. Ben, this is my partner and best friend Hunter. Hunter, this is my friend Ben. Now shake hands and get along."

They're reluctant, but they do shake hands. Hunter is the first to speak. "It's nice to finally meet you. Brynn doesn't shut up about you."

"Hunter!"

He turns and shrugs. "It's the truth."

Ben actually smiles and walks over to me, bending down to kiss my cheek. "I've got to go, but I'll leave you two to talk about me some more." He turns to Hunter. "It was nice to meet you."

I wait until Ben's out the door, but I pick up the throw pillow and chuck it at Hunter. "Stop being my older brother! I don't need to worry about being embarrassed every time you two are together."

"Hey, it got him to chill out, didn't it?" He walks over and plops on the sofa. "So, what are we doing today?" He picks up the remote and turns the television on.

I grab it out of his hands and turn it off. "Working. I thought you were bringing files with you."

"Yeah, I did. They're in the car. You had an unusual car in the driveway. I wasn't hauling that shit in here just to haul it back out." He jumps up. "I'll go get the stuff, but put a bra on. Your boobs are distracting." He turns quickly and snaps his fingers. "Do you need help?"

"Go!" I shake my head as I walk to my bedroom. I can manage a sports bra on my own.

"I'm getting another drink. Do you want anything?" I look at the laptop as another email message comes through.

"Nah, I'm good." Hunter takes the laptop to check the email as I go to the kitchen. "Hey, it's the list of known drug dealers Travis has interacted with."

I walk back into the living room drinking water. "Good. We can compare names, but I really doubt any of the ex-boyfriends are going to be on that list."

"At first glance, you're right." He puts the laptop back onto the coffee table. "I'm tired of hitting brick walls with this fucker."

I pick up the laptop and look through the list. I don't recognize anyone else, either. "Well, it was a good try, but now we're running out of options."

"I'm sure there are options we've not considered very thoroughly."

"Like what? We've investigated every angle we've been given."

"No, *we* haven't, but I have." Hunter shakes his head. "I've been investigating Porter since we saw him on that surveillance video. I don't trust him at all."

I close my eyes, trying to keep calm. He never should've started an investigation about anyone without me, but especially one of our own. "You've been doing what?"

"I've been digging into Porter's life." He scoffs. "If that's what you want to call it."

"What have you found out?"

"There were a few girls who'd gone missing when he was in college. He was never a suspect, but I don't like the coincidence." He starts pacing again. "And why doesn't he ever want to go to the crime scene? I think he's already seen it."

"You can't be serious." My head can't stop shaking my disagreement. I don't believe a word of what he's saying.

"Think about it. He fights us every step of the way, but doesn't transfer out. He makes our lives miserable because he enjoys it."

"He's one of us, Hunter. He isn't a killer. He doesn't even know her!"

"This guy doesn't know any of his victims. We can't connect them to anything. The only thing they have in common is that they each have been to bars at least a few nights prior to their death if not the night they died, but even the bars aren't connected."

He sits down next to me. "Just think about it. All he does is bar hop. I don't know why he would do it. I haven't worked out a motive, but if we can't rule out the ex-boyfriends or anyone who loved these victims, then we sure as hell can't rule out an asshole who treats women like disposable objects."

I point my finger in his face. "You can't say anything to anyone unless you have solid evidence, Hunter. This could ruin him. I won't do that on a hunch."

"No matter how much this should be discussed with SAC Matthews, I'm not saying anything to anyone. Hell, I didn't even tell you until now. I'm only telling you so you'll be careful around him."

I cringe when I think of last night. Things are still a little foggy, but I remember Porter just walking in. I wonder what would've happened had Ben not been here.

"What?" He looks at my hand. "Are you in pain?"

"Porter came over last night."

"What did he want?"

"I don't know. He said he just wanted to check up on me, but Ben was here, and they got into a fight because Porter walked in without knocking."

"What the fuck, Brynn! How often does he do that?"

"That was the first time."

"You need to keep your fucking doors locked! This world isn't safe. You should know that better than anyone, but you just fucking ignore it. I'm sick of it."

"You're not my dad or my keeper. I can handle things myself."

"One of these days, Brynn, you're going to find yourself in a bad situation, and I can only hope and pray I'll be there to help you. You can't take on the world alone. No one can. When are you going to realize that?"

"When are you? You hold everything in and try to take on *the world* and your problems alone when I'm right here." I place my good palm on his cheek and make him look at me. "Don't hold anything in again. It makes you cranky, and you're not my Hunter when you do. I promise to be more careful and keep my doors locked if you promise to not shut me out."

He holds my hand and smiles. "Your Hunter?" He takes my palm and kisses it, never breaking eye contact. "You've got a deal."

CHAPTER 10

SHADOW

I KICK BACK ANOTHER DRINK and take a look around, wishing I had more time to seek someone out tonight. It keeps me on edge when I don't get the fix I need. Things are too busy to take the time to properly plan, and there's no reason to get sloppy now.

Brynn and Hunter are too much on my mind to think straight. I need to be more careful around them, but I can't help the anger I feel. They think I'm a fool, but I know I'm being watched. They'll never catch me, but I will keep them running in circles.

Brynn

The field is a big part of my life, but I've gotten used to lounging in my pajamas all day. Now that my hand is better, it's time to get dressed and work from the bureau again.

It was a much-needed vacation, even though I still poured over notes and statements trying to find some connection to these victims. There has to be something we're overlooking. Maybe it's something simple, and we're putting too much thought into it.

Those who went to college didn't attend the same colleges, and the rare occasions they did, they didn't seem to have any of the same classes.

None of them were friends with each other on social media nor did any of them have any similar hobbies. It seemed as if this was truly a random act each and every single time, except for the fact that random acts don't usually occur in murders like these.

The women were seduced, and that takes time. They had to be comfortable enough with the killer to let their guard down. There were no other injuries anywhere on their bodies, so a struggle didn't take place.

The act of strangling alone is a personal one that takes time and effort to do. There aren't any drugs in their systems by the time we find the body to say he's drugging them, but the lack of physical evidence screams they aren't conscious when he kills them. There would be more physical wounds from victims who fight back. These victims don't for whatever reason.

"Hey." Porter walks up to my desk and stands with his

crotch inches from my face. "What's on the game plan for today?"

When he rocks on his heels, pushing his hips closer to me, I snap and hit him in the bulge that's a little too close for comfort with my pen. "Back it up. I don't want to catch something."

He starts rubbing himself where I hit him, causing me to shake my head and look back at the computer. "Watch it! A lot of women depend on me and expect me to be injury free."

"Well, unless you want to be penis free, keep it out of my face."

"All right, calm down." He grabs the chair next to the desk and sits a little too close. "What are you looking at?"

I sigh, knowing he isn't going to leave or even back up out of my personal space. It'll just be quicker if I tell him and let him move on. Plus, I'm starting to tell him a little more to see what kind of reaction I'll get out of him. Maybe I can tell we're getting close to something if I keep him in the loop and just watch how he reacts.

"I'm just going over the phone records again."

"They didn't have any numbers in common that weren't ruled out already. The common numbers were delivery places. Everyone's ordered food. There's no lead there unless you're going to ask if they ordered the same toppings on their pizza."

"Most of them had numbers we can't explain. There has to be a connection to that."

"They're prepaid phones. We already looked into them." He stands and puts the chair back. "Quit wasting time on dead ends and do something useful."

I'm seething when he tells me I'm wasting time, but I may

have just had my first reaction that can do some good. I will be looking more into these numbers, but now I need to do it a little more discreetly.

I kick off my shoes not caring where they land and lie down on the sofa. Mindless television is what I need. Just as I'm about to grab the remote, there's a knock on my door. Pretending not to be home is an option, but the knocking isn't stopping. I wish I didn't listen to Hunter and lock the door, because now I have to get up.

"Coming! You can cool it with the knocking now." I open the door and hang my head, wishing I had pretended not to be home.

"Come on. You should be glad to see me." Porter and his smirk are the last things I want to see tonight.

"I'll be glad to see you tomorrow morning back at work, but not in my living room." I walk back to the sofa and grab the remote. I need to drown him out.

He shuts the door and sits next to me. "So, what's for dinner?"

I don't hide my irritation when I look his way. "Whatever *you* have for dinner isn't going to be in *my* living room. What are you even doing here?"

"I think I hurt your feelings today."

A scoff is the only reaction I have the energy for tonight.

"No, really. The phone number angle is a good one, but Lopez and I already went through them all. There just isn't a trail anywhere, and none of the phones have been on for months."

"So it's possible that the killer used those to contact his victims."

"It's probable, but not all of the victims had numbers that weren't explained."

"I know. I'm just not buying that this guy is as random as he lets on. Everything is planned meticulously, right down to how they're laid out when we find them."

Porter shakes his head. "The fact he's going to kill isn't random. He knows that night that he'll have another victim. He just doesn't know who it is yet."

"I don't believe that." I get up to get a beer. This conversation needs alcohol.

"Why?" He gets up and follows. "There's nothing to connect them to anyone to think they were having an affair. You have them all living a double life."

"But they did. They willingly had sex with him before they died. I can understand the single girls taking him for a spin, but the committed ones? Why would they risk their loving relationships to hook up with some random stranger?" I walk back to the living room without handing him a beer. It may be rude, but I'm not going to invite him to stay.

He grabs one anyway and catches up to me in the living room. "Committed girls want one-night stands just as much as single girls do."

"Then none of those relationships are as solid as the men claim they are."

Porter shrugs. "Are they ever?" He turns to face me and lays his arm on the back of the sofa. "Look, I've been with plenty of girls who have boyfriends." He shrugs as if there's no apology to be made. "If they're married, I have second thoughts, but just boyfriends? No way. Those girls are begging for excitement, and I'm just the man to give it to them."

"Obviously, they did because they do have sex with him, but I just don't understand it."

"Come on. You're committed to the suit, right?"

"Committed? No, we're just dating, but I still wouldn't go sleep with someone I just met at a bar."

Porter runs his eyes over my body. "I'm not calling you a liar, but you're a liar. I know women, and I know you would—and probably have—slept with someone you just met."

I don't answer and take another drink of beer. "What about you? Don't you feel guilty for breaking people up?"

"Who says they break up? Sometimes a girl just needs to be noticed." He sets his beer onto the coffee table. "Sometimes she just needs to have a night be all about her." He inches closer. "And sometimes," he leans in to whisper, "she just needs to be fucked."

I remove my gun that I haven't taken off yet and jab it in his ribs. "I'd say you're the one close to being *fucked*. Back off."

He slides back to where he was sitting with his hands in the air as Ben walks in. He slams the door and has Porter off the sofa before I can put my gun away.

"What are you doing to my girlfriend?" Ben's fists are gripping Porter's shirt and keeping him up a few inches to where Porter has trouble touching the floor.

"Ben." I'm by his side in just moments. "Just put him down and he'll leave. I swear I'm fine."

Porter stumbles to catch his balance as he's dropped from

Ben's grip. "I can't go. I've had a beer and could be arrested for drunk driving."

Ben reaches into his pocket, pulls out a business card, and flings it at Porter. "Call me if you do. I'll have the charges changed to harassment."

Porter bends over and picks up the card. "I should arrest you right now for assaulting a federal agent."

"Porter, just go!" I turn back to Ben as he and Porter glare at each other until the door closes. Touching his face, I turn his attention back to me and smile. "Hi."

His breathing is heavy, and his muscles are tense. Loosening his tie and sliding it out of his shirt, I try again to get him to talk to me. "It's just us now."

"I don't want him here unless someone else is here. I don't like him."

I step up on my tiptoes and kiss his lips, even though he isn't kissing me back. "I didn't invite him over." I try kissing him again.

He finally kisses me back and grips my face. "I don't want anything to happen to you."

"It won't. I promise." I smile at him again as I try to undress him more by unbuttoning his shirt.

A smile spreads across his face. "I guess I should be your knight in shining armor more often."

I shake my head. "That isn't why I want you right now."

"Is it the suit? I didn't have time to change since the meeting ran late."

I back him into my bedroom and throw his shirt across the room. "No, it's because of what you said."

He allows me to push him onto the bed and straddle him,

but he won't let me continue further than that. "What is it then? I've got to know what turns you on like this."

I lean down to his ear and whisper, "You called me your girlfriend." Just saying the words brings another smile to my face until his sharp inhale cuts through my excitement. My smile fades as silence sets in. *Did I not hear him right?*

I close my eyes as my chest aches and my cheeks warm. It must not have had the same meaning I gave it. I roll off him and look to the ceiling. I blink tears away, determined to not let him get to me. I may have jumped to conclusions and made a fool of myself, but he said it. I know he said it.

I focus my energy on being angry and ignore the hurt I feel. "What, did you forget my name and say the first thing that popped into your head?" I get off the bed. I need another beer.

"No, that isn't it." He grabs his shirt before he follows me out to the kitchen.

Hunter's assumption that Ben wants to be more than a one-night stand is growing on me. The thought of having someone steady in my life is starting to appeal to me. When he called me his girlfriend, I felt something I'd never felt before. And I liked it. Until I realized he hadn't meant to say it.

"Well, it obviously wasn't what you meant to say, so maybe I'll forget you said it. In fact, I'm so tired that I've already forgotten it! Good night." I go back to the bedroom and slam the door before he's able to walk through it.

I hear him place his hand on the door, but he doesn't open it. "I hadn't realized I said it, but it doesn't mean I don't mean it."

I try to drink the beer to stop myself from crying, but it's only delaying the inevitable. This hurts. I try to compose myself as much as possible and try to get him to leave. "It's fine, Ben. I'll talk to you tomorrow." I clench my eyes closed, trying to ward off the tears for just a moment longer. "Please lock up when you leave."

I hear his hand slide down the door before I hear his footsteps walk away. I get into bed and turn the lights out. I really do just want to go to bed and forget this night ever happened. Once I see the lights to the living room go out, I cover my head with the blankets and let go.

I haven't cried like this since my father died. I guess it's about time, but I don't like feeling so weak and alone. Nothing good comes from that. I'm too lost in my self-pity to hear Ben come back inside, but I do feel the bed dip and sit up to push him away.

He wins the match as we wrestle for control and puts his big arms around me. "Please don't cry. I want this next step for us, but I don't want the reason it came up to be because I lost my cool with that asshole. Will you just forget about it long enough for me to properly ask you sometime?"

I nod into his chest, unsure if I should really believe him or if he just feels guilty. At this point, I'm too tired to care. I just want to go to sleep.

CHAPTER 11

Brynn

"**G**IRL, WERE YOU UP ALL night, or what?" Porter's over-
ly zealous remarks about my appearance just may
get him shot today.

I ignore his innuendo that I was up all night having sex
and sit at my desk. Hunter narrows his eyes at me. Shaking my
head, I let him know now isn't a good time to talk. I just want
to work the case.

We chase the same tiring leads as we've always chased.
Witness lists, employer records, friends, family, and co-work-
ers. No one is cross-referencing over each case. I feel the tears
coming again, but this time it's more out of frustration and
exhaustion instead of being hurt.

"Come on." Hunter stands and makes me get up. "Let's go
grab some lunch."

"Where are we going?" Porter stands and stretches.

"Eat shit for all I care. You're not coming with us." Hunter doesn't give him any time to respond and ushers me outside.

I stretch and look to the sky as soon as we're free of the stifling, stale air in that room. It feels good just to stand outside. Maybe this is really why smokers smoke.

"Come on." Hunter tugs on my sleeve. "You want him to catch up?"

We get into his car, and he drives off before we're even buckled. "What's the hurry?"

"I just don't want him following us, and you were taking too long."

I finally get the seat belt fastened and look at Hunter. He isn't going to like the update I need to give him. "He came over again last night."

He looks at me with a scowl. "Porter? What the hell did he want?"

"Back at the bureau he told me I was wasting time looking at the list of the unidentified phone numbers. He claimed he felt bad and wanted to apologize. Then we ended up talking about the case."

"Anything good?"

"I don't know if I'd consider it good or not, but I am looking at this from a different point of view."

Hunter parks at the taco truck and turns to me. "Well? What's the new point of view?"

"These women were looking to get fucked. They hadn't planned on getting killed, but sex was definitely on the agenda."

"You got that from Porter?" He starts shaking his head.

"Of course, he's going to tell you that. Whether he's the killer or not, it's his hobby to make women think they want to sleep with him. These women probably feel guilty after giving in, so he has to justify it to sleep at night." He opens his door and hops out.

"Well, I didn't fall for it. He got a gun to the ribs for his efforts with me."

He leans back inside the car. "If he laid a fucking finger on you, I'm going to kill him, and then I'm going to kill you for not calling me."

"He didn't touch me. He was just trying to sweet talk me, and I wanted to make my feelings clear."

"How he can sweet talk anyone being such full of shit is beyond me. Sit tight. I'll be right back."

Hunter thinks it'll be best if I take time off from the numbers I've been searching through. As much as I hate to give up on something, he's right. Sometimes a little distance gives a fresh perspective.

"This is stupid!" Hunter throws his pencil onto the desk. "Look, I'm just going to say it, and if it makes me a sexist pig, then so be it." He stares at me until I look at him.

"I already know you are, so why the big announcement about it?" I smile, even though I try not to. It's too much fun not to mess with him when he's in a mood.

"Well, good. I don't have to worry about it." He packs up the papers on his desk and hands the folder over to me. "It's all yours."

"What is this?"

"The last three weeks of the victims' shopping sprees. I don't recognize half of the names on there." He gets up and grabs his coffee cup. "I'm so glad I'm not a woman."

"Oh, believe me. We are, too."

"You know, I was going to offer to get you a refill, but not now that you hurt my feelings." He stomps off in the most feminine fashion I've ever seen him display.

I sit back and just watch him for a moment. The guys are going to razz him about this, but he doesn't care. I've been cranky, and it's just like him to help me get through it and make me smile, even at his expense.

Taking a deep breath, I look down to the folder he handed me and get started. As I suspected, it's a mess and out of order. It's going to take me longer to straighten it out than it will to actually look for similarities. I should've asked for that refill.

"Here, crybaby." Hunter's pouring coffee from his cup to mine when I look up.

"Thank you." I'm already lost to the folder in front of me that I don't respond to the crybaby remark.

I look at the first victim's list of transactions and just like before, nothing stands out. None of these women were what I would consider a shopaholic. Their transactions were modest and within their means. Most of them had minimal credit debt, with the exception of a few.

"Wait." I shuffle through the pages.

Hunter walks back with his own refill and perks up as he watches me. "Did you find something?"

"Yes." I keep flipping through the papers. "Maybe."

"Well, what is it?"

"It's just they all visited the same shopping center a few days before their death."

His eyebrow arches as if to ask if I'm serious. It may not be a big clue, but if the killer was in the area and met his victims there, it was worth checking out.

"Did they all go to the same store?"

"Not exactly, but there isn't anything else that these women have in common. They all live in different areas, so even their pizza places aren't the same." I hold up the folder. "However, each one of them visited the same shopping center within days of being killed."

"You think the killer is in that area." We are both out of our seats before he finishes his sentence.

We're out the door and to his car without another word. It may be a stretch since most of the city's population has been at that shopping center at least once, but it's the only lead we haven't looked at yet.

"You're welcome." Hunter looks quite smug as he pulls out of the parking lot.

"Are you just now responding when I thanked you for the coffee?"

"No, of course not. I'm telling you that you're welcome for handing this lead to you."

I smirk and shake my head. "Of course, you are."

"Where do you want to park?"

"Just pull over right here."

"Here?" He glances at me with his eyes narrowed.

"Yes and shut up."

He pulls over and looks around until he spots what I already have. Porter is running up the steps to the building across the street. He is supposed to be on the other side of town. I grab Hunter's arm as he opens his door. "Don't."

He looks back to me, nodding as he shuts his door and drives back out onto the street. "You're right. We don't know what he's doing. Let's see if he's honest later about his afternoon."

"Exactly. Plus, I want to run through some of these stores before they get too busy."

The first two stores are exactly the same—dead ends. The victims look familiar, but the associates see too many faces to notice anything. One does recognize a victim as being in her store shortly before she was killed, but said she doesn't remember anything particular about the transaction.

"Wow." Even Hunter's impressed by the clothing in the third store we walk into.

"Hi." I smile at the woman behind the counter. "I'm Special Agent Bennett, and this is Special Agent Williams. We'd like to ask you a few questions."

"Do you have a warrant?"

I tilt my head. "Do we need one?"

"Whether it's about customers or our business practices, it's all confidential."

I want to pull her by the bun on the top of her head and snap her back to me when she walks away, but I hold my cool. "In that case, I'd like to speak to the manager."

She doesn't even bother to turn around. "I am the manager."

Hunter shakes his head when I open my mouth and asks his own question. "Are you the owner of this store?"

"No." She turns and gives him a look that would've sliced

his balls off if it were capable. "I would've thrown you out if I were."

"Then we'll take the owner's information."

She turns back to the rack she was adjusting. "I'm sure you have your ways to find out. Good day."

I walk over to a rack of dresses that are clearly out of my price range and start to look through all of them. "Do you have a fitting room?"

"For people who can afford to pay, yes."

"You don't take credit cards?"

She looks my way briefly before continuing with her task. "You do dress with style, I'll give you that. I still don't believe you can afford the clothing in that section." With a nod of her head, she directs me to somewhere else. "How about a nice scarf?"

"I can't afford this section, but my boyfriend can."

This piques her interest and has Hunter walking toward the door. "Are you seriously going to shop right now? We need to get to the other stores before they close and see if they'll be decent enough to answer our questions. Families are waiting on answers."

I shrug. "I know, but they're already dead. What's another day going to make?" I turn back to the rack. "Do these run true to size or small?"

She seems to be interested in the banter between Hunter and me the moment we mention dead victims. "You're here about people who died?"

"Yes. There are a few who seemed to have shopped here shortly before they were murdered, and we'd like to know if they were here with anyone."

"No."

Both Hunter and I look at her as she takes a step back, realizing she just answered a question. We take a step forward to continue the questioning.

She looks at me. "The one I recognized from the news wasn't with anyone."

I step forward, leaving Hunter behind a little. "Do you remember what she bought?"

"I know it wasn't much. She had a date and wanted to look nice, but we were kind of out of her price range."

"And you're sure she wasn't with anyone?"

"Positive."

Hunter softens his attitude. "What else did she say about the date?"

"I just remember her being so happy about it. She said it was going to change her life. I remembered feeling that way when I met my husband, and it was so depressing to see her on the news a few days later."

I signal to Hunter to give us a few minutes, and he takes my cue, walking to the far corner to give us an appearance of privacy. "So, why were you afraid to answer our questions when we first asked?"

"We get a lot of jealous spouses who come in to fish for information. It isn't the first time a *special agent* has been in to ask how someone got a dress or who someone has been sending dresses to. Hired private detectives are not very creative."

I nod. "But she wasn't in that kind of situation?"

"Not that I could tell. She wasn't acting like a woman hiding anything."

I take the folder out from under my arm that I tucked there

when looking at the dresses. "Which woman was it?"

She selects the first victim. "I'll never forget her long black hair."

"Thank you for your time." I hand her a business card. "Please, call me if you think of anything else."

She nods, slips the card into her pocket, and goes back to the rack she's already adjusted twice. Hunter and I walk outside before he starts speaking.

"Do you think she'll call?"

I shrug. "If she remembers something, I think she will. I'm just not sure there's anything to remember." I look around and focus on the building Porter went into. "I think the killer is from this area. I think he saw the victims here and picked them out. He followed them until he was in a place he could make a move. People here are sober and would remember too much about him."

"Do you think he was the date she was referring to in there?"

"I don't know. She wasn't killed after a date, so it's hard to say." I take a deep breath and sigh. "I want to make a timeline of days and times of transactions to see if there's a pattern of when he would look for victims. Let's head back."

It's getting late and Hunter and I want to call it a day, but we are seeing when Porter will walk in to let us know how his afternoon went. I start rubbing my eyes. The information is starting to blend together.

"We should just go. He probably won't even come back

tonight." Just as Hunter stands, Porter walks in.

"Who won't come back tonight? Were you all waiting on me?" Porter winks at me. "That's so sweet."

Hunter sits back down and shakes his head. "Not everything's about you, Porter. Since you're here, what did you find out today? Amaze me with your sleuthing."

"There's a lot about me that could amaze you, Hunter."

"I bet."

"Boys! It's getting late, and I'm getting cranky. Porter, did you find anything out?"

"Nope. Ran a couple of leads, but nothing solid yet. We'll get it, though. What did you two do today?"

"We went shopping." I allow him his chuckle as he walks to the coffee machine, but his back stiffens when I say where.

Hunter and I share a glance. "Yeah, we went shopping late this afternoon and picked up a few tips. Nothing solid, but we think we're in the right area."

"That's really great." He walks back to his desk and doesn't say much as he turns to his computer.

"All right, well, I've had enough fun for today." I look at my watch, close my eyes, and sigh. I hadn't heard from Ben all day. The girlfriend slip must really be bothering him.

CHAPTER 12

Brynn

J UST AS I GET THROUGH the door and slide my jacket off, my
phone beeps. I look at the ceiling and raise my fists since
all I want to do is put my feet up and watch mindless television. If it's another murder, I'm going to kill the murderer
when I find him.

I close my eyes until the phone is in view. "On the count
of three, I'll look but only because I have to." I take a deep
breath and count. "One . . . two . . . three."

"Who are you talking to?"

I turn and throw the phone at the person behind me.
"Ben!" I walk over and touch his chest where the phone made
contact. "What are you doing?"

"Right now? Trying to figure out why my girlfriend threw
her phone at me."

I pull my hand away. "That isn't funny." I pick up the phone and walk to the sofa to put my feet up. I check the message, and it's just Hunter reminding me to let the case go for tonight.

"Neither is getting a cell phone to the chest, but I'm trying to make the best of it. You have quite the throw."

I'll respond to Hunter later. I toss the phone onto the coffee table and pick up the remote. Ben sits next to me and waits until I flip through seven channels before he takes the remote from me. "Are you going to acknowledge me for more than target practice, or should I just leave now?"

"Last night you freaked about calling me your girlfriend, and here you are just twenty-four hours later being blasé about it. How am I supposed to react?"

"I'm sorry. I thought about it today, and I reacted poorly yesterday. I said it, and I meant it. You are my girlfriend. I just had a more romantic way of making that official statement than throwing some asshole out your door."

I look at him, but cross my arms. "That's kind of romantic. Protecting me and claiming me as yours. Actions like that can get me hot. I was all over you after that, if you remember."

"I do remember." He slides closer to me. "And I was an idiot to let that moment pass."

"Oh?" I feign interest and lean on the arm of the sofa. "What would you have done differently?"

He grabs my hips and pulls me under him on the sofa. "For starters, I wouldn't have stopped you, but I would've taken over."

"Only if I let—" He kisses me silent and puts his thigh between my legs. I rub my hands down his back and hope he isn't teasing me again. My hands make their way down to his ass as I pull him into me, letting him know I want more than just heavy petting tonight.

"Let's move this to your bed."

I hold his face as I look in his eyes. "After the day I had, we'd better not go in there unless you're serious about this."

"We'll talk about your day later." He stands and holds out his hand. When I take it, he bends down, picks me up, and tosses me over his shoulder. "Right now, there are other pressing matters."

The laugh he gets me to make melts away some of the stress from the day. He doesn't let me go until we're through the door and he kicks it shut. His hands touch every part of me when I slide down, and before my feet touch the floor, I want to attack him.

He holds my face and kisses me softly. "I want to make love to you. I've wanted you since I saw you in the bar, and I was insanely jealous of the men around you."

I whisper, "You were?"

"Yes." He continues his light kisses down my neck as he unbuttons my shirt. "The thought of anyone near you makes me crazy."

My shirt drops to the floor, and I look up at him. "There's no one else."

"Good. Let's keep it that way."

I place my hand on his chest to stop him. "For you, too." It isn't a question.

"You're the only one I've ever wanted this much."

I reach behind me and unfasten my bra. "Then take me."

His hands slide down my body as he backs me up to the

bed. As the rest of my clothes are stripped away, so are my worries that he'll stop this before it starts again. The hunger in his eyes matches mine, and I know it's only a matter of time before he loses his self-control.

I can't wait.

I get on the bed and lift one knee to allow him a better view. I need him to catch up and get undressed. "I'm feeling a little alone up here."

He grabs my ankle and pulls me back to the edge of the bed just as he drops to his knees. I barely have time to register what's about to happen before he takes his first taste. It's a long lick that has me shaking for more before he rests on my clit. As with anything he does, subtlety is not involved with this. He knows what he wants, and he's taking it.

He sucks as soon as my clit is between his lips, and I fist the sheets. "Oh, damn!"

He takes two fingers and enters me, curling up. He's making quick work with this orgasm, and I'm not complaining. As his fingers work me from within, his mouth is still sucking on my clit. It's almost too much, but I don't want it to stop.

"Just like that. Please don't stop."

He increases the speed of his fingers and changes to flicking me with his tongue. I can't hold out anymore. My back arches as I cry out. "Fuck, yes! Oh, God."

He stands and smiles at his performance, taking his time to take his shirt off. I'm left helpless to watch the slow, painful torture of him getting undressed. As soon as his erection is free, I sit up. I've felt him through slacks or jeans, but it isn't the same as seeing it, and he doesn't disappoint.

He takes the condom from his wallet and tears open the

package. Watching his hands slide it on only gets me worked up even more. He gets on the bed and backs me up to the pillows.

As he hovers above me, he strokes the hair out of my face. "You're so beautiful." He kisses me and teases me with his hips.

I try to lift my hips, but he holds me down. "Ben," I plead, "I need this."

He props himself up on his elbow as he looks at me. "And you'll get it. I want to take my time. Let me worship you."

I get lost in his kiss while his hand roams my body. I'm not hungry for slow, but his touch helps my craving. His fingers lightly run over my breast, and I gasp when he pinches my nipple. I can feel him smile against my lips before he takes the kiss deeper.

His kiss gets more urgent as he brings his hand up to hold my face. I can feel him getting in place, and I adjust my hips to help him. There's a bigger gasp as he slides inside. I wrap my arms around him and cling to his back as he tortures me with slow, steady strokes.

My walls clench around him as I try to get him deeper. "Oh, you feel so good. I need more."

He adjusts his hips and goes even deeper. "You're amazing."

He kisses my neck as he works his hips faster. My hands slide to his hips and grip. "Yes, faster!"

He props himself up on both of his elbows and looks down at me. Our eyes connect as he picks up the pace. I feel the tension building and don't want to let go yet. I need to feel him just a little bit more.

As if he has the same thoughts, he shifts his hips and slows down. He chuckles as I protest. "I can't let go of you yet. I'm going to do this all night."

I lift my head and whisper into his ear, "Then maybe I should do some of the work." I laugh as I try to brace myself when I'm suddenly on top. I sit up straight and raise my eyebrow. "Are you ready for this?"

He nods as I start my slow movements, but there's no way I can compete with his self-control. I simply don't have it. I start riding him harder and place my hands on his chest. His hands go to my hips, and I think he's going to slow me down, but he helps me to speed up instead.

His hands cover my breasts as I arch my back and ride through my orgasm. He pinches my nipples, sending more shockwaves through my body. He sits up, wrapping his arms around me and going even deeper as he kisses my breasts.

My hands fist his hair, and I keep him close to me. "Oh, God." I pull his head up to me so I can kiss him. My legs shake as I start to ride him again. "Ben."

He lays me down at the foot of the bed and takes over while I wrap my legs around him and don't let go. "You've got one more in there for me, don't you?" He pumps a few more times until he feels my walls clench around him. "That's it. Give me just one more, and I'll be right behind you."

He puts his hand between us and rubs my clit. I grip his arms as another wave tears through my body. He thrusts a few more times and collapses on top of me, completely out of breath. I wrap my arms around him. I don't want him to ever get up.

He kisses my shoulder. "Well, what do you say?"

"Yes. Let's do it again."

He laughs as he rolls over, pulling me with him. "No, I wanted to know if it was worth the wait."

I manage to get up on my elbow and look him in the eyes. "Yes, it was worth the wait. Just don't make me wait that long again."

CHAPTER 13

Brynn

I T'S AMAZING HOW A FEW orgasms can change your perspective. Make that a few orgasms with the right partner. Just having them on your own isn't as fulfilling, but I'm completely satisfied as I get ready for work. I may actually be ready before Hunter shows and be waiting for him by the coffee pot instead.

"Damn!" I hear the door and grab my watch. "I was almost ready before you for a change." I turn the corner and see Hunter pouring his cup of coffee.

"Oh, yeah? What's the occasion?" He turns and looks at me with narrowed eyes. "You, uh, had company last night, huh?"

"I did." I put my hand on my head and suck in a breath. "I forgot to respond to you last night. I'm so sorry."

"No problem. I figured you went off the grid for the night. You knew I'd come get you if anything happened. I guess the action happened here." He hands me a cup of coffee. "So, where are we starting today?"

"Before I forget, I won't need a ride tomorrow."

"Well, you don't *need* a ride any day, but I like to pick you up." He shrugs. "But whatever. I'll just meet you at work."

I nod and take a sip. He was right when he said things would change when Ben and I got closer. I enjoy my rides in to work with him, but I spend all day with Hunter. Ben wants to take me to dinner and back to his place. I'd really like to see his place.

"Hey, I don't know where this is going with Ben, but I need to see where it can go. I hope you understand."

"Of course, I understand. I'm just going to miss my friend. I'm sure things will work out great between you two." His smile is genuine, but there's a pull behind it that doesn't let it reach his eyes. I know he means well, but I also understand he's going through a lot of changes already.

He reaches around me to place his coffee cup into the sink and leans down to whisper, "I guess you no longer need me to confirm if you're sexy or not." He slaps my ass and heads out the door.

I shake my head as I grab my stuff and walk after him. "You've got a lot to learn there, stud. A woman can never be told too many times that she's sexy."

I sift through text messages, emails, and social media accounts from the victims. It's a way to get to know each victim and how they interacted with people, but it gets me nowhere closer to the killer and how they interacted with him. He's smart. I have to give him that.

There is no trail, virtual or otherwise, that leads me to him in any form. The spell he must cast over these victims in the brief moments he talks to them is unnerving. How does he do it, and does he do it alone?

"Hey, did you ever look at those numbers?" I toss my pen at Hunter when he doesn't respond.

"What? I'm in concentration mode here." He tosses my pen back.

"Numbers? Did you check them?"

"Yeah, I got nothing." He wheels away from his desk and comes over to my side. "You should let me look through the sexting ones. You're already getting enough action."

"Bennett's getting action?" Porter's attention is of course piqued when my sex life comes up for discussion. I shoot Hunter a dirty look.

His screwed-up face tells me he realizes his mistake as he rolls back to the safety of his own desk. He mouths the word, "Sorry."

"Bennett, Bennett, Bennett." Porter's head is shaking while he walks to my desk. "Holding out on details, are we? I thought we were a big happy family here." He sits on the corner of my desk. "So, did the suit fall flat, or did he rock your world?"

I don't get embarrassed often, but I feel my cheeks pink at the thought of last night. I can't look up and make eye contact with anyone or even respond to Porter, so I continue to flip through the pages of social media in front of me.

Out of the corner of my eye, I can see another pair of slack-covered legs approach Porter. Hunter's going to do something he'll regret if I don't stop him. This is my fight, not his. I look up just in time to see Ben shove Porter off my desk, and I hurry to get between them before fists start flying.

Ben takes a step forward, pointing in Porter's face as I push on his chest. "If you ever get within two feet of my girl again, I will—"

I cover his mouth before he can say anything else, but Porter barks back and pins me between them.

"You'll what, Grandpa? Come on and say it. Give me a reason to throw your ass in jail."

"I'll do more than throw your ass in jail!"

I'm trying to push them apart, but it takes Hunter and Lopez pulling on them to free me from between them. I've had all I can take. "Enough!" I pull my jacket back down and brush my hair out of my face. "You don't like each other. I get it. I think the entire world gets it now."

Porter's face is still hard while he stares Ben down, but Ben looks disappointed in himself after my outburst and lowers his head. I walk up to him, touch his face, and smile. "Hey, there." I reach up and kiss him, not caring who's looking.

His hands slide around my waist as he pulls me closer. "I'm sorry I lost my cool."

"It's okay. It's kind of romantic." I smile when he finally makes eye contact and smirks. My hand slides around the back of his neck to pull him down so I can whisper, "I told you that gets me hot."

He pulls me closer to him. "I came to take you to lunch,

but I'm afraid I'm the only one who'll be eating."

I slide my hands down his chest and grab his lapels. "Don't make promises you can't keep."

He removes my hands from his jacket, taking one in his, and leads me out without another word. I try to reach for my bag as he walks by my desk, but he doesn't slow down to let me grab it. I look at Hunter, but he's back to work at his computer, avoiding my eye contact.

Ben isn't slowing down on the way out to the car. It's exciting to think he could be serious, but I don't get my hopes up. A regular, old-fashioned lunch sounds great, too.

Then I see the limo and stop. "Ben?"

He turns to me and takes my other hand as he walks backward, leading me to the limo. "I want to spend your lunch break with you, not driving you." He tugs on my hands to get me closer to him.

I nod my thanks to the driver who opens the door for me as I get inside. Lunch is already waiting for us like a picnic, but after that scene in there, I'm not sure there will be much time left for food. At least I hope not.

Ben slides in next to me and presses the button to slide the privacy glass in place once his door is shut. He isn't moving or saying anything, causing the tension to build inside me. If that's his intent, he's doing a damn good job. I'm afraid to move, but I let my eyes look in his direction. The sound of the driver's door closing startles me.

Ben's deep laugh takes over the space as he pulls me close. "Is someone nervous?"

"I would say anxious. I'm not sure what we're doing here."

"It's simple." He slides me down the seat and lies on top of me. "I'm going to eat my lunch."

"Ben." He kisses me as he presses his body into mine. "I do have to go back to work."

His hands slide down to my belt to unfasten it. "Then we have no time to waste."

I lift my hips to help him undress me, but I feel a little exposed in the limo. "Are you sure he can't see anything?"

He directs my face to look at him instead of the privacy glass. "You are mine now. No one else, remember?"

I nod and watch him as he slides down my body. Just the thought of what's about to happen has my breath quickening. He parts my legs and kisses my thighs. I may not need the extra build up, but I'll take it. My thighs are pressed further apart as his tongue inches closer. He seems to be just as impatient as I am for this, but his self-control is winning out.

Both of his hands are on my body, opening me up to him. I try to reach down to help, but he puts my hand underneath me. "Patience."

I nod and continue to watch his hands. He slides his middle finger along my slit, but he doesn't touch my clit. I cry out in need. He chuckles, but leans in and flicks my clit with his tongue a few times before pulling away again. "Don't stop, please."

The pinch on my thigh is unexpected and a little painful, but it makes me want him even more. "I will give you what you crave, but it will be my way." He slides his middle finger in and out, slowly as he tests me. He holds his wet finger up and smiles. "I think my lunch is ready now."

"It's been ready." I inhale as I speak the last word when

he sucks on my clit. "Oh, God." I search for something to grip, but finding nothing, I place my hand on his shoulder.

He slides two fingers in and out of me, and I start to rock my hips. He swirls his tongue around without making contact again, and I want to scream from frustration. Just as I open my mouth to say something, he flicks my clit, and I moan.

He doesn't stop moving his fingers as he looks up to me. "I'll give you what you need now since we're limited on time, but tonight, I call the shots, and I will take my time."

I don't have time to nod my agreement before he presses his tongue against me. The pressure and the flicks of just his tongue alone are enough to drive me crazy, but his fingers thrusting in and out are sending me over the edge. I search for something to hang onto again, but go back to his shoulders.

"Oh, fuck. Don't stop." I rock my hips to the rhythm he's creating. I arch my back and grip the jacket on his shoulders.

He gives me a few more flicks with his tongue before he starts sucking again. It's too much. My entire body starts to tremble as he's pulling another wave of pleasure from me, and this time I try to push him away.

My body finally starts to relax as he eases up and slides his fingers out. I can't catch my breath or move. I'm not sure how I'm going to work the rest of the day without a nap.

He makes his way back up my body and smiles when our eyes lock. "You need to eat. I hope your lunch is as good as mine was."

"Can't move." I close my eyes and smile when he kisses me.

"I do have something else that can keep you awake, but unfortunately, I don't have condoms with me. Poor planning on my part, but it's for the best. You need to eat."

He sits up and coaxes me into getting dressed after he's cleaned up and taken care of me. He wants me to eat lunch, and while I am hungry, I'm also very tired and would rather sleep the last twenty minutes of my lunch break, but he's right when he says I should eat.

I sit up and look around as I try to regain my composure and balance. I've never lain down in a moving vehicle before, and it's a little unsettling to change positions. I look out the window to get my equilibrium to catch up with the moving limo and come face-to-face with Porter. He's on his motorcycle next to us and glances over every so often.

"Your colleague needs to be careful. I could start to build a case of harassment against him."

I look at Ben. "How long have you known that he's been next to us?"

He goes on to fix my plate for lunch as if nothing is bothering him. "I've watched him try to catch a peek in here for a while, but he can't see in the windows. I thought you and Hunter were closer than you and Porter."

I look back out the window. "We are. I don't know what Porter's problem is." I look back to Ben as he hands me a full plate that I'm no longer hungry for. "Thank you."

CHAPTER 14

Brynn

THE LAST COUPLE OF WEEKS have been some of the happiest I've had since my father died. I've spent every free moment with Ben, and he's been great to split our time between our separate homes. I'm sure he's more comfortable at his place, but I started to feel as if I was moving in, and I didn't like feeling that this early.

His house isn't as big as I thought it would be, but he has a beach house we're going to this weekend. He may have more money than I'll ever see in my lifetime, but he doesn't flaunt it, and I think that's part of his charm. I can't date someone who isn't down-to-earth and has entitlement issues.

Hunter snaps his fingers in my face. "Hey, we're talking here."

I shake my head. "Sorry."

We've moved to the conference room to spread out and place each victim in her own section. I'm not sure how long we'll have the conference room, so I need to start focusing on the job and stop daydreaming about my life.

"Cut her some slack, Williams. Our girl is in love."

Hunter's patience is running thin with Porter. He still thinks there's something going on with Porter and continues to watch every move he makes.

"I'm not in love. I'm just enjoying Ben's company."

"You know there's a name for women like that, right?"

I grab Hunter's arm as he starts toward Porter. "Just let it go."

"You have commitment issues, Bennett." Porter spreads his arms out. "That's all I'm saying. Or maybe he isn't the right guy for you."

As if Porter would know the right guy for me. "Let's just get back to the case."

"This case is dead." Porter sits down and props his feet onto the table. "Let's face it; until he makes another move, we're just wasting our time."

I take a deep breath and try to ignore his laziness. "Then let's talk about him. What do we think we know about him?"

"He's older." Porter seems bored.

Hunter glances my way, and I know he's going to challenge some of Porter's beliefs. I tilt my head to let him know to tread lightly. There's nothing tying Porter to these crimes.

He makes it seem as if he's just discussing the case, but I know Hunter's trying to get him to give something up. "I think he's younger. He's able to leave victims in popular public spots without being seen. You need to be fit to carry them alone."

"I agree, but he doesn't have to be in his twenties to do it. I think he's pushing forties, if not over it."

"These women are young. Why would they be attracted to an older man?"

Porter looks my way. "Care to take that one?"

I cross my arms. "Ben isn't that much older."

"Oh, come on! He could be a grandfather!"

"He isn't that much older, and you need to cool it with the gramps bullshit!"

Hunter pulls me back as I start for Porter. I'm feeding into what he wants, which is changing the focus off the case. I shake my head and walk to the other side of the room. I need to get it together.

"Let's forget his age." Hunter's trying to get more info from Porter. "What else do you think about this guy?"

"He's got pick-up skills. He's a smooth talker who can easily get women to trust him." Porter looks around the room at the different victims. "None of these women were into one-night stands and yet," he motions with his hand as he speaks, "here they are."

He stands up and walks to a victim across the room. "Hell, she was practically a virgin. Two boyfriends before this loser and never had a one-night stand in her life. Part of me thinks he promised her something else, but I can't figure out what."

"What do you mean?"

"She didn't even own any toys, Bennett. How many single women do you know who don't take care of themselves when the urge strikes?"

"Actually, there are a lot of women who don't buy toys. There are other ways to take care of things that don't involve batteries."

He shakes his head. "She wasn't sexual. Nothing about her appearance or her life said she was into sex. Her friends said she didn't go to the bars that often. The clothes she owned were very modest. Fuck, even the books she read were young adult. No sex. I just don't know how he got her to go with him."

"It's easy, isn't it?" Hunter steps forward. "I mean, you do it all the time. You say something to make some woman think she's the only one in the room, and the next thing you know, you're at the very least getting your dick sucked in the parking lot."

"The difference between this guy and me is that I wouldn't go after girls like this one. I only approach the ones who are looking to suck someone's dick in the parking lot. I wouldn't have gotten that vibe from this victim."

"Maybe she needed to feel that." I surprise both of them by the looks on their faces. "You said it yourself. Women are sexual beings. We want orgasms just as much as the guy hitting on us does, but maybe men don't hit on her because she doesn't know how to show that or isn't confident enough to show it. Maybe he watched her and saw her reactions to things."

Porter nods in agreement. "The bar they went to is definitely a more bump-and-grind kind of bar. There's a sexual energy there, for sure."

"How many of these bars have you been to?" Hunter's back to interviewing Porter.

"I've been to all of them."

"How many on the night our victims were killed?"

Porter walks toward Hunter. "What are you trying to say

there, buddy?"

"I want to hear you lie to me. I want to look you in the eye when you lie to my face."

"Boys." I take a step toward them.

"I don't answer to you, Williams. When you get SAC in front of your name, then we'll talk."

"We're talking now." He takes another step forward. "How many? Be careful of your answer."

"SAC Matthews knows. He's the only one who needs to know."

"I know for a fact you've been to one. We have you on video."

Porter backs up. "Then you already know everything, big shot. If you'd have gone to SAC Matthews as you should've, you would've been told he was already apprised of the situation."

I try to defuse the tension before it gets worse, but still move forward with questioning him. "Why would you hide it from us? You had to know we'd find out."

"You two don't make it very easy on a person here. Why would I come to you and say I was there?"

"We're investigating a murder, and one of the investigators was caught on video at the bar the victim was picked up at. You don't think at the very least we would want to discuss it?"

"Fine, let's talk about it. I was on the prowl for a good time. I wasn't looking at the men. And as I said before, she wasn't someone I would've given a second look to, so I don't remember seeing her there."

"Why hide it?"

"I didn't hide it. I went to my superior and discussed it.

He didn't warrant it as a big deal and said I could stay on the case."

"Okay, why not tell us? As Bennett said, we were bound to find out."

"Why tell you, asshole?" Porter sits in the chair and props his feet onto the table again. "You don't seem to believe anything I say anyway. I think the killer is older; you think he's younger."

"Okay, let's get back to work." I walk over to the victim he was just talking about. "I think you're on to something with this one." I flip through a few pages of notes.

"See, I'm more than just a pretty face." He looks at Hunter. "Maybe you should hear what I have to say more often."

Hunter still can't let things go. "Maybe you should stop hiding things from us."

"We're all hiding something. Isn't that right, Williams? Care to lay it all out there? I'm game if you are."

I look between them and settle on Hunter. "What's he talking about?"

"It's just hot air, trying to divert the attention away from him."

Porter scoffs and turns back to the case work in front of him. I look at Hunter, but he only holds my gaze for a moment before he moves on to another victim's section. I decide to talk to him about it later. He won't say anything in front of Porter.

It's been a long day. Things got a little better when Lopez joined us, but the tension between Hunter and Porter was still high when they walked out of the conference room at the end of the day. Porter had a few good points about the victims and potentially good points about the killer, but why he held on to them for so long was lost on me.

I'm still going through notes on my desk as my phone rings. "Bennett."

"Hey, beautiful." Ben's voice makes me smile. "I'm going to be a little late tonight. Do you think Hunter can give you a lift home?"

I look across the desk at Hunter's empty chair. I'll take a cab. "I thought we were going out?"

"Yeah, I'm sorry. I'll be at your place as soon as I can. This meeting is running a little bit later than I thought it would."

I lean my head on my hand. I was looking forward to going out. "Sure, no problem."

"Tell Hunter I owe him."

"I'll see you later?"

"Of course, but grab dinner because I'm not sure how long I'll be."

I hang up the phone and lay my head on the desk. I was looking forward to going out, but just going home does actually sound better. It's been a tiring day.

"Need a lift?" Porter stops at my desk on his way out.

"I can manage."

"I didn't say you couldn't, Bennett. I just asked if you needed a lift."

I weigh my options and glance at my bag. A ride sounds so much better than waiting for a cab, but Porter's track record while we're alone hasn't been the best.

"I bet if anyone else here had offered you a ride, you'd be

in their car by now."

"This is true, but they have cars. You have a motorcycle."

He smiles and tips his head. "That's true, but they forecast rain today, so I do have my truck."

I point to him. "No funny business. It's a ride in your truck, not permission for any other kind of ride. Got it?"

He crosses his heart with two of his fingers and holds them up. "I swear."

I grab my bag and stand. "Okay. I'd really appreciate it."

"Good." His smile is genuine, which is rare. "But if you attack me when we get to your place, I can't be held responsible. I am a man after all."

I shake my head as I follow him out. I knew the smile was too good to be true. "Sometimes I don't know why I put up with you."

"I'm irresistible!"

"I wouldn't go that far." I get into the truck and buckle up. If I'm going to be alone with Porter, I'm going to use it to my advantage. "Can I ask you something?"

"Sure."

"When you said Hunter and I didn't make it easy, what did you mean?"

"Williams doesn't make it easy for me to talk to him. I can talk to you a little more. However, you two are partners. You're usually a package deal."

"I can understand that, but you don't make it easy to talk to you, either. You've got a big chip on your shoulder, and frankly, we'd all like to knock it off."

"Are you trying to psychoanalyze me?"

"No, that's way too much work." I look at the street he

just drove past and look back to him. "Why didn't you turn there?"

"Because I'm taking you out." He glances my way. "I want to show you how I think the killer operates."

I'm a little nervous being alone with Porter now, but I'm intrigued as to how he thinks the killer operates. Hunter will not be happy when he hears I've gone with him alone and without backup, but I'm not sure Porter would attempt killing one of his own, even if he is the killer.

"Have you worked it through yet?"

"Worked what through?"

"If you can trust me or not." He laughs at my silence. "Text SAC Matthews if you want and tell him you're checking something out with me."

"Matthews?"

"If you text Williams or Ben, they'll be there before we get there."

"Good point." I send a text to Lopez instead. He's aware of the tension, and there's no reason to pull SAC Matthews into it.

Porter pulls up to the same bar the victim we were discussing earlier had been to right before her disappearance and murder. I look around the parking lot, and it looks a little different when it's packed. Business suffered a little at each bar when it was announced victims had been at the establishments, but they all bounced back within a few weeks.

"Come on. I'm sure Williams hasn't thought of doing this."

"You're right, but he's a different kind of guy, isn't he?"

"Yeah, the boring kind."

He jumps out of his truck and heads to the door. I shake my head, jump out, and catch up. "No, I'd say the gentleman kind."

"I thought you didn't need anyone." He smirks and opens the door for me when I don't have a response. "Ladies first."

I walk inside, and it's loud, crowded, and intimidating. How victim two ever made it through the door, I'll never know. Porter takes my hand and weaves us through the crowd to get to the bar. He orders two beers and uses the time it takes to get them to look around. I look around, but I have no idea what I'm looking for.

The dance floor is crowded, but no one seems to mind. Dance partners are blurred as everyone appears to dance with whoever is standing next to them. I'm unsure how you would stay with your date in all of that.

"Come on." Porter takes my hand again and leads us to a table. "Could you look a little less like law enforcement?"

I look down at myself and then back up at him. "What do you mean?"

"Loosen up, will you?" He motions around. "Everyone is having a good time. You look constipated."

"Maybe my date sucks."

"Good one." He smiles and comes around to my side. It's a tall table without chairs, and I contemplate going to the other side, but I don't want it to look like I'm trying to get away, even though I am.

"No funny business."

"Relax." He reaches his arm around me and puts his hand on my hip. "I won't go lower or higher than this, but we should look more comfortable with each other. These people know me here. They'll expect me to hang on you."

He leans down and whispers, "Plus, I can tell you things easier this way."

"They'd better be really important things." I put my hand on his to keep it in place.

"Look around. What do you see?"

"A lot of drunk people bumping into each other."

He scoffs. "That's obvious. Look again."

I scan the room and look at the people individually instead of the crowd. I try to make my mind into that of a killer looking for his next victim. There are a few whom I see as easy targets, but our guy doesn't go for easy. That would be Porter's angle.

"What do you see?"

"I see exactly what I would expect to see—drunk people trying to hook up." I remove his hand from my hip and turn to face him. "So, what's your point with all of this?"

"My point?" He shakes his head as he grabs his beer. "I just wanted a drink."

"You're a douche."

He grabs my jacket when I start to walk away. "Look, our guy is slick and calculated. Do you see anyone slick and calculated here?"

I'm looking at the only guy who fits that description. "What do you suggest we do?"

"I don't suggest we do anything. I'm just telling you what I'm doing."

"What are you doing?"

"Looking for the slick and calculated."

"You mean to tell me that you're here looking for the killer?"

"Yes, actually. You and Williams went to the shopping center looking for him, didn't you?"

He has a point, but going to crowded bars when there's no rhyme or reason to which bars he chooses seems like a waste of resources. It will take sheer luck to run into the killer on the night he decides to make a move again.

"I'm tired, and I want to go home."

He sets his beer down and takes a deep breath. "Okay, let's go."

"You stay and look for the killer. I'll just catch a cab."

"No, I'll see you home."

We walk back out to his truck, but this time he doesn't hold my hand through the crowd, and I struggle to keep up. I give him a little space once we reach the door. I don't think he's happy to leave this early.

I get inside and buckle up without saying anything, but I have so many questions. Porter speaks first. "I'm good at my job, and I will find this guy. I have the bar scene down. You and Williams don't."

"I'm not sure that sitting in a bar, people watching is the best move for this. Everyone in there is trying to be slick."

"You're right, but most of them aren't."

"What are you going to do if you find someone who is actually slick?"

"Follow them."

"Seriously?" I turn as much as the seat belt will allow me. "This is why you disappear?"

"Yes. It's also what I was doing in that building across from the shopping center." He looks at me. "I will follow up on any lead I see fit, and I don't need to clear it with Mom and

Dad."

I assume he means Hunter and me. "Just don't do anything stupid."

"Don't worry. I won't jeopardize the case." He pulls out into traffic.

"I meant you."

He glances my way a couple of times. "Did you just say you care for my well-being?"

"You are part of the team, and you're taking dangerous measures going at this alone. I don't need you going off half-cocked and getting killed."

He reaches over and takes my hand. At first, he squeezes it as if to say thank you, then he places it on his lap. "I'm always fully cocked."

I take my hand back and roll my eyes. "If you weren't driving, I'd punch you in the balls. In fact, stay in the truck when you drop me off. Your balls still aren't safe."

CHAPTER 15

SHADOW

ALL I CAN DO IS watch for now. It pains me to not touch anyone, but the stakes are too high. I risk losing it all for a moment of weakness. I'm stronger than this and will keep myself in line.

I scan the room one more time before going home and lock eyes with the sweetest thing that's walked in all night. She's fending off an asshole I know all too well. They're the same type to try to get into her pants or at the very least get her into theirs, but they don't know the first thing on how to treat a lady. It'll be great fun to take her away from this asshole. He clearly doesn't know the first thing about the woman before him.

Her short dark hair is as straight as she probably is. She hasn't cut loose yet, but she wants to. Her skirt is flirting above the knee, but she keeps tugging it down. She needs to be shown that she's as desirable as she's trying to be, but he's coming off too strong.

She looks away from me a few times but always comes back to my eyes. I never stop looking. I arch an eyebrow and tilt my head to the empty chair. If she comes to me, she's mine. I usually like to play a little longer than I will with this one, but I need the fix, and who am I to turn down an opportunity?

She clears her throat and feels her cheeks. She's embarrassed by my obvious desire for her, but I think it's a turn on for her, as well. The internal battle they go through is fascinating to watch, but they usually head over my way.

I smile and sit up straighter as she walks over. I stand and pull her chair out for her. As she takes her seat, I breathe in her scent and lean in to whisper, "You're so beautiful."

"Thank you." She avoids eye contact for as long as she can, but it doesn't take long before she starts stealing glances my way. "I'm not sure what I'm doing here."

"I think you know exactly what you're doing here." That gets her to look at me. I reach under her and pull her chair closer to me between my legs. I slide forward on my seat a little to let her knees touch the crotch of my pants. "You're a woman with desires, but you don't know how to set those free. You came here thinking you could find someone to help you, but these boys are all the same, aren't they?"

She squirms in her seat until I lean forward and place my hand on the back of her chair. I take my phone out of my pocket and hand it to her. "Call yourself."

Her hands shake as she reaches for the phone and does as I say. She looks around the bar when she hands it back. "I don't do this."

"But you want to." I take her chin and make her look at me again. "Are you here alone?"

"No, but they're dancing."

"You don't like to dance?"

"All the boys are the same."

I smile. "Not all of us are still boys. There are men who know how to treat a lady with the respect she deserves and who can satisfy the desire she craves."

I scoot back and look her over again. "You have my number. Use it when you want a man."

I get up and toss a couple of bills onto the table. My phone is ringing before the bar door closes behind me. "Tell your friends you're leaving. I'll wait for you."

It doesn't take her long to come outside, but she's still hesitant as she walks over to me. If she were too eager, I'd leave her in the parking lot. She can hardly keep eye contact, but she can't look away.

"I don't know what I'm doing."

I hold out my hand and pull her close when she takes it. "That's okay. I do." I lean down and she thinks I'm going to kiss her, but I kiss her neck instead. When she starts to moan, I walk backward, pulling her to my car.

The ride home is the trickiest. They have a lot of thoughts going through their minds and can decide to call it off at any time. This is when it's most important to keep them engaged sexually. I adjust my pants a few times, letting them think I'm hard and my desire for them is uncontrollable.

My next move is to rest my hand on their knee and never slide up their leg without an invitation. I rub my thumb over the top of her knee to give her extra attention and keep her mind occupied with thoughts of me touching her.

"How." She clears her throat. "How much further is your place?"

She squirms in her seat, which causes my hand to go up her leg a little, but I slide it back down to her knee. I can see her chest rising from the corner of my eye as her breathing increases right before she takes my hand and slides it further up her leg.

I take the invitation and slide my hand under her skirt. I keep up the gentleman act and only touch her through her underwear, but I can still feel how soaked she is for me. She presses her hand against mine to get me closer to her.

I smile and look at her. "I want to take my time with you, but you're going to make that difficult. Do you know how desirable you are?"

She shakes her head as she looks at my pants. She's making this difficult to keep my control. I finally pull into the driveway and turn to her. "You are so beautiful, and I'm going to show you just how crazy you're making me."

She latches onto my arm when I open her car door for her and hangs on until we get inside. She lets go to look around while I lock the door. I walk up behind her, brush her hair away from her neck, and start kissing where I know it drives most women crazy. She is no exception. She leans back against me and hugs my arms that I've wrapped around her.

"I want you so much," I say between kisses.

"Then take me."

I take her hand and lead her upstairs to my bedroom. Once the door is shut, I turn her around and press her against it, kissing her hard and fast. She doesn't seem to mind.

I take my jacket off and toss it across the room. I take a couple of steps back and start to undress. It's important to make yourself vulnerable before asking someone who's unsure of what they're doing to be the first one to make that kind of move.

She stays with her back against the door as she watches my shirt fall to the floor. Her gaze is fixated on my hands as they unbuckle my belt. There are just a few more steps before she sees what she's been eyeing most of the night, but I'm not going to show everything at once.

I get down to my boxers and take a step back when she reaches out for me. Shaking my head, I smile. "Your turn."

She steps away from the door and looks down at herself. "With the lights on?"

"How else am I going to see that beautiful body you're hiding from me?"

I reach out and pull on her hips to get her closer to me. I kiss her neck to get her to relax before I unbutton her blouse, making sure I kiss down her body with each section of skin exposed, but keeping away from her breasts. Her shoulders and torso down to her belly button will get her hotter than just going for the obvious, and I promised to take her like a man. I refuse to grope her like an immature boy.

I'm on my knees in front of her skirt, and I reach behind her to unzip it. Her hands are on my shoulders when I look up to her and continue looking into her eyes as I slide her skirt off. She steps out and kicks it to the side.

I stand, never breaking eye contact until I lead her back toward the bed. I finally allow myself to look at her and smile when I see the matching red lace set. "You are so beautiful."

I reach behind, unfasten her bra, and sit on the bed so I'm eye level with her breasts. I need to take my time no matter how much I want to devour them. Once I'm inside her, I can unleash my full desire, but I need to play it cool until then.

"Is something wrong?"

I look up and shake my head as I lean forward and take one nipple into my mouth. She sucks in a breath when I bite. I place my thumbs in her waistband and pull down, exposing all of her to me. I continue to work my mouth over her nipples, teasing each one as I slide my hand between her legs. She's so slick and ready for me.

I stand and turn her around. "Lie down for me."

She gets in the middle of the bed and watches me as I slide my boxers down. I pump myself a few times to show her how hard I am for her and reach over to the nightstand for a condom. She seems fascinated on my cock and how the condom slides on. I watch as she moves her hand between her legs.

"Do you feel how wet you are?"

I startle her, and she looks down at her hand as if she hadn't realized she had started masturbating. I smile as I lie next to her and put her hand back to where she had it before. I slide down to get a better view. "Show me what you like."

She's hesitant, but as soon as she starts touching herself again, she can't stop. I follow her fingers with my tongue and lick everywhere she's touched. She lets me continue without her as she grips the comforter.

When I move my tongue faster and start pumping my fingers into her, she reaches up and clutches the headboard. I need her to have this orgasm. I need her to want to be fucked as much as I want to fuck her. There can be no marks other than the one around her neck, but I'm too worked up to take my time with her. I need the release she can give my cock and my soul, but it has to be done right.

She's quiet when she orgasms, but I'll get her to scream before the night is over. I slide back up her body and get her to look at me. "Did you enjoy that?"

She nods.

I smile and kiss her so she can taste herself on my lips. "Then I need you to tell me how much you're enjoying it. I don't know what you want me to do next."

She looks down, embarrassed to say the words.

I grab her chin and get her to look at me again. "I need you to say it." I put myself between her legs and rub my cock against her slit. "It's so easy for me to fuck you right now, but I don't hear anything."

It's quiet and barely a whisper, but she says it. "Fuck me."

"What?" I lean my ear down to her mouth. "I can't hear you." I stick the tip in and slide it back out, causing her to groan.

"Fuck me." It's louder, but still not loud enough.

The tip goes a little further this time, but still not enough to satisfy either of us. "I think I hear you, but I'm still not sure."

"Fuck me! Please, please, please. Just fuck me!"

I slam into her, holding myself as far in as I can manage. She's so tight, and I've waited too long for this. I place my head on her shoulder and try to compose myself. This may be the last time I get to take someone for a while, and I need to make it last.

I start to thrust my hips and get up on my elbows to watch her face. She's wide-eyed looking at me for guidance. I kiss her, still pumping my hips. "I'm going to fuck you now."

She nods her head.

I sit up on my knees and pull her hips on my thighs. I look up to the headboard and back down to her. "Grab onto the headboard. You're going to need it."

The fear and hesitation that were once in her eyes have been replaced by excitement and desire. I know now she's ready. I barely wait for her to grip the headboard before I start thrusting. I can't hold back any longer.

It doesn't take long for her next orgasm to hit, but I'm a selfish bastard, and I want more of them. I need her to strangle my cock just like she'll be strangled before the night is over. It's new to her to be taken so hard and fast, but her body revels in it and is hungry for more. I'm willing to give it as much as it will take.

The third orgasm is almost too much for her, and she begs me to stop. I don't. Not yet. She got what she wanted, and now it's my turn.

I lie back down on top of her and move my hips slower. "I need just one more thing from you. Do you think you can do that for me?"

She barely nods her head. She's exhausted after the work-out I just put her body through, but I think she'll be up for one last ride.

I reach down between the mattress and the headboard and pull out the rope. I put it around her neck, and as I thought, she perks up. "What are you doing?"

"Shh. It's okay."

She struggles to get it off her neck, and I back up, sliding out of her. Once she sits up, it slides the board behind the headboard in place and locks her to her fate.

"It won't last forever." I get off the bed and discard the condom. "In fact, it will be over before you know it."

She starts to fight, but the rope tightens each time she moves. She's a quick learner and stops moving. "Just let me go. I promise I won't tell anyone."

The tears start, and I sigh. It's always the same thing. They think it's about them. "It can't be helped. I gave you what you needed and showed you how desirable you are. Now it's my turn to get what I need."

I stand at the foot of the bed and watch as she struggles again, causing the rope to get tighter. "It really is for the greater good. You're saving a life by taking her place. I can't bring myself to kill the one I need to, so I have to find others to fulfill my legacy."

I start to stroke myself as she gasps for air. I close my eyes and imagine the one who should die lying in my bed taking her last breath. I fall to my knees as the orgasm hits. It gets stronger each time I imagine her death. The end will come soon whether I'm ready to let her go or not. It has to. It should've already, but I'm too selfish to let her go.

CHAPTER 16

Brynn

I SIT UP AND GRAB the phone before it wakes Ben. "Hello?"

"There's another one." Hunter sounds just as tired as I do.

"Fuck." I throw the covers off, grab my robe, and head to the living room. "When?"

"I just got the call. Where are you?"

"I'm home. Come get me. I'll be ready in twenty." I hang up and turn, running into Ben's chest. I clutch the phone to my own. "God, you scared me."

"Who was that?"

"Hunter. There's been another murder. Go back to bed." I try to kiss him, but he backs away.

"Why did you leave the room to answer his call?"

"I didn't want to wake you. There's only one reason Hunter calls at four in the morning, and it isn't to chat." I walk by to get ready. I don't have much time, and even if I did, I don't have the patience for jealousy.

"It just looks odd to leave the room."

"It looks odd to let you sleep?" I walk into the bathroom, start the shower, and take my robe off. "Go back to bed. I don't have time to talk about this right now, but the next time I get a call, I'll make sure to wake you up so you hear every word." I get into the shower and close the curtain in his face.

When I get out of the shower, Ben's gone and so are his clothes. I shake my head and get dressed. I can't think about him or his attitude today. I need to focus on the job. I wonder who it is and what we'll find, if anything.

I walk out to the kitchen to start the coffee, but smell it's already brewing as I hit the hallway. When I turn the corner, I see Ben and Hunter talking.

"I thought you left." I accept the coffee Ben hands to me and the kiss, but turn so he kisses my cheek.

Hunter takes another drink of his coffee before he puts the mug into the sink. "I'll wait outside." He shakes Ben's hand. "Thanks for the fuel."

"Anytime." Ben turns to me. "I'm sorry. I know he's your partner, but it drives me nuts to think you want to hide things from me."

"When have I hidden anything from you?"

He shakes his head. "You haven't. I have no excuse. I'm sorry."

I take a drink and set the cup down before wrapping my arms around him. "There's nothing to hide." I kiss him. "Hunter is my partner and my friend, but unless it's sensitive information about the case, you can hear anything I say to him."

"I probably don't want to know much about these cases anyway."

"You're probably right." I kiss him again. "I've got to go."

"Let me know where to pick you up."

"Oh, I don't know if I'll be home tonight. It depends on what we find. We can go a couple of days without much sleep."

"So, the beach house?"

"Fuck." I look to the ceiling. "I'll see what I can do, but I don't think I'll be able to make it this weekend."

He takes a deep breath but nods. "I understand."

I really hope he does. I walk over and give him one more kiss before I leave, but I can tell he isn't happy. I'm not happy about it, either. I was looking forward to enjoying some downtime with him at the beach, but this is too important to walk away from.

I get into Hunter's car and put my head on the headrest. "Let me guess, fucking joggers found her."

"Yep. Buckle up so we can go." Hunter looks over at me. "It's a bitch to be in a relationship with this, isn't it?"

"How did Jamie deal with it?"

"She wasn't crazy about it, but she understood. I hope Ben understands."

"He will. If not, he isn't the one for me, is he?"

"You seem to be a little sober about that. Is everything okay?"

"Yeah, it's fine." I look out the window.

"That's really convincing. What's going on? I need you to be all-in at this crime scene. I can't have you distracted."

"I just miss going out." I look at Hunter. "It's a stupid

thing, isn't it? He's a homebody, and I like to go out."

"It isn't stupid, but you do need to compromise."

"And the jealousy!" I regret it the moment I say it.

"Jealousy?"

"He just doesn't like me talking to other guys, including you." I sigh when he glances my way. "I went to the other room when you called this morning because I didn't want to wake him. He, well, I don't know what he thought exactly, but it wasn't good."

"It's difficult. If we were two guys, it wouldn't matter, but in some ways, we're closer to each other than we will be to our significant others. Since we're of the opposite sex, that kind of closeness is a threat. It may not be sexual, but we do have an intimacy they can't understand."

"I guess you're right." I look out the window. "I just don't want to have to explain my every move."

He reaches over and holds my hand. "It'll get better."

We get to the crime scene, and the reporters have already set up shop. I sigh and shake my head. "Just once I'd like to be here before them."

"We should start investigating them and see if they're so quick to show up the next time."

"Are you kidding?" I get out and walk around the front of his car. "I don't want to talk to them any longer than I have to."

"You've got a point there." He looks around and takes a deep breath. "Body?"

I nod. "Body."

Crime scene, interviews, social media, phone records, and surveying her apartment and desk at her job have taken up the majority of the last four days. Hunter and I sleep when we can, but mostly in shifts and at the bureau.

We've gone home to shower and change twice in that time period and are still where we were when we first started—nowhere. All we have to show for our efforts is another grieving family who can't make sense of the crime and another young victim who fell for his charms.

We're combing over the video frame by frame again because it's apparent that's where she met him. He didn't stick to his usual pattern and call her days prior to her death. He called her less than an hour before she left the bar.

"Something happened to spark this. I just wish I knew what it was."

"I think it was pure opportunity." Porter sits at another monitor looking at a different angle with Lopez while Hunter and I watch another.

I hit *Pause.* Hunter hates it when I listen to him, but Porter has made good points. "How so?"

He pauses his video. "You see when he catches her eye. There's no recognition when she looks at him. She just likes what she sees."

"We can't see him, so we don't know that he's the one to catch her eye."

"Give me a break, Bennett. She isn't going to hit on two different guys. She likes this guy, and unfortunately for her, he's the killer. Unfortunately for us, he's sitting out of camera shot."

"I don't know." I shake my head. "I see a lot of guys I like, but I don't walk up to them."

"She's hesitant, but intrigued. This is what I was trying to tell you the other night."

Hunter sits up. "What other night?"

"Pick your boxers out of your ass because they're riding high, my friend." Porter turns back to me. "He's slick and calculated. You can see women looking his way all night, but he doesn't give them the time of day.

"He only zeros in on the one who looks controllable. Those other women wouldn't be complacent enough. He'd have his hands full, but this one . . ." He shakes his head. "This one is struggling to find her sexuality, and that's who he goes for."

Hunter dismisses his theory. "Not all of them have been like that."

He shrugs. "He's getting lazy, or he doesn't have time to make them controllable. I agree that things have changed for him, but it could be something as easy as his workload increasing causing him to have less time, or maybe he's getting a divorce and doesn't care about taking his time anymore." He straddles the chair and starts to watch his video again. "Either way, it's a matter of time before he fucks up or before he enters a bar that videos every fucking corner. This guy hiding is starting to piss me off."

The door slams open, and SAC Matthews walks in. "Porter, my office now!"

Porter jumps up and looks just as puzzled as we do. "What the fuck?"

"Don't question me. It'll be even worse for you. Now get your ass to my office." He looks around at the rest of us and scowls. "The rest of you head home."

"But—" Hunter points to the monitors.

"Do it. You all are stinking up the bureau. Go home, get cleaned up, and rest. You're going to need it."

The three of us sit and stare at each other. Lopez is the first to get up. "Hey, if the boss man tells me to go home, I'm not going to question it. I'm going to see my family."

I look at Hunter. "Any idea?"

"No, but I'm sure he deserves it." He stands. "Let's go."

I smell my shirt as I follow him out. "We don't really stink, do we?"

"Just like a girl to get that out of what just happened."

"Hey! I'm going to Ben's tonight. I don't want to go over there if I smell."

He turns and looks at me on the way out. "Take a shower and don't worry about it."

"It's a good thing he doesn't expect me off so soon. I'll be able to shower before I head over."

He opens his car door for me and walks to his side. "So shower with him. Problem solved."

"I don't like shower sex."

Hunter's eyes are wide as he gets inside and looks at me. "I didn't say anything about sex, but I love shower sex. Maybe you just haven't had the right partner yet."

My mind goes to Hunter in the shower, and I lick my lips. It's a good thing he's looking out the other window for traffic, or he would've seen that. I shake my head and look out my window.

"No, there's nothing sexy about the shower. You get water in places you don't want, the tile is always cold, and it's too damn slippery. Someone is bound to fall and break something."

"You are doing it wrong."

I narrow my eyes. "I don't think there's a right or a wrong way to have sex. I just prefer to do it out of the shower."

"What about the bathtub? You don't have to be in the shower."

"Water sloshes out all over the floor. You just like to make a mess."

He stops at a red light and looks my way. "I will say sex done right is messy at best, but a little spilled water shouldn't stop you from having one of the best nights of your life."

"It wouldn't stop me if the moment came up, but I'm not going to go into it thinking sex in a bathtub."

The light turns green, and he starts to drive again. "So, what do you like? What's your perfect idea of a roll in the hay?"

I look at him. "I don't think that's very appropriate."

He laughs and glances at me. "It isn't, but you brought up sex."

"How did I bring it up?"

"I just said to shower with him. You're the one who made it sexual."

"Whatever." I look out the window.

"Fine. If you're too afraid to answer, I won't hold it against you."

"Afraid?" I shake my head. "Listen, I'm not afraid of anything, but there are some things I need to keep private."

"Even from your best friend?"

"Yes, when my best friend is a dude, absolutely."

He laughs. "Suit yourself, but that could've been a great conversation."

"Yeah, for you." I hop out of the car and turn before I shut the door. "Thanks for the ride. I'll see you tomorrow."

I head inside and go straight to the bathroom. I really want that shower, but when I turn the water on, the pathetic trickle that comes out doesn't look very inviting. Ben's is so much more powerful than mine, and my shoulders are screaming for powerful after being hunched over a monitor all day.

I pack a bag, spray some perfume in case I do smell, and head to Ben's. My mind is occupied with shower sex, but I'm not sure I'm up for that tonight. It's best to try it when I have more energy. I'll shower alone tonight, but maybe I'll be more adventurous tomorrow.

I walk up to his door and wonder if I should've called first as I knock, but when Ben answers, his smile melts away my worry.

"Hi." He kisses me, and I lean against him. I'm so tired. "I didn't think I would see you tonight."

"You'll probably only see me sleep, but I wanted to be with you. I hope that's okay."

"Of course, it's okay. I love having you with me."

I wrap my arms around him and try to not freak out that the word *love* has come into play. It wasn't directed at me, but it was close. I'm not ready to say I love him yet, and I'm most certainly not ready to hear it.

"Are you hungry?"

"Starved."

He wraps his arms around me and walks me to the kitchen. "It's going to be a little while before dinner is ready, but do you want to take a nap or something? I just started it."

I smell my shirt again. "Maybe a shower."

"Sure." He leans down and kisses me. "I'm so glad you're here tonight."

I kiss him back and hold his face. "So am I."

I head upstairs and undress as I go. I throw the clothes I've taken off onto his bed and finish undressing before I head to his bathroom. I can't wait to have hot water beat my muscles into submission.

I turn the water on and wait for the right temperature before getting inside. It's heaven, and my shoulders thank me for coming here.

I take his soap and breathe deeply. I've missed Ben's scent. He isn't one for cologne, but who needs it when you buy soap that smells this good?

I start to lather up and look around. I smile thinking that Hunter loves shower sex. Reaching over, I feel the tile and shake my head. It's cold. It's always cold, and it's always the woman who's pushed up against it.

I run my hand over my breast and feel my nipple. I wonder what Hunter would do differently. He said I must have been doing it wrong when I gave him my complaints about it.

I shake my head and turn toward the water to rinse off. I shouldn't be thinking about Hunter in the shower. I remember the time he caught me showering, and I smile. If shower sex is his favorite, then it's no wonder he was sporting an erection for so long. Poor guy couldn't get any relief.

I close my eyes as the water runs over my body. I imagine Hunter joining me that day instead of running away. What would he have done? I move my head to the side to allow the water to hit my neck and imagine it's him kissing me. "Fuck, don't do this."

I grab the shampoo and wash my hair. I think about the last four days and the case, but nothing is getting the image of him in the shower with me out of my mind.

By the time my hair is washed, conditioned, and the rest of me is squeaky clean, my mind is filled with dirty thoughts of Hunter, and my body is screaming for a release. I look to the door and up to the ceiling. It's just a fantasy.

I run my hands down my body and feel where I ache the most. My clit is so sensitive to my touch; I know it won't take long. I place my other hand on the tile wall and steady myself as I rub my clit.

I close my eyes and imagine Hunter behind me, and I spread my legs a little more. I can almost hear him whisper. "That's it. Open up for me."

I slide a finger inside and moan. I add another finger and lean forward more on my other hand. I bend over as if Hunter is behind me, driving into me. "Oh." I work my hand faster and brush my thumb over my clit.

"Oh, God." I stay bent over, but bring my other hand to my breast as I imagine Hunter pinching my nipple. "Fuck." I spread my legs further and increase the speed of my fingers thrusting as I slide my other hand down to rub my clit with the same intensity. It doesn't take long to feel the orgasm pulse through my body.

I place both hands on the tile wall as I try to catch my breath. That was one of the most intense climaxes I've ever had, and he isn't even here to share it. Maybe there is something to shower sex after all.

CHAPTER 17

Brynn

WE'RE ALL SUMMONED TO SAC Matthews' office first thing the next morning. Hunter, Lopez, and I wait in silence for him to get here. We aren't waiting long.

"Porter's been removed from the case and is on paid leave." He doesn't even wait until he's seated to spring it on us. "And you three are a close second."

"Why us?" When Hunter's pissed, he doesn't mince words no matter whom he's talking to.

"Why didn't you come to me when you found him on that video?"

"He said you already knew."

"I did, but if you suspected something, you should've come to me."

"I told him not to." I'm not going to let Hunter take the

blame for hiding things from him. "I didn't want to ruin his reputation on a hunch that Hunter had."

"You know how bad that sounds, don't you?"

"I suppose it does, but I didn't believe Porter was the killer. Are you suspecting him now?"

"All I'm saying is there are things that don't add up. You will be reassigned to a different case, and you will hand over everything you have on this case. Is that clear?"

I touch Hunter's arm before he speaks. "Crystal."

"Get out and clean up the mess you've made. Hand over your shit and take a few days. I'll call you when I have a new assignment." We all stand and start to leave. "And, Williams, play nice with these guys taking over."

"Play nice?" At least he waits until we are clear of SAC Matthews' office. "He wants us to hand over all of our work to these assholes? Fucking ridiculous."

"Hunter, we'll talk about it later."

"If I hadn't listened to you, we wouldn't be in this fucking mess."

"Me?"

"Yes! I wanted to go to him earlier, but no, you didn't want to believe he was the killer. Do you believe it now?"

"No."

He stops throwing things into boxes and puts his hands on his hips. "No?" He scoffs before he starts throwing papers from his desk into boxes again. "Maybe it's good to take a few days off."

I glance at Lopez, and he's just as stunned as I am for the developments this morning. I really don't believe that Porter is capable of this, but isn't that what everyone says who's close to the killer? They never saw it coming.

"I'm out. This is bullshit. You can sit here and hand over the case if you want, but I'm fucking out."

I watch Hunter storm out as I sit back down to finish packing up our desks. He has every right to be angry, but he usually doesn't take his anger out on me. I hope that passes when I visit him later.

New suits walk in just as I finish packing Hunter's desk. I haven't seen them before, so they must've brought an entirely new division in who's never met our team. It makes sense, but it's going to make it harder to get info out of them. If they were people we've worked with before, I may have been able to stay in the loop.

I grab the bag out of the backseat and the case of beer I bought at the store. If anything can make Hunter feel better, it's free beer. His car is home, so I know he's here, but he won't answer the door. I try the handle anyway.

"Huh, lecture me about leaving my door unlocked." I push it open and walk inside to silence. I don't like silence. I place the beer and the bag onto the counter and take my firearm out as I head down the hallway. The main floor is empty, but I hear grunting coming from the basement the closer I get to the door.

I open and listen a little more before I call out, "Hunter? Are you decent down there?"

I hear him set weights down. "If I say no, will you go away?"

I walk down the stairs and put my firearm away. "I was

kind of worried about you. You left your front door unlocked."

"Yeah, well, I figured there'd be this annoying girl I can't shake no matter how mean I am to her." His smirk tells me he's not mad anymore, but he does feel guilty.

I look around his gym in his basement and back to his bare chest. "You've worked out enough frustration to have a civilized conversation yet?"

"No, but I don't have a girlfriend for the level of frustration I need released."

I smile. "I hear Porter's got a lot of free time on his hands. Maybe he can be your wingman at the bar."

Hunter gives me a disgusted look.

"Too soon?" I look at his chest again. "Can you put some clothes on?"

He grabs his shirt, wipes the sweat off his face and torso, and throws it across the room when he's finished. "Does a well-defined set of abs make you uncomfortable?"

"No. It makes me feel guilty. I brought you beer and snacks."

He shrugs and shakes his head. "Why didn't you say so?"

He's back to the fun-loving Hunter I'm used to, but we still need to talk about what he said to me. "Hunter, I'm sorry I kept you from going to SAC Matthews."

"Nah, I wouldn't have gone without something more concrete anyway." He gets off the weight bench and walks over to me, placing his hands on my arms. "I'm sorry I lost my shit back there. I don't like being taken off the case."

"Neither do I."

He bends down and hugs me. "I was actually worried he was going to split the team up. I don't want a new partner."

I wrap my arms around him. "I don't want one, either."

He pulls back and looks at me, but still hangs onto my arms. "I have a serious question. Will you answer it?"

I nod.

"Where is this beer you speak of?"

I smile. "Follow me."

"Anywhere."

We head upstairs, and he runs up to his bedroom to get a new shirt. I kind of like looking at his chest, but it is probably best to be fully dressed before the beer comes out. I take the beer and the bag of snacks to the living room to wait for him.

I throw my jacket onto the chair, sit on the sofa, and take the remote before he has a chance to decide what we'll watch. I probably should go home, but my days are spent with Hunter. I don't know what else to do.

Hunter comes back into the room and plops down next to me. "No girl shit."

"Girl shit?"

"Yeah. Nothing with lost puppies, kids, and definitely nothing about falling in love."

I nod and turn back to the television. "I second the falling in love."

"I thought things were going well for you two." He looks into the bag and goes straight for the chips. He hands the opened bag to me, but I turn it down. "No romance and no chips? Wow, what happened last night?"

I think back to the shower when I masturbated to his image, and my cheeks grow warm. I lean forward and open a beer.

"That must have been some night." He crunches a chip.

"This isn't helping my frustration level."

"Shut up. I have a question." I hesitate, but I need the answer. I'm really feeling guilty for my shower last night. "What do you consider cheating?"

"That's a hard question to answer. There are so many levels to that." He puts the chips down and sits up. "Did he cheat on you?"

"No." I groan, sit back, and cover my face. "I was thinking about someone else when I should've been thinking about him."

"Pfft. People do that all the time. I'm sure it would hurt his feelings if you told him you were fantasizing about someone else while he was doing the deed, but I bet he's got his own celebrity crushes going on. We all do."

I let him continue to think it was during sex instead of when I masturbated. "So, if Jamie had fantasized about someone else, you wouldn't have cared?"

"I'd almost bet she did. There was one time—"

I cover my ears. "I really don't need the details."

He starts talking louder. "There was this one time after the movies, we barely," he smiles and lowers his voice when I uncover my ears, "made it to the car before she attacked me. I don't care that she was thinking about the actor. I'm the one who got laid." He eats another chip. "The good old days."

"Why aren't you dating yet?"

"Because." He leans forward and looks into the bag. "Jerky! You love me."

"I do, but why aren't you dating yet? You don't want to be with Jamie anymore. It's been months since you broke it off. I can understand her hesitation to move on, but you?" I shake my head. "I don't understand."

"The same problem that came up with Jamie would just come up with the next girl."

"You don't know that."

He places another beer onto the table for each of us and picks up the rest of the pack. "I'm going to put this in the fridge."

I get up and follow him. "Talk to me. What's going on?"

"I broke it off with Jamie because I knew I would've cheated on her if given the chance."

"Wow." I never would've thought he would've been the cheating kind.

He leans onto the island and hangs his head. "I like someone, but she's with someone else."

"Have you told her?"

"No. I don't want to complicate her life. She seems happy. I've already broken one girl's heart."

"Who is it?"

He looks at me and stares a little too long. "It isn't important. She's with someone."

"You don't want to tell me?"

"Who did you fantasize about last night?"

I look away. "Good point."

Hunter laughs and heads back into the living room. "Are we really staying off this case?"

"Yes." My answer doesn't match the shake of my head. I'm not giving up this case that easily. Hunter smiles and pulls out some notebooks.

Hunter and I spend the day writing down everything we can remember. We may not have gotten every name right for witnesses or friends and family, but we do have a starting point to work from.

Since I have more time now, I decide to cook for Ben. It may not have been the best idea, but he's cooked for me so many times. I hope this passes as edible.

He walks in as I set the salad onto the table. "Hey, there."

I smile and accept his kiss. "Hey, yourself."

"It smells really good."

"Thanks." I head back to the kitchen to pull the steaks out, and when I bend over to reach into the oven, I feel him grab my hips and press into me. "I see you brought dessert."

I put the pan onto the stove and turn around to kiss him. I would love to be distracted and have dinner later, but I need to tell him about the case, and I'd rather eat while it's hot.

I pull back and smile. "Dinner's going to get cold."

"You're right." He helps me take the things to the table and grabs the wine. "How was your day?"

"Interesting. We've been taken off the case."

He drops the glass he was about to pour wine into, and it shatters onto the floor. "I'm so sorry."

"It's okay. They weren't special or anything." I walk over to grab the broom and dustpan.

"Why? Usually that means some sort of misconduct."

"They have their reasons, but it wasn't my misconduct." I tilt my head. "Well, maybe a little."

I start to sweep while Ben holds the dustpan. "Are you going to tell me about it, or am I going to read it in the papers?"

"Another good question. So far, it's out of the media, but

I hadn't thought of that. I guess it depends how far their investigation goes."

"Do I need to be your attorney?"

"No." I finish dumping the broken glass into the garbage and grab another wine glass before walking over to him and wrapping my arms around him. "They suspect Porter of being the killer."

He laughs so hard I let go of him. "That little punk?"

I smile. "Yes, that little punk. You don't think so?"

"I guess anything is possible, but he doesn't have what it takes to kill someone."

"Oh? You're the expert on this?"

He chuckles and shakes his head as he sits at the table. "No, but I equate killers with patience, common sense, and intelligence. He has none of those qualities."

"Common sense?" I sit next to him and accept the wine he's poured.

"Well, maybe common sense isn't the right term, but he's a hothead. He wouldn't think things through as one would think a killer would. He'd be sloppy, don't you think?"

"I suppose you're right."

He puts his knife down. "Do you believe he did it?"

"I don't know what to believe."

The mood shifts, and Ben scowls. "You aren't seeing him anymore." It isn't a question.

"There's really no reason for me to see him right now, but I can't say I won't ever see him again."

"You're still working this case. I know you. Behind the scenes or front and center, you won't give it up, but you will not see him. Is that clear?"

"Clear?" Dinner hasn't tasted too badly until now. I've lost my appetite. "I'm a federal agent. I know how to take care of myself, and if the investigation leads me to asking Porter questions, Hunter and I will ask Porter questions. If you don't like who I am or what I do," I point to the door as I finish my sentence, "there's the door."

He takes my hand in his and puts it back onto the table. "I'm sorry. I don't want anything to happen to you. It's one thing to think you're out there investigating criminals, but it's another to think you'll be face-to-face with one." He kisses my hand and goes back to eating dinner.

It's a little harder for me to be as forgiving of his outburst. "Don't you have faith in my ability?"

"Of course, I do. I don't want anything to happen to you. Agents get killed. You can't deny that."

"I don't, but this is my job. It's what I love to do."

"What are you going to do when you get married? What happens when you have children?"

"If marriage and children happen, it will be with someone who understands this is who I am."

"You won't change jobs when you get married?"

"I hadn't planned on it. To be honest, I haven't really given it much thought."

"Are you against it?"

"Not at all. My parents were very much in love, and I would consider marriage, but I don't think the time is right for me now."

This conversation is taking an uncomfortable turn. I think he's more ready for marriage than I am. I clear my throat and take my plate to the sink.

"It's Friday night. Let's do something fun."

"What did you have in mind?"

I turn to him, shrug, and lean against the counter. "Just a couple of drinks. Maybe a couple for me and just one for you."

He puts his plate into the sink behind me, leaning in and wrapping his arms around me. "I just get one?"

"Well, someone has to drive." I reach up and kiss him.

"We need to stock your bar so we both can enjoy some drinks."

I look at his chest and run my hands over his shirt. "It's more about going out. We can talk just like we talk here, but we aren't staring at the same four walls."

"But I can't kiss you in public as much as I can kiss you here." He leans down and kisses me.

"We can kiss plenty when we get back home."

He puts his forehead to mine. "I suppose I do owe you a night out. Do you have somewhere in mind?"

CHAPTER 18

Brynn

BEN LOOKS AT HIS WATCH and finishes his drink. He's bored and making me bored by watching him check the time every ten minutes. "Ben, we just got here." I look at my drink. "I haven't even finished half of this yet."

"I think it's better to stay home where I can hold you and not talk across the table in a crowded bar."

I look to my left and contemplate downing the last of my drink just to go home, but it would be to my home, and I would go alone. Maybe we're spending too much time together.

I narrow my eyes and tilt my head when I see Jamie across the room. She's laughing a little too loudly and hanging on some man who obviously has trouble with his eyes. They can't seem to look above her chest. When she stumbles, he promptly puts her onto his lap.

"Uh, I've got to take care of something." I get up and walk over to her. "Hey, Jamie."

Her smile and carefree attitude disappear when she sees me. "Fuck. I was having such a good time, too."

"I see that. I just wanted to say hi and see if you needed a ride home."

The dumbass behind her thinks he is getting an easy lay. "I've got her covered."

I look back to my table where Ben is checking his watch again and wish I had kicked back my drink before walking over here. There's no way I can finish it now. I look back to Jamie and see her kissing the dumbass.

"Okay, it's time to go home." I pull her off his lap and start to take her to our table. He stands and pulls on her other arm. I stop and take a deep breath before turning around to face him. I've officially run out of patience.

"She's having fun and wants to stay." He tugs on her hand again. "Aren't you, baby?"

"I really am." Her pout and overzealous nodding tell me she's too drunk to make this decision.

"It won't be fun in the morning, Jamie. I'm taking you home."

He tugs her out of my grip and wraps his arms around her. "I said I'll take her home."

I grab the nearest chair, twist it, and prop my foot up on the seat. Lifting my pant leg, I show the piece I have for back up and tilt my head. "Is a drunk chick really worth getting your balls blown off?" I point to Jamie. "I mean, she's beautiful, and I know you'd never get her while she's sober, but are you willing to risk your balls?"

He lets go of her. I shake my head, adjust my pant leg, and turn the chair back to the table before grabbing her hand again. I turn back to Ben to see him finish another drink. He was only supposed to have one, so now I get to drive. I tug her arm again to get her to move faster.

"Ben, where are your keys?"

He looks at Jamie and back to me. "I've called for a driver to pick us up." He signals for the waitress again.

"No, we need to go." I sit Jamie on the chair and grab my handbag.

"You just complained that I wanted to leave too early, and now you want to go?"

"I don't want to go, but . . ." I look at Jamie, who's finishing my drink, and back to Ben. "No, actually, you're right. I do want to go now. I need your keys."

"Why?"

"You can't drive."

"I'm perfectly capable of driving."

"You've had more than one drink. I'm not comfortable with that." I hold out my hand for his keys.

"What are you doing with her?" He nods to Jamie.

"Taking her home." I sigh and put my hand down. "Fine. Jamie and I will catch a cab."

"I'm not feeling well." Jamie puts her head on the table.

I sigh even harder and look up to the ceiling. "Maybe a cab is a good idea." I tuck my handbag under my arm and put her arm around my shoulders. "Good night, Ben."

"Wait. I'll go with you." He takes money out of his pocket and hands it to the waitress who finally shows up. He hands me his keys and picks Jamie up. "Let's go."

"Thank you."

He carries her to the car and helps to get her buckled. He sits in the back with her in case she does get sick, but for the moment there's just a lot of groaning coming from her. It's going to be a really rough day tomorrow for her, but I assume most of her days are rough since Hunter left.

I glance in the rearview mirror and wonder if I should call him. It wouldn't be fair to her to have him help her, and it wouldn't be fair to him to ask him, but I'm not sure she should be alone tonight.

I pull into her driveway and rush to unlock the door while Ben gets her out of the car. I step inside to find the light and take a step back when I see her living room. It's loaded with wedding stuff.

There's a kick at the door, and I turn to open it. "Sorry." I don't feel as bad when Ben walks inside and has the same reaction I did.

He turns with her still in his arms and looks at me. "She needs to get rid of this shit."

"That's the least of her worries right now. Let's find her bedroom."

"I thought you'd been here before."

"Yeah, but I didn't take the tour." I walk upstairs and turn lights on as I go. "Here. I think this is it."

Ben walks through the door, sets her onto the bed, and turns to me. "Now what?"

"Now you go downstairs and wait while I get her into pajamas."

"Are you going to leave her?"

Jamie answers him, "Why not? Everyone leaves me." She

turns and starts crying into her pillow.

"Oh, fuck me." I cover my face in frustration and stifle a scream. This night of fun and relaxation has been anything but. "Just go home, Ben. I'll call a cab."

"Nonsense. I'll stay as long as it takes. I'll just stay downstairs." He kisses my cheek, leaving me with Jamie.

"Where are your pajamas?" I head over to the dresser and open a couple of drawers. I turn to her. "Do you have pajamas?"

She points to a chair in the corner that appears to have a shirt on it. This doesn't look good. I walk over, and as I suspected, it's one of Hunter's T-shirts. I pick it up and put it right back down. "No, Jamie. You're not going to get over him by wearing his shirt to bed or keeping all that wedding shit in the living room."

I walk to her closet and look for one of her T-shirts to change her into. I know she's too wasted to even remember this conversation, but it will make me feel better to get it out. I've wanted to say these things to her for a while.

"It sucks to not be with the one you love, but he wasn't right for you. Why would you want to spend the rest of your life with someone who doesn't feel the same way? You'll find the man of your dreams. It just doesn't feel that way right now."

"It's easy for you to say. You've got two guys."

I motion for her to sit up and end up pulling her up myself. "Come on. The quicker you get dressed, the quicker you can get into bed. And what do you mean by two guys? I'm only seeing Ben."

"It doesn't matter. I realized something tonight, and I feel shitty for celebrating it."

"This is you celebrating? Honey, you're going to feel a lot shittier tomorrow about this celebration."

I help her out of her shirt and grab her other shirt while she unfastens her bra. I hold the opening of the shirt so she can stick her head through it and help her to guide her arms through, as well.

"I'm a terrible person." The drunk tears have started, and I put my palm to my forehead and try to keep my composure. I just want this night to be over.

"You're not a terrible person, Jamie. You're just going through a terrible time."

"I was happy because Hunter is unhappy. That's what I was celebrating." She unfastens her jeans and sits on the bed with tears running down her cheeks.

"What?" I coax her into shimmying out of her jeans, and I tug on the ankles of her pant legs. "Why is he unhappy?"

"I realized he finally knows how I feel."

"He's always known how you feel. He feels terrible for everything." I fold her jeans and throw them onto the chair with Hunter's shirt.

She stands up and tries to pull the covers back, but can't keep her balance. I wrap an arm around her waist and use my shoulder to keep her up while taking my other hand to turn her bed down.

"No, I mean he knows how I feel because he feels it, too."

"Jamie, I don't think he's getting back together with you."

"I know that!" She starts crying harder. "I know that."

"Then what were you celebrating!" It's wrong to raise my voice to someone who clearly isn't thinking right, but I'm so frustrated I can't keep it bottled up anymore.

"That he hurts just as much as me!" She crawls into bed and struggles with the covers until I help. "He's hurting just as much as I am, and it made me happy."

"Why is he hurting? He hasn't said anything."

"Because he can't have the one he loves, either."

"Okay, Jamie. Go to sleep and let's hope you'll feel better in the morning."

"You don't see it, do you?"

"See what? That you're drunk and delusional? Hunter isn't in love with anyone."

Her laugh is that of a woman gone mad—hollow and lifeless. "He's in love with you! He left me because he loves you too much to marry me, but he can't have you because you're in love with Ben! Do you get it now?"

I take a step back. "Hunter isn't in love with me."

"Just get out, Brynn." She rolls over and turns her back to me.

I walk out just as she starts to sob and quietly close her door. I slide down the wall outside her bedroom and sit on the floor, stunned by what she just told me. I had no idea I was the reason he broke up with her.

My mind shuffles through everything Hunter's said to me the past few months.

"I'm not in love with her."

"You are beautiful and desirable. Don't you ever doubt that again."

"I like someone, but she's with someone else."

I bring my knees up to my chest and hug them as I whisper, "Holy fuck."

CHAPTER 19

SHADOW

"TAKEN OFF THE CASE." I scoff while the same thoughts keep running through my mind ever since I was told. I throw the phone I used for the last victim across the room and watch it shatter as it hits the wall.

Pacing is all I can do these days. I thought everything would've been cleared up and things would go back to normal, but they haven't. If they think they're going to keep my girl and me separated, they've got another thing coming. I will keep up the chase whether they like it or not.

The only good thing that could've come from this isn't happening, either. She's still spending every fucking day with him. What do they have to talk about so much? There's no new case to work. They seem to have gotten a little too close. Maybe it's time to separate them for good.

Brynn

I place my hands on my knees and bend over as I try to catch my breath. I gave up running when I met Ben, spending all free time I had with him. Now, I need to run to clear my head. I'm not sure what to do about Hunter. If I tell him and it isn't true, it'll embarrass both of us and cause him to be angry with Jamie. She doesn't need an angry Hunter after her.

If I do tell him that I know and it's true, I have no idea how to handle that. I stand up and look to the sky. I've run my route twice already, and I'm exhausted, but I take off running again.

Before Ben, I would've jumped at the chance to be with Hunter. He's everything I thought I wanted in a man—aggressive, confident, and rugged. However, Ben has opened my eyes to a different kind of man. He's kind, and he likes to take care of me. I didn't think I'd be the type of woman who wanted to be taken care of, but now that it's happened, I like it.

Halfway through my run, I stop and sit on a bench in the park, leaning my elbows on my knees to put my face in my hands. I'm not sure what to do or how to handle it. If I ignore it and Jamie tells him . . . I sit back, still covering my face and let out a frustrated scream.

"So, this is what Bennett is like on her downtime."

I look to my right and see Porter sitting there. "You have no idea what I'm like on my downtime."

"You're right. You never let me get close enough to you." He looks my way. "Not near as close as Williams does."

"He's my partner. I trust him with my life. Of course, we're going to be close." I may be a little more defensive of our relationship than I need to be, but I don't like his tone.

He faces forward again. "There was another one."

I cross my arms and look to the sky. "I've been staying away from the news."

"Aren't you going to ask me if I did it?"

"What makes you think I'd believe you even if you did answer?"

He leans forward. "Good point."

"What do they have on you?"

"Not much."

"It has to be something to get all of us thrown off the case."

"You guys got thrown off the case because you didn't come forward when you saw me on the video." He sits back and extends one of his legs. "I guess SAC Matthews didn't like my confession about being at a couple of the bars the night some victims were killed. He thought it was too coincidental, so he launched his own private investigation on me."

"What did he find?"

"Bitter ex-girlfriends." He stands and starts pacing. "Have you heard of autoerotic asphyxiation?"

"You're kidding, right?"

"It was something an ex and I played around with when we were younger. She told them she broke it off when she got scared." He shakes his head. "I broke it off because her best friend was hotter and wanted to fuck."

He sits back down and grips the seat of the bench. "I'm an asshole, but I'm not a killer." He looks at me. "Brynn, you have to help me clear my name. I'm not going down for this."

I get out of the shower and wrap a towel around my body. I bend over to wrap another towel around my hair and stand up. I miss working cases, but I'm starting to enjoy taking my time getting ready now.

I need coffee after the last couple of days and especially after the encounter with Porter this morning. I'm not sure what to believe anymore. I've heard autoerotic asphyxiation can be addictive, but it's more so for the person whose orgasms are intensified instead of the person who's administering the choke hold.

I round the corner to get my much-needed coffee and scream when I see Hunter. It startles him and causes him to splash coffee onto his hand. "Fuck." He sets the mug down, shakes his hand, and runs cold water over it.

"What are you doing here?"

"It's Monday. I thought we were still working the case."

"Yes, but I locked the door."

He looks at the door and back to me while he dries his hands with the dishtowel. "It was unlocked."

I notice the flowers on the table and point. "Did you?"

"No, they were here when I walked in."

We both look at each other and back to the flowers. "How did—" I look at the door and start to walk toward it.

"I'll look to see if it was messed with. You look at the card." He looks down my body and up to my head. "I don't think you want to go to the door like that."

I look down and groan. "I would've gotten dressed had I known you were out here." I walk over to the flowers and look at them, plucking the card out of the middle. "They look nice."

"You don't know what kind they are, do you?"

"Flowers aren't really my thing, but I can still appreciate them."

"Your door looks fine. You probably forgot to lock it." He nods my way. "What's the card say?"

"'We won't be apart for long.'" I look at Hunter. "It isn't signed."

"Ben's a real romantic, huh?"

"Well, he didn't want to leave this morning." I look at the card again. "It doesn't say where they're from."

"You want to find out what the flowers are, don't you?"

"No, I want to know why they entered my home without permission."

"Maybe Ben brought them."

"He had a big meeting, or he would've stayed in bed." I look at Hunter. If he is in love with me, I can't say things like that anymore. "Sorry, I didn't mean—"

"It's okay." He waves me off. "You're a couple. You're going to be in bed. You're concerned about this, aren't you?"

I look at the flowers again. "I know I locked the door. I *know* it."

Hunter picks up my phone and hands it to me. "There's only one way to find out if Ben brought them in himself or not."

I take my phone and text him while I head to the bedroom to get dressed. Hunter sits on the sofa and turns the television on. At least I won't have to worry about him waiting on me.

He's made himself at home.

I turn before I shut my bedroom door and look at him. I haven't talked to him since Jamie's confession Friday night, but I don't sense any awkwardness. If she had told him what she told me, I'm sure he would've felt awkward. At least, I do.

I shake my head and go into my bedroom to get ready, but I need to finish my text to Ben first. A simple *thanks for the flowers* should be enough to know if he's the one who sent them.

It doesn't take long before my phone rings. "Hello."

"Did I mess up?" Ben sounds frantic.

"No, but what about your meeting?"

"We're on a break. Did I forget your birthday?"

"No." I look to the ceiling. "You didn't send the flowers?"

"No, you really got flowers?" There is a long pause. "And you thought I sent them?"

"Well, yes. Who else would send me flowers?"

"Was there a card?"

I sigh. "It just said we won't be apart for long. I thought it was you because you had such a hard time leaving this morning."

"I wish I had thought of it, but it wasn't me. It wasn't signed?"

"No."

"Who delivered them?"

"Well, I kind of hoped you had."

"No, I mean the company."

I switch hands when my towel starts to fall. "They were on my table when I got out of the shower. Before you yell at me, I did lock my door. I wasn't expecting anyone."

"I'm coming home."

"No, finish your meeting. Hunter's here. I'll be fine."

"This is bullshit. I want to be the one to take care of you."

"Tonight. Take care of me tonight."

He lets out a slow, steady breath. I know he's battling this in his mind, but he has to know that I'll be fine. "Okay, but you need to keep me updated. Text me the minute you know anything. I don't like this at all."

"I promise. I'll keep you posted. I'm sure it's nothing. In fact, I bet it's the wrong address."

I hang up with Ben and finish getting dressed. I need to have this discussion with Hunter, but telling him I met with Porter this morning isn't going to go over easy after these flowers.

I ease out into the living room and sit next to Hunter. He glances my way a couple of times before turning the television off. "Well?"

"He didn't send them."

He sits up and tosses the remote onto the coffee table. "Now you've got my attention." He gets up and looks the flowers over again. When he can't find anything there, he heads to the door to look at it again.

"Maybe they sent them to the wrong address."

He looks my way, but doesn't believe me. "I'm checking the perimeter. Are you going to call this in?"

"There's nothing to call in. We already both handled the card and the flowers. Let's not jump to any conclusions. It could be an honest mix-up."

"I still don't like it."

"That isn't everything you won't like."

He stops halfway out the door and comes back inside. "What haven't you told me?"

"I met with Porter this morning."

He slams the door and storms over to me. "Without me? You really do have a death wish, don't you?"

I back up. "It was on my morning run. It isn't as if I had set up the meeting. I sat on a bench to rest, and he sat next to me. What was I supposed to do?"

"The first thing you do is text me that you're with him! That's what we've always said. We'll text each other even if it's just a period to get word to the other that we're in trouble. And what about after your little meeting? You were too busy to clue me in then?"

"You're right. I'm sorry."

He's furious with me, and he has every right to be. "I'm going to walk outside to calm down, but when I get back, you're telling me everything you know."

I nod as he slams the door. I would be furious with him if he talked to Porter without me, but it isn't as if I had set out to meet him. He just showed up. I shake my head and grab my laptop.

While I wait for Hunter to check the outside, I look up info on autoerotic asphyxiation. I know what it is, but I don't know much about it. I would bet money that Hunter doesn't, either.

My eyes are wide after reading some things, but it's the videos that make me uncomfortable. I jump and close the laptop when Hunter comes back inside.

"Are you watching porn while I look out for your safety?"

"Uh, not exactly. Did you find anything?"

"Nothing as interesting as you seem to have. I did call the flowers in, though. I want them looked over." He points to the laptop. "What were you watching?"

"What do you know about autoerotic asphyxiation?"

"I know it's dangerous and something I'd never be able to do to a woman. I'd rather not have it done to me, either. Why?" He sits next to me on the sofa and takes the laptop from me.

"Porter said that an ex told investigators that she broke up with him because he scared her with this. It would make sense that this could be the cause of death. The killer could feel guilty for the accidental deaths, and that's why he displays them with so much respect."

"I don't buy it. I think he's killing them to kill them. He wouldn't take trophies if it were an accidental death."

I nod. "That's true."

I watch as Hunter lifts the laptop screen and presses *Play*. As much time as I've spent with Hunter and as much television we've watched together, we've never seen actual sex together. There's the appearance of sex in movies or television, but there's no denying what these people on my laptop are doing. It's a little uncomfortable.

I look over at him, and his eyes are just as wide as mine were when I watched it. "Holy shit." He looks at me. "Have you ever tried this?"

I shake my head. I look back down to the laptop that's in Hunter's lap and see he's getting turned on by the video. I get up. "I'm getting something to drink. Do you want something?"

"Whatever you're getting is fine. Thanks."

He can't or won't tear his eyes away from the laptop. I think I've created a monster. I realize he isn't getting much action now, but it's awkward to know how he feels about me and sit next to him while he's so turned on. If I'm being honest, it turns me on, too. I'm afraid to sit that close to him in this state.

CHAPTER 20

Brynn

B EN TALKED ME INTO GOING to the beach house with him. It was long overdue anyway. We'd talked about coming out for a while, but things kept getting in the way.

I smile when I feel him kiss my neck. I can get used to waking up like this. "Hi."

He whispers into my ear, "Good morning, beautiful."

He's made me breakfast in bed each day we've been here, and today is no different. I sit up and accept the tray he's offering.

"You're too good to me."

"I'd do more if I could."

I touch his face and smile. I believe him, but he already does so much. "What's on the agenda today?"

"Well, since we only have a couple of days left, I'd rather

stay in bed all day, but I think you want to go out, so maybe shopping?"

I nod. "I could stand to check out the stores. In fact, shopping makes me very tired. I probably would need a lot of recovery time in bed when we're finished."

"Then shopping it is." He kisses my forehead since I've taken a bite right before he kissed me. "I'm jumping in the shower, but I promise not to use all the hot water."

I think about the shower sex conversation with Hunter and the fantasy I played out in Ben's bathroom. I take another bite. I need to stay away from shower sex for a while.

My phone buzzes, and I reach over to grab it, careful not to spill the tray. It's Hunter. "Hey, what's up?"

"When are you coming back? I'm bored."

"Bored? I thought you and Lopez were going to look into a few things while I was gone."

"We did. I'm still bored. Lopez isn't as fun as you."

"I'm going to tell him you said that."

"I already did. Really, when are you back?"

"We're coming back Sunday night. Ben could only get one week off."

Ben comes out of the bathroom with a towel around his waist and narrows his eyes at me. "Who's that?"

I put the phone to my chest to answer him. "Hunter."

"Well, eat up. I need to get you tired so we can get back to bed." He smiles and grabs his clothes to get dressed.

I put the phone back to my ear. "I'll talk to you Monday, okay? I'm sure you can find plenty to keep you occupied until then."

"If I have to."

I hang up and smile. I miss him, too.

It's been a great day of food and shopping, and it's times like these that really remind me what a great guy Ben is. It's the sitting at home staring at each other that I have a problem with.

I may have been teasing about needing recovery time in bed, but after shopping as long as we have, I really am going to need it. I fall face first onto the bed.

I feel the bed dip next to me and feel Ben come close to my ear. "Are you telling me that I out shopped a woman?"

I turn my head to look at him, but move nothing else. "If you want people to think you're the girl in the relationship." I smile.

He laughs and lies down with me, holding his arm open so I'll snuggle up next to him. "I'll be whatever you want me to be."

I move into his arms and place my head on his chest. "Just give me a few minutes to sleep, and I'll rock your world when I wake up."

He wraps both of his arms around me. "I'm sure you will. Take as long a nap as you need. I'm not going anywhere."

He starts to rub my back, and I close my eyes. I place my hand on his chest and feel his muscles. They flex when he moves his hands up and down my back. I slide my hand under his shirt to feel his muscles against my fingers instead of through the shirt. I'm not so tired anymore.

I lift myself up on my elbow to hover over him and look at him. He arches an eyebrow before I lower my head and kiss him. I straddle him and never break the kiss when he sits up, wrapping his arms around me.

 We struggle out of our shirts and toss them aside before kissing again. He makes quick work of my bra, and it's added to the shirt pile. Our kiss is getting more frantic as he cups my bare breasts, and I unfasten his pants.

"I want you so much." Ben's never been worked up this much, and I'm excited for the possibilities.

I stop kissing and look at him. "Take me."

He flips us around and places me on my back. I weave my fingers in his hair as he sucks on my nipple. He sucks and bites until it's painful and moves to the next. I reach down and unfasten my pants. I need him in me now.

He takes the hint and helps me out of the rest of my clothes, but moves my hands away from his pants. He slides down and spreads my legs. If he gives my clit half the attention he gave my breasts, I'm going to be in trouble.

I grip the sheets and arch my back. "Oh, God."

He sucks hard and then caresses me with his tongue. The sensations are magnified when he sucks to a painful point and flicks with his tongue again.

I run my fingers through his hair and hold him to me a little longer. I need to be filled, but the desire he's pulling out of me is incredible. "Don't stop."

He takes two fingers and enters my pussy, searching out that spot that makes me scream. It doesn't take him long to find it. "Fuck." I move my hips and try my best not to squeeze my legs together.

I give a slight tug on his hair, but he won't stop licking and finger fucking me. I abandon his hair and move my hands to the headboard. The buildup he's giving me is intense, and I need to hang onto something I can't hurt.

"Ben!" My legs are shaking. He goes faster with his tongue and his fingers. "Oh, God. Don't stop." He switches to sucking my clit again, and I explode. "Fuck! Yes! Don't fucking stop."

I sit up, placing my hands behind me and grinding myself into his face. I need more. "Fuck me, Ben. I need to feel you inside me."

He looks up, and his eyes are dark. Where was this Ben hiding? I slide over to the nightstand and grab a condom while he finishes undressing. I sit up against the headboard and motion for him to come to me. I want to put the condom on this time.

He gets back onto the bed and walks on his knees to me. I wrap my hand around him and stroke his cock. He doesn't let me do this too often because he usually can't wait to get inside me, too, but I'm taking the opportunity to rock his world as he rocks mine.

I put the condom on the bed next to me and guide him to my mouth. Wrapping my lips around him, I flatten my tongue against the underside of his cock and hear him hiss. He needs to hang on tight because I've only just begun.

I move my mouth faster up and down the length of his dick, hitting the back of my throat. I stop every few strokes to suck. Each time I stop, I increase the intensity of the suction. He's going to know what it's like to be sucked to a painful pleasure.

He grips the headboard and groans. "I'm not going to last much longer if you keep doing that."

I suck harder one last time and swear I hear the headboard crack under his grip. He reaches down for the condom and pulls out of my mouth. He moans as he slides it on and hangs his head.

"I'm so fucking sensitive I almost lost it from the condom." He backs up a little and pulls my legs to slide me down the bed. Hovering over me as he leans on his hands, he smiles a wickedly sexy smile. "I'm going to fuck you."

I smile innocently and say, "Yes, please."

He reaches down and thumbs my still sensitive clit to make sure I'm ready for him right before he slams into me. I arch my back, and he takes that as an invitation to suck my breast again.

I rock my hips with his and hold his head to my breast. "Oh." I can't breathe or think.

He kisses his way up to my mouth, but never slows his hips. I wrap my arms around him and hold him to me. I need more of this Ben. "Don't stop."

I reach down and squeeze his ass, urging him to go faster. This is consuming me, and I can't get enough. I want more.

I think back to the videos Hunter and I watched and wonder if this is how those women felt. Were they okay to try strangling during sex to achieve more? Is that how he talked them into it? I hold Ben's face to make him look at me.

He slows down and looks worried. "Everything okay?"

I can't believe I'm going to ask him to do this, but I want to try it. I need to try it. I need to experience what those women experienced if this is how they died. I need to be placed in their situation to understand it. "If I ask you do to something, will you do it?"

He narrows his eyes. "That depends."

I take a deep breath and tell him. "I want you to choke me."

He slides out of me and sits up on his knees. "What?"

"It's to heighten the—"

"I know what it's for." He rubs his face. "I didn't know you were into that."

"I'm not. I'm just curious." I sit up and wrap my arms around him to pull him back down. If I tell him it's for the case, he won't do it. "Please. I won't ask again. I just need to do it this once."

I reach down and guide him to me and wait for him to slide back inside me. He looks into my eyes, down to my neck, and back to my eyes. He moves his hips and slides inside me again, but doesn't go as fast as he was before.

He places his forehead to mine as he picks up the pace. "I don't want to hurt you."

"You won't."

Keeping his forehead to mine, he looks into my eyes. He starts to move his hips faster. "Punch me, slap me, or rip my face off to get me to stop if you can't say stop."

I nod, getting more excited at the possibility that he'll go through with it. I start to move my hips with his, encouraging him to fuck me like before.

He traces my neck with his finger before wrapping his hand around my throat. He kisses me and moves his hips even faster while his hand gets tighter. I stop kissing him when I can no longer breathe.

He fucks me harder as his hand tightens even more, and he moves his other hand to my clit. I'm trying to breathe, but no air is coming in. I grip the sheets as I feel my orgasm starting. I move my hands to his back and claw. The pain he feels makes him tighten his hand even more and causes him to pump his hips at an insane speed as his fingers pinch my clit. It's all I need to spiral into the most intense climax I've ever had. I only hope I remember it as I start to pass out.

I try to shove him off me, but he's lost to finding his own orgasm. I struggle to stay awake and manage to claw at his hand and slap his face, even though it isn't as hard as I would like. I feel my body go limp as darkness takes over.

CHAPTER 21

Brynn

I LOOK AT THE BIG ugly yellow bruise that's wrapped around my throat. I asked him to do it. It was stupid. We had no idea what we were doing. I can't fault him for how far it went, but we're both struggling with it.

I wasn't out for too long before he got me to wake up again, and my body still buzzed from the intense orgasm he gave me when I came to, but I never want to go through that again. It was terrifying, and I think of the women who were killed that way.

I swipe the tear that fell away and reach for my scarf. I'm seeing Hunter today, and I need to hide the bruise. It isn't light enough to just use makeup, so I have to accessorize and hope he doesn't tease me about the scarf. Normally, I'd just take it off when he did that, but I can't do that today.

There's a light tap on the door, and I know Ben is on the other side of it. It isn't his fault we tried it. I asked for it, but the fact he didn't stop bothers me. I know he didn't mean anything by it and that he feels immense guilt, but the experience has shaken me.

I open the door and look at him. He leans in to kiss me, and I allow the quick peck, but I don't stay for long. I walk out and get my much-needed morning coffee.

Ben is slow, but he follows me. "I need to get to the office. I'll call you later and finalize plans for tonight."

"Okay. That sounds good. Have a good day." I take a sip of coffee when he steps toward me. He nods and walks out.

I hear conversation outside when I walk to the living room and know that Hunter must be here. I check my scarf to make sure it's still in place and sit on the sofa. I look over to Hunter when he walks in and try to smile.

He smiles back and heads to the kitchen for his coffee. "How was the beach house?"

"It was amazing." It truly was amazing until the night we left. After I woke up, I couldn't stay with Ben in that bed anymore and needed to get home.

Hunter comes in and sits next to me. "So, I should look into buying one?"

I smile. "Did you win the lottery while I was gone?"

"What's on the agenda today?"

"How far did you and Lopez get?"

He takes a deep breath and shrugs. "It's hard to say. We talked to the ex-girlfriend. I think she's lying about Porter. They definitely played the game, but I don't think she was an unwilling participant. She had photos from what she said was their time together, but you can't prove it.

"It's just that when we told her that he was being inves-tigated for the murders of these women, she seemed shocked and regretful. It didn't help that Lopez told her she could go to jail for lying."

"Yeah, that will make her stick to her story."

"It still doesn't clear him of the crimes. He still could have the desire to do it and get carried away."

I take a sip of coffee. It's harder to discuss this than I thought. Ben got carried away, so I can see how normal people would.

"Did you guys have a fight?"

I shake my head. If he finds out I asked Ben to do this for the case, he'd kill me. "No, we haven't fought." I clear my throat. "You know how it is when you spend a lot of time with someone. You tend to get on each other's nerves. It'll be better in a few days."

"Okay." He rubs his hands on his legs. "Oh, I talked to Jamie, and she said you helped her out of a tricky situation."

My morning just keeps getting better. "It was no big deal."

"To her it was." He nudges me with his arm. "To me, too. Why didn't you tell me?"

"Honestly, I didn't want you to get pissed at her. I'm sure she felt bad enough the next morning to not have to deal with your cranky ass about it, too."

"She's a grown woman who can make her own deci-sions." He turns his head and looks at me. "But I do thank you for looking out for her."

"Why did she tell you anyway?"

"She went looking for you at the bureau and then called

me when they said you took leave."

I raise my eyebrows in surprise. "Why was she looking for me?"

"To thank you." He laughs. "I guess she went back there a couple of nights later, and he tried to hit on her again. She didn't realize what an asshole he was."

"I'm glad I was there for her."

He puts his hand on my knee. "I'm glad you were there for her, too. When she told me about it, my first thought was this case and what if that nut job had been there. I don't think I could've handled her being killed like that. The thought of her scared and helpless rips through me."

My eyes start to water, and I try to sip coffee to keep them at bay. It doesn't work. I lean forward and place the mug onto the coffee table and lean on my elbow on the arm of the sofa to look out the window. I need to get this weekend out of my mind.

Hunter squeezes my knee. "When are you going to tell me what's wrong?"

The dam breaks, and he pulls me into his arms as I sob. I climb onto his lap, straddling him, and burying my face in his neck as I cling to the front of his shirt. I don't break under pressure often, but I'm glad my best friend is here to help me when I do. Only, I don't want to tell him what's wrong, and I don't think he'll let me keep it to myself.

He rocks me while his big arms surround me, protecting me until the tears are more under control. "Please, talk to me. I need to know you're okay."

It's pointless because tears are still falling, but I try to wipe them away anyway. "I'm okay."

I try to sit up, but he doesn't let me go far. I look down when he reaches up and pulls the scarf off my neck. He puts my chin between his thumb and index finger and lifts. I close my eyes and start crying again when he lets out a slow, steady breath.

"I told him to do it."

He leans down and kisses my neck. It's unexpected, and I open my eyes. I shouldn't, but I tilt my head to give him better access and wrap my arms around him. He gives me light, feather-like kisses until he reaches the other side of my neck. Once he starts to make his way back across, he lays me down and his kissing intensifies.

I shouldn't allow this. I still need to work things out with Ben, but the way I feel right now with Hunter is too good to stop.

He moves up to my mouth, and I don't hesitate to kiss him back. I wrap my leg around him when he starts grinding his hips into me. He cups my breast through my shirt and squeezes. My hips start to move with him. God, I want this man.

He reaches down and pulls my other leg up and around him so when he stands up he takes me with him effortlessly. We kiss until we reach the bedroom. As he looks into my eyes, we're both breathing hard, turned on, and we both know it's wrong. I slide down his body, and he lets me go.

I touch my lips and look at his. "I'm so sorry."

He shakes his head, still trying to catch his breath. "*I'm* sorry. I just meant to comfort you." He holds my face and leans in for a soft, quick kiss before he leaves.

I've been avoiding life and mail since the weekend with Ben and the morning with Hunter. I've stopped talking to both of them until I can figure out what I want. I still don't know what I want, but I owe it to Ben to give him another try. We were still together when Hunter and I kissed. It was just at a weak moment when I allowed it to happen.

Ben's in the kitchen making dinner while I attempt to go through my mail. He wants things to get back to normal as quickly as possible. It's sweet, but it's going to take more than making dinner and bringing my mail to me for me to get back to normal.

However, looking through the mail does bring a sense of normalcy back to life. At first, anyway. It's mostly bills and junk mail, but there are three cards that catch my attention. I sit up when I open the first one.

I'M STILL
HERE,
WAITING.

It's on cardstock paper, cut to size with one of the earrings from the victims hanging from it. I snap a photo and send it to Hunter before opening the second envelope.

THE CHASE ISN'T OVER.

Ben comes in, wiping his hands on a towel. "Dinner's almost finished." He looks at me while I snap another photo. "What's that?"

"Don't touch that!" He jumps back when I yell, but I don't want anyone but me to touch these. "I'm sorry, but dinner's going to have to wait."

He comes around while I open the third and reads it over my shoulder.

COME FIND ME BEFORE I FIND YOU.

"What the fuck is this, and what's with the one earring on all of them?"

"Ben, I need you to stay calm about it."

"Calm?" He throws the dishtowel on the chair. "When were you going to tell me this shit was happening?"

"I didn't know it was happening until right now." I pick up the phone and answer it.

Hunter sounds pissed. "Is that what I think it is?"

"Yes, there's a third that I couldn't send you yet."

He sighs. "What does that one say?"

"'Come find me before I find you.'"

"Well, that's just fucking stupid. He already *found* you if he's sending you shit. I'm on my way."

I hang up and turn to Ben. "These need to be taken in, so Hunter's coming over to get them."

"I don't like this. You're not staying here anymore. When

he leaves, we're leaving. You're staying with me, and that's final."

I don't argue with him because I'm a little freaked out. So much has happened since the flowers that I almost forgot about them until the cards showed up in my mail.

I shiver and feel Ben's arms wrap around me. "We'll figure this out."

I turn and wrap my arms around him. I sure hope so.

Hunter brought the new investigators with him when he came to look at the cards and earrings. He was right to bring them with him. It needs to be handled by people who aren't close to it.

SAC Matthews had been called and also came out to my place to see for himself what was happening. He told Hunter and me to be in his office first thing this morning. That's where we are now—waiting on SAC Matthews.

Hunter reaches over and puts his hand on my knee to stop it from bouncing. "Everything will be fine."

SAC Matthews comes in and sits on the edge of his desk, looking straight at me. "Any idea who this could be?"

"No."

"Okay, well, I'm officially taking you off active duty until this is figured out."

I sit up. "But that can take forever!"

He stands and looks at me. "Do you not have faith in your fellow FBI agents?"

I look at Hunter and close my eyes. "I have faith."

"Good." He turns to Hunter. "Your new duty is her." He points to me.

"You want me to protect her?"

"No, I want you to make sure she doesn't investigate this case anymore." He walks round his desk and sits. "You both are on paid administrative leave as of this moment."

Hunter sits up and takes a deep breath before sitting back in the chair. We didn't become FBI agents to sit on our asses and wait for others to do our jobs.

He points to both of us. "If I catch either of you sniffing around this case again, you'll be out of jobs. Is that understood?"

Hunter sits up straight again to defend me. "She wasn't even in town when I interviewed people."

"That may be, but she's back in town now, isn't she?" He looks at both of us and waves us out of his office. Before we leave, he has one last piece of advice. "Just because you two are off a case right now doesn't mean you can get soft. I expect you back to work as soon as this shit settles. Stay prepared."

I turn back and look at him. "Are you saying you're close to solving the case?"

"Good day, Bennett."

Hunter and I share glances before we walk outside. We're quiet until we reach our cars, and then the awkwardness creeps in. I'm the first to speak. "You don't really have to babysit me."

"It wouldn't be babysitting. We spend our days together anyway."

I look down to the concrete and back up to him. "I'm not sure what to do about the other day."

"I'm sorry about that." He looks at my neck. "It's cleared up, so that's good."

"Yeah, really good before he saw it."

He nods, and there's more silence. I open my car door to throw my bag in and when I turn to him, he's walked up to me.

"You said once that you haven't been running since you started seeing Ben. What else haven't you been doing?"

I shrug. "Pretty much everything. When I'm with Ben, we just talk or watch something. I don't work out anymore." I look down at myself. "Why? Can you tell?"

"Stop. I didn't mean that. It's just your cardio and strength training can't really be sacrificed for this relationship. You need to keep yourself in top shape in case some psycho decides to come after you." He smacks his forehead. "Wait! Someone already is."

"Fine. I'll start working out again."

"Good. Be at my house every day with comfortable clothes, and I'll get your ass whipped back into shape." He smacks my ass as he walks back to his car. "Let's go. We start today."

CHAPTER 22

SHADOW

GLARE AT HUNTER WHEN he hits her ass. He needs to be taught a lesson on where to keep his hands because they shouldn't be on her. That isn't for him to touch. I know he broke his engagement off because he's in love with Brynn. I wonder if he's told her yet.

They get into separate cars, but head the same direction. I start my car and follow. It looks as if they're heading to Hunter's. I need to keep my cool and stay back so they don't see me. Years of training on how to follow people go right out the window when I'm following her. I need to keep my head on straight and not get so close.

It's just so hard to stay away. I have to. It isn't time yet.

Brynn

"Are you trying to kill me?" I grit my teeth as my legs burn from the wall squat he's making me do. We've been through so many different exercises, and he's running circles around me. Not that I could ever keep up, but I did a better job of faking it before I started dating Ben than I do now.

"Just a few more seconds." He puts a five pound hand weight on each leg.

"Hunter!"

"You can handle it. You're just in pansy mode since you haven't done this for so long." He takes the weights off and signals that I can get up.

I stand and rub my legs. I really need to sit down. I will be better for this training we're going through, but at the moment I don't care too much for it.

"My turn." He takes a spot on the wall and eases into position. He raises his eyebrow when I scoff. "What?"

"You make it look too easy, and I hate you."

He blows kisses. "You'll love me when this is how we prefer to watch television."

"Oh, no. I'm not watching anything sitting in an invisible chair. That'll be a table for one, sir."

"Well, I get bored when I sit like this."

"Why don't you put any weights on your lap?"

He looks at the weights and back to me. "Go grab some weights for me." He watches as I look to the five pound ones and back to him. "I'd need the fifty pound weights if you want it to matter."

I look over to the weight bench and contemplate getting them, but I'm not sure my jelly limbs will allow me to carry fifty pounds. "You want fifty pounds for each leg? Isn't that a little much?"

"You don't think I can handle it?"

I look at Hunter, unsure if it was a challenge or not. I smile and walk over to him. I need to sit anyway. I'll kill two birds with one stone. I straddle his lap and sit on his knees. "Let's see how long you last now."

"I can go all night."

My breathing picks up as I realize the position we're in and the innuendo he just made, and I look down to his lips. I start to stand, but he grabs my hips and pulls me further up his lap.

"You were sitting on my knees. If you want to be effective, you need to sit on my thighs." When he speaks, his breath warms my already heated cheeks.

I look down and place my hand on his chest. It would be so easy to fall into a relationship with Hunter, but I'm already in one with Ben. I love working with Hunter. Can I give that up? What would life be like if I switched from days with Hunter to nights?

I touch his face, and he leans into my hand. I'm already as close as I can be, but he squeezes my hips and pulls me closer still. I place my forehead to his.

"I can't do this anymore, Brynn."

I hold his face with both of my hands. "You don't mean that." My heart sinks.

"I think it's fair to warn you that I'm falling."

"Hunter, I—" I'm cut off mid-sentence as he falls off the

wall, landing on his ass. It throws me forward and puts us chest to chest. We're both stunned, but I start laughing.

He wraps his arms around me and holds me tightly. "I told you I was falling." He stretches his legs out. "My butt is going to hurt. Are you going to rub it for me?"

I sit up as much as he'll allow me to and look at him. "Uh, no. Our partnership does not include butt rubs." I struggle to get up, and he lets me go.

"I'd rub your ass if you needed me to."

"Yes, but my butt is cute."

His expression changes to shock—complete with blinking eyes and an open mouth. "Are you saying my butt isn't cute?" He touches his hand to his chest as if I've wounded him.

The sound of footsteps coming down the stairs causes both of us to turn. "I'm the one with the cute ass. Isn't that right, Bennett?"

Hunter jumps to his feet as Porter comes down the stairs. "You're trespassing. Get out."

Porter puts his hands out in front of him. "Calm down. I'm sure your ass is cute, too."

"Porter, what are you doing here?" I stand in Hunter's way when he starts to go after him.

He places his hands into his pockets and rocks back on his heels. You can tell he hasn't slept much. The circles under his eyes make that unmistakable, but the age his face is showing tells me how stressed out he is.

"If Hunter would return my calls, I wouldn't have to be here."

I look at Hunter. "Why didn't you tell me he's been calling you?"

"I'm not listening to his lies, and you shouldn't, either."

Porter looks as if he's about to break in two. He threads his fingers through his hair and grasps his head. "I didn't kill those women!"

Hunter walks up to him and puts his face in Porter's. "Then prove it to me! Don't just deny it; prove it!"

"I'm trying! You won't listen!"

The standoff between them is intense. They're nose-to-nose with fists clenched. I want to break them up, but I'm afraid of disturbing the peace. It feels as if there's one small movement, they will each start swinging.

Hunter backs up. "Brynn, head home. You're going to be late meeting Ben."

"No, I want to stay."

He looks my way, but doesn't move beyond that. "It isn't up for debate. I want you nowhere near this case. If I feel it warrants our involvement, I'll fill you in. What I'm not going to do is let you listen to his bullshit and risk getting you thrown off the team for good."

"But—"

"Go. Ben's waiting. I'll call you later."

Porter looks relieved to finally have someone listen to him. I would listen to him, but Hunter's dead set against it. If this is the only way he'll hear Porter out, I'll leave.

I turn to Hunter before I go up the stairs. "I'm leaving because I don't think you'll listen to him otherwise, but if you don't listen to him, Hunter, I will. He's still a member of our team, and that alone gives him the right to be heard. Promise me you'll hear him out and not just kick him out when I'm gone."

"I promise I'll hear him out."

I pull up to a security van outside my place. Ben isn't here yet, so I get out and approach the men standing outside. "May I help you?"

"We're waiting for Benjamin Drake."

"Well, I live here, so you can talk to me."

He looks at his paperwork and back to me. "Brynn Bennett?"

"Yes."

He holds his hand out, but I just look at it. "We're here to discuss installation of the video cameras for you."

"What?" I look behind me as Ben pulls up, and I cross my arms while I wait for him to come up to us.

"Sorry I'm late." He kisses my cheek and shakes the guy's hand. "Shall we get started?"

"No." They both turn to me. "I don't want cameras."

"It's for your best interest." Ben leads me away from the security men.

"What's in your best interest is to discuss these types of things before scheduling appointments. I don't want to be filmed coming and going in my own home."

"No one will be watching except you. I don't like all the things that have happened to you lately. It's either this or moving in with me until the guy is caught."

I look back to my home and then to the ground. I don't want to move in with Ben. Cameras may be a good idea, but I would've preferred he discussed it with me first. "How much is this going to cost?"

"Let me take care of it."

"If I get the cameras, I'm going to pay for them."

"I've already paid for them. They're here to go over the installation."

I place my hands on my hips and look at him. "I don't need you to take care of it. I'm perfectly capable of taking care of myself. Is that understood?"

"Yes, but you don't take care of yourself or worry about your safety, do you?"

I can't deny that, but it still pisses me off that he's taking care of things for me. I walk over to my car to get my gym bag, and he follows. "I should send these men away, but the cameras are probably a good idea." I grab the bag and shut my door before turning to him. "Don't ever set something like this up again without talking to me."

He looks down at the outfit I'm wearing and looks at the gym bag. "Did you go to the gym? I didn't know you belonged to a gym. We could go together."

"Changing the subject is not going to get you off the hook, but I went to Hunter's. His basement is practically a gym, and he's helping me to stay in shape and ready for work when we're called back on a case.

"As for these guys, I'm going to take a shower and ignore the fact that they're here. You paid for it; you can deal with it."

I shouldn't be so bitchy about it, but it angers me that he's taking care of things without discussing them with me. We aren't in that place in this relationship where decisions can be made for each other.

I walk inside and head straight for the bedroom, locking

the bedroom door behind me. I need a shower. I want to know what's going on with Hunter and Porter, but I need to be patient.

I turn the water to hot because my muscles are already starting to feel sore. I'm not sure I'll survive Hunter Boot Camp. I stand under the spray and let the water consume me.

I hear tapping on the bedroom door and regret locking it. I don't want to get up to unlock it. I groan as my muscles protest the movement.

"Is everything okay in there?" Ben sounds concerned, but there's no reason to be.

I unlock the door and turn back to the bed. "Everything is fine. I'm just sore." I plop face first in the same position I was in before I had to get up.

"What did he have you do?" I hear the door close behind Ben.

"Are they gone?"

"Yes, the cameras are installed. I'll show you about them later." The bed dips as he sits next to me. "Maybe you overdid it today."

"No, I'm just really out of shape. I used to run and take better care of myself, but I started dating this really great guy and decided to spend my time with him instead."

"Really? Well, I hear this really great guy you're dating is really great with massages."

He hasn't touched me since the last night we spent at his beach house. We've both been treading lightly with the physical contact, but a massage sounds really good. It might be a good way to ease back into the physical part of our relationship.

I turn my head and look at him. "Don't play with my emotions or in this case my sore muscles."

He starts to roll up his sleeves with a wicked grin across his gorgeous face. "I assume you're nude under the robe?"

"There's only one way to find out."

He slides his hand under me and finds the sash to untie it. He peels back the top of the robe and uncovers my shoulders. He's careful when he straddles my body and makes sure not to touch me more than he needs to.

When his fingers make contact with my shoulders, I can't help but let out a moan. He knows exactly what to do. I close my eyes and let him work on the rest of me.

CHAPTER 23

Brynn

A s I PULL UP TO Hunter's place, I can't believe what I'm seeing. His car that means more to him than his own life has been keyed violently. I'm not sure they even used keys to do it.

I sit in the car for a little while and just look at the sad sight in front of me. I glance to the house a few times, wondering if he's seen it yet. I take a deep breath, swallow hard, and get out of my car.

I walk slower than I normally would, because I don't want to be the one to break the news to him. It will kill him. If he's already seen it, I'm sure it would be in a body shop right now and not still in his driveway for the neighbors to see.

He opens the door just as I step up, and he's smiling. He hasn't seen it. "So, you're a little sore from yesterday, huh?

Can't get your legs to carry you any faster out of fear?"

The sympathy I felt before for him vanishes as he mocks my fitness level. I step out of his sight line to his car. His reaction is what I had suspected it would be. He does a double take, drops the coffee mug he was holding, and runs out to his car.

"What the fuck?" He walks down the passenger side of the car, shaking his head in disbelief. I should've warned him. "What did they use? A fucking chainsaw!"

"You didn't hear anything last night?"

"No, I didn't fucking hear anything! They wouldn't have survived had I caught the fuckers!"

I walk out to him and place my hand on his arm. "You need to calm down. I know you love this car more than anything."

He stops cold as he rounds the driver's side. "Almost more than anything." He threads his fingers through his hair and fists his hair. "I do love this car, but there are things I love more, and those are what I need to focus on."

"Wow."

"I still need a minute." He walks past me and goes inside. I look at the car once more and follow him.

I'm not sure where he goes, but I give him the space I think he needs—the space I would need if something like this happened to me. I wonder what he's going to do about it. There really isn't much that can be done about it. I clean up the mess from the broken coffee mug before grabbing a cup of coffee for myself to wait for him on the sofa.

It doesn't take him long before he's back out in the living room with me. "SAC Matthews is sending someone over to look at it." He sits next to me.

"Really? I wouldn't hold out much hope for them to find whoever did this."

"After they take the car, will you take me to a rental place? I'm going to be without my car for a while."

"You already called a body shop?"

He reaches over and grabs my hand. "You didn't look at the entire car, did you?"

"No. I figured it was all scratched up on the other side, too." I take my hand back and stand, but he grabs my hips. "Let go, Hunter. I'm going to see it now or when they get here, but either way, I will look at it."

He lets go, and I rush out the door, only stopping when I round the front of the car and see his side.

BRYNN IS MINE

I cover my mouth with my hand. This happened because of me. His car is scratched up because of me. Hunter walks up next to me with his hands in his pockets. "I'm so sorry, Hunter."

"It isn't your fault. It's clearly a message for me since it's only on my side of the car." He starts to take his hands out of his pockets, but puts them back inside. "I want to put my arm around you, but I don't know if he's watching."

"You need to get cameras, too."

He looks at me and tilts his head. "Too?"

"Ben had cameras installed at my place last night. That's why we had to meet."

He rubs his chin. I turn and narrow my eyes at him. The investigators pull up and stop our conversation for now, but I'll try to find out what he's thinking later.

"I can't believe you got this car." I look at the SUV Hunter picked out as we walk by it while I follow him up to his house.

He opens the door and lets me in. "What's wrong with it?"

"Nothing, but I thought you'd go with something else."

He grabs a bottle of water and throws one my way. "Nothing else had leg room. Did you see those cars?"

I laugh and shake my head as I set down the water he tossed me. "I guess I didn't think of that."

"Besides, if I pick up some hot chicks, the seats fold down."

I stop laughing and clear my throat. "What are you? Fifteen?" I don't like the smirk on his face, so I grab the bottle of water and head to the living room.

"That's what the guy said. Did you not pay any attention in there?"

"Well, no. I had other things on my mind."

"Like what?" He sits next to me and nudges me with his knee. "What's going on in that pretty head of yours?"

"When are you going to tell me about Porter?"

He groans and leans back on the sofa, stretching his legs out. "I feel for the guy. I do. If he's innocent and truly hasn't harmed anyone, then I feel for him." He tilts his head to look at me. "I'm just not so sure he's innocent." He looks back to the ceiling. "But, I'm no longer feeling that he's as guilty as I thought he was."

"So, we're going to look into it?"

He sits up and places his elbows on his knees. "The thing is, Brynn, no one is comfortable with you being part of this anymore."

"No, no, no! You are not going to keep me out of this. This is my case, too!"

"We can go over things here or at your place, but I'm not going to let you go with us if we go into the field."

"Goddammit, Hunter! I never thought you'd treat me like this. I can take care of myself." I slam the bottle onto the coffee table and stand. "I'll find this guy before you clowns do."

I start to storm off, but he grabs me around the waist and pulls me onto the sofa. He lies on top of me and fights me to put my hands above my head.

"Dammit, Brynn! Shit like that will get you killed. Do you want to be his next victim?"

"Don't treat me like I can't handle this case."

He looks at me and adjusts himself, slipping his thigh between my legs. "I know you can handle it, but I can't. If anything were to happen to you . . . I can't handle that." His voice gets quiet. "I can't handle that, Brynn."

He sits up at the other end of the sofa and downs the rest of his water. I sit up and try to figure out what to say next. I understand what he's saying, but I don't want to stop working this case, especially if I can help a teammate.

"Your mom died at the hands of a crazy man. Is that how

you want to end up, too?"

"That isn't fair. This isn't the same thing."

"Isn't it?" He turns to me. "It's exactly the same thing. Someone had gone after your family, and your mom is dead. All because your dad was working a case. It's exactly the same damn thing."

"You're asking me to stop doing what I do. I can't. You'd be going just as crazy as me. In fact, you have been since we've been taken off the case. You're working out like a mad-man trying to keep busy. I need to solve this, too!"

He puts his elbows back on his knees as he runs his fingers through his hair. "I know what I'm asking you to do. Believe me, I know. I want you out there with me, but it's safer if you stay out of it."

"I didn't start with the FBI because I wanted to feel safe."

"No." He turns to me with one hand on his knee. "You started with the FBI because you have a hero complex or a death wish. You think you can solve every case when there are thousands of unsolved cases every year. Even your mom's isn't solved, but you think you can solve that one, too."

He stands and paces the living room. "These are the facts, Brynn. This guy is after beautiful twenty-something women." He stops and points at me. "That's you." He starts pacing again. "Now, I don't know when his obsession with you started, but it escalated when you were taken off the case. I won't have it escalate further if he thinks you're back on it, and he got what he wanted. We aren't playing a fucking game here.

"Our best option is to ignore it and work the original case. If it weren't for the trophies being attached to those cards, I wouldn't have even been so sure that it was the same guy. It's just weird."

I have to admit that he has a point. If he were truly obsessed with me, he would've made some sort of contact with me prior to me being taken off the case. I'm not sure what the game is that he's playing, either.

Hunter sits next to me and places his arm around me. "We'll figure this out, but I need you to stay safe for me."

I nod. "I understand, but tell me what's going on. You said you'd let me help from here, so let me help."

"Okay." He leaves for a moment and comes back with a notepad. "This is what Porter told me. The first murder that happened after we were taken off the case is the one with the most connection to Porter. He's slept with her before and was seen that night talking to her again."

"No one saw them leaving?"

"There's proof he didn't leave with her. That's why he hasn't been arrested yet."

I nod. "Okay. What else?"

"The murderer is getting more violent. The victims aren't in as pristine condition as they once were. Something has set him off."

"That's why you still think Porter did this."

"That and the fact there's suddenly an obsession for you." He looks at me. "If he were truly obsessed, he would've contacted you before you were separated from the case. He would've made some move to get your attention. He didn't.

"The way I figure it, Porter needs us to think he's being framed. What other explanation would there be for this to suddenly point at him perfectly?"

"Does he have an idea who it is?"

"You believe that someone is trying to frame him?"

"At this point, I don't know what to believe. I would like to know if he has a list of suspects himself for this, though. It's a wild accusation to say someone is framing you, and it's even a more incredible accusation to say he's doing it himself."

"He has a list of people, but it's full of ex-boyfriends of women he's bed."

I scoff. "Of course, it is."

CHAPTER 24

Brynn

I GET OUT OF THE workout today, but I'm promised a brutal one tomorrow to make up for it. The car took up most of the morning, and by lunch we were knee deep in the case again. It feels good to have actually worked on something for a change. I stop halfway down Hunter's driveway when my phone rings.

"Hey, Ben."

"Hey, beautiful. When are you free for the evening?"

I start to walk to my car again. "I'm actually leaving Hunter's place now."

"Do you need another massage tonight?"

"Well, I don't *need* one, but if you're going to offer I won't turn it down." I get in and start my car. "Uh, I'm sorry I fell asleep on you last night."

"Any time I can get my hands on you is a good night in my opinion." There's a brief pause. "Did you have dinner with Hunter already? I was calling to see if you were up for dinner."

"Hunter and I didn't have dinner, but I'm always up for food. You should know this by now."

"I see no safe way to answer that."

I try not to, but laughter erupts out of me. "You're probably right."

"So, I'll pick you up?"

"Sure. I need to go home and change, but I can be ready soon."

"It isn't anything fancy, so just dress comfortably."

"Okay. See you soon." I'm a little disappointed because I enjoy getting ready for fancy dates, but at least we're going out.

I just put the finishing touches on my outfit when Ben knocks on the door. I walk out to the living room to see him enter and shake his head. I'm going to be lectured again about leaving my door unlocked, but I don't want to hear it. I walk up and kiss him when he turns around before he has a chance to say anything.

He wraps his arms around me. "With a greeting like that, you're going to make me second guess going out."

"It's just a preview to later." I kiss him again. "Where are we going?"

"I feel like Italian tonight. Does that sound good to you?"

"Sure."

He takes my hand after I lock up and walks me to his car. "You should do that more often when you're inside, too."

I squeeze his hand. "I can handle myself." I don't want to argue this anymore.

We get into the car and buckle up before he backs out. I'm waiting for more arguing about locking the door, but he surprises me and changes the subject. "What's new with your case?"

"Not a whole lot. There are a few more things that lead investigators to believe that it's still Porter, but nothing concrete."

"At least you're not denying the fact you're still working it."

I slip my hand on his thigh. "Well, not to my boyfriend. I'll still deny it to anyone else, though."

He puts his hand on mine. "What do you think?"

"Do you really want to talk about this?"

He glances my way. "What I want is to have my girlfriend at dinner, so what I'm hoping is that by talking about this now, we can enjoy each other's company and not be distracted by it."

"I do that, don't I?" I turn to him. "I get distracted and ignore you. I'm sorry."

"It's okay. I understand. I'll probably be the same way sometimes when I have a situation with a client, but I'd really like to talk about us at dinner and not the case."

Us? I'm not sure I'm ready for the "us" talk. I still don't know what I want for us to have that discussion.

He puts his hand back on the steering wheel when I take my hand back. "I should've waited until we made it to the restaurant." He glances my way again.

We get to the restaurant and are seated before either of us says another word. We look at the menu, and while it all looks so good, I don't have much of an appetite with the butterflies in my stomach.

"I'm going to get the veal. Do you know what you want yet?" He's talking about food, but I hear an undertone in that question.

"I really don't."

He puts his menu down and smiles. "It's okay. I'll wait."

I try to give a little smile and go back to the menu. I see him over the top of the menu looking around. I want to look around, too, but keep my eyes on the menu.

"Why haven't we ever done that?"

I lower the menu and look around. "Do what?"

"Take photos." He points to the couple in the corner.

"It never occurred to me to take them. I guess I feel a little silly sticking my arm out at a restaurant with my phone attached to the end of it." I go back to looking at the menu.

He scoots next to me, and I look at him. "We'll have the waiter do it. We'll use your phone because it has a better camera."

I put the menu down, amused that Ben wants a photo of us. I place my hand on his knee and scoot in closer. "A photo would be good. Why the sudden interest, though?"

"People are starting to think I made you up. They were getting on my case about not dating, and now that I am, I've never introduced you to them." He looks at me. "I feel I'm failing at this boyfriend thing."

I pull his face to mine and kiss him. "You're not failing."

The waiter walks up, and I hold out my phone. "Would you take a photo of us, please?"

"I'd be happy to."

I groan as I sit in the car. Ben turns to me. "Is everything okay?"

"Too much food."

His laugh makes me smile even if it is at my expense. "I knew you'd love it here."

"A little too much. Next time, don't let me have so much bread before dinner."

"I'm not stopping that train." He puts the car into reverse and starts to leave. "Besides, we'll work it off later."

"The dinner was good, but I don't know if it was *that* good for you to get dessert."

He smiles. I enjoy teasing him, but we both know sex is going to happen. I slip my hand on his thigh and inch my way up. He stops me. "I need to make a stop somewhere. I'd rather not walk in and get arrested for lewd behavior because of my erection."

"We're not going home?"

"It'll be a quick stop."

I take my hand back and lean back in the seat, closing my eyes. My stomach is really full. It's going to be a little while before I can do anything with him anyway.

I'm comfortable with him, and the sex is great, so why am I having such a hard time committing to this? I turn my head and look at him. He's everything I would look for, and I'm happy when I'm with him. We don't have the exact same interests, and he likes to stay home more often than I do, but there are compromises with any relationship.

Can I see myself with him in five years? What about twenty? I look back out the passenger window. I'm not sure I've ever seen myself settle down. Is that something I even want?

He pulls into the drugstore, and I laugh. "You really are sure of yourself." He gives me a funny look, and I tilt my head. "Aren't you here for more condoms?"

"Oh, I really should pick those up, too." He looks at my belly. "Do you need anything?"

"You came here for my indigestion?"

"No, but I'll get something for you if you need it."

"No, I'm good. I'm going to stay in the car, though."

"Sure." He leans over and kisses me. "Keep the car locked. I'll be right back."

I lay the seat back a little to accommodate my stomach and moan. I may lie down when I get home. I close my eyes and wait for Ben.

Someone slaps their hands on my window and makes me jump. I open my eyes and see Porter laughing. Bloated stomach or not, I'll kick his ass. I get out of the car.

"What the fuck?"

"I just thought I'd say hi." He waves like a moron. "Hi."

"What are you doing here?"

He looks at the drugstore and back to me. "Shopping."

"You don't live over here. Are you following us again?"

He tilts his head. "Again? That implies I've followed you before."

"We both know you have."

He rubs the back of his neck. "Have you talked to Hunter?"

"Every day, but you already know that."

He looks at the car behind me. "Still dating Gramps, huh?" I turn to get into the car, and he grabs my arm. "I'm still talking to you."

I look at his hand on my arm and back to him. "We're done talking, and you need to be done following us."

Ben comes out of the drugstore, and the moment he realizes who I'm talking to, he runs our way. "Get away from her!"

Ben shoves Porter, knocking him back hard enough that he almost falls. Porter rushes Ben, causing him to drop the sack from the store. I pick it up and throw it into the car.

"Stop!" I try but can't separate them. They're each landing blows to the other, and they aren't holding back. Porter gets the upper hand and throws Ben to the ground then gets on top of him. Ben's arms are up, trying to block Porter's punches to his head.

I take my gun out and wrack back the slide to chamber the bullet next to Porter's ear. The noise is enough to stop him. He understands there's a loaded gun next to his head.

"Get up." I keep my gun on him as he gets up and backs away. "You're going to leave us alone. You're going to stop following us. And you're going to never contact me again."

"Brynn."

"No, Porter. Enough is enough. You've gone too far this time."

He looks at Ben and back to me, nods once, and backs away. I keep my gun on him until he gets to his motorcycle and takes off. I look at Ben, but he's up already and leaning against the car.

Men can be sensitive when they get their asses kicked, so I try to not make a big deal out of it, but I have to know how hurt he is. I put my gun away as I walk up to him.

"Hey, are you okay?"

"Yeah, my pride is hurt more than anything else."

I touch his face and move his head to look him over. "Maybe I should drive you home."

He stands up straight and starts to panic, looking around the car. "Where did it go?"

"What? Your sack?" I reach in and take it out of the car. "I tossed it inside when you two started your scuffle."

He leans against the car again and sighs. "I think I'll just take you home if that's okay."

I stand between his legs and wrap my arms around his waist. "Come home with me and let me help."

"I'll take you home, but I'd like to figuratively lick my wounds in private."

He stands and walks to his side of the car. I'm sure he's embarrassed that Porter was able to gain the upper hand and that it took me to get Porter off him, but Porter's had training that Ben has not.

I allow him to take me home and don't bring up him staying again. I'm surprised he comes inside with me when we get to my house. "Did you change your mind?"

"No, I'm sorry. I just have something to give you first."

I let him in and turn the lights on. He walks past me to the living room, but in the full light of my home compared to the street lights outside, his face looks terrible. I hide my reaction while I shut the door. He feels bad enough already.

I turn and see him holding a framed copy of the photo we had just taken. It's difficult for him to smile, but he's giving it his best shot.

I smile and walk over to him. "That's a great photo." I take it from him and look at it. His smile in the photo is huge. There's no doubt how he feels about me. I place it on the mantel and turn to him. "Thank you."

I slide my arms around his waist and hug him carefully. I would kiss him, but his mouth is swollen. I know how it feels to be punched in the face, and kissing isn't on the top of the list to do.

"I'm glad you enjoy it. I'm also glad it was taken before the fight."

I laugh and look up at him. "It's good you're joking about it so soon. Are you sure you don't want to stay? Let me help you get cleaned up."

I try to take his hand, but he pulls it away from me. It's a bloody mess, but I'm not surprised by the way Porter looked.

"No, I really want to get home and try to figure out how to get the swelling down. If I stay here, other things on me will swell, and I'll forget about trying to fix this." He motions to his face. "Clients won't really trust their attorney if he looks like this."

I want to make a joke about trusting attorneys, but I refrain. "Well, if you're sure. I'd like to play nurse, though."

"See, things are starting to go in a direction they really shouldn't tonight."

"Oh, fine. I'll play nurse another night." I walk him to the door and kiss his cheek. "Thank you for a wonderful dinner and for my photo of us. I'll take it to bed tonight."

He nods and leaves. I watch as he walks to his car. He really seems hurt. I don't think he needs medical attention, but he isn't used to getting the shit kicked out of him, either.

CHAPTER 25

SHADOW

STAND IN THE ALLEY waiting for the trash to be thrown out. Tonight's going to be a little different. I'd planned on going for the hunt, finding my next victim with the cat-and- mouse game, but I'm too eager for the kill. I need the feeling of control. Only, I hope it isn't the bartender who takes the trash out tonight.

The door opens, and I step back into the shadows a little more until I see who it is. It's the girl I've been waiting for. She a sexy little number, but she isn't like the rest. She'll be a fighter and tonight, I want that fight.

"Dani." I watch as she looks around. I step forward a little. "Over here."

We've had sex before, so I know she'll be up for a quickie. The sex is amazing. I'll miss it, but I saved her life for this moment. Killing her will give me the power to keep going. It will re-energize my soul and remind me what I'm supposed to do with my life.

"What are you doing back here?"

I pull her into the shadows with me when she's close enough and press her against the wall. "I'm glad it's you instead of Joel who was on trash duty."

She rubs my cock through my pants. "I'm glad, too. I could use this a whole lot more than Joel."

I take the condom out of my pocket and put it between my teeth. She knows the drill. She turns around and bends over while I take care of the condom. It helps that she rubs herself to get ready for me. It also helps to get me even harder as I watch her do it. This isn't our first ride in the alley, but unfortunately, it will be our last.

I use my thumb to pull her panties aside and thrust inside. She braces herself against the brick wall with one hand as she continues to rub her clit with the other. I take her hips and start pounding into her. I almost regret what I have to do, but it must be done. I'll find another pussy like hers one day, but I will miss it until the replacement is found.

She stands up and grips the back of my pants. It's her signal her orgasm is close. She wasn't kidding when she said she needed it. She isn't usually this quick to finish. It suits me fine because thinking of what I'm going to do to her is giving me a hair trigger on my orgasm, too.

I reach behind me and take the rope out of the back of my pants and the moment her orgasm hits, I quickly wrap it around her throat. I pull tightly and push her against the wall when she tries to fight me. Her pussy is still milking my cock with the orgasm she's feeling, and it's all I can do to hang on. As I knew it would be, it's the best fuck of my life so far.

I give in to the orgasm and pull tighter on the rope. Her body goes limp, and I put more pressure against her to hold her up against the wall. I'm not stopping until my dick is fully satisfied.

I'm out of breath and exhausted when my cock is finally empty. I let go of the rope and place my hands against the wall. I pulled my truck into the ally because I knew I'd be exhausted after this, but I underestimated just how much. I don't have much time before they come looking for her. She was only supposed to be gone a few minutes.

I pull her face to mine and look her over. She really was quite the beauty. I wish it didn't have to end so soon, but it was one hell of a last ride.

I slip out of her and stand with my shoulder against her back. I tie the condom off and slip it into my pocket to discard where it's safe. After I zip up and place the rope back into my pocket, I turn her around and throw her over my shoulder. A quick toss into the back of the truck, secure the covering so no one can see, and I'm on my way.

Brynn

It was bound to happen. The second I crack the egg and get it on my hands, the phone rings. I abandon breakfast and wipe my hands on a dishtowel to answer the phone on probably the last ring. "Hello?"

"Hi." Ben's mood sounds good, but his lips sound swollen with the way he's talking.

"How are you feeling?"

"Not great. I'll get there, though."

I lean against the counter. "Are you going in to the office today?"

"I have to."

"I thought maybe you could come over and stay in bed all day." I turn to the door as it opens and wave when Hunter walks inside. I turn my back to him to finish my conversation with Ben. "I could still play nurse."

"As much as I would prefer that, I really shouldn't. I'll take a rain check for tonight, though."

I watch as Hunter picks up the bowl with the egg and sniffs it. It's difficult to not laugh, so I turn my back to him again.

"Definitely tonight. I may even go shopping today."

"If you're getting a naughty nurse outfit, I may need to open my afternoon up and come home early."

I laugh and jump when Hunter shoos me out of the way of the coffee pot. It's hard to have a sexy conversation with Hunter around. "Don't clear your afternoon yet. I'll let you know if I find one."

"Okay. I'll talk to you later and say hello to Hunter."

"Okay. Wait, how did you know?"

"I heard the door, and you keep lowering your voice when we talk about the naughty nurse."

"Well, do you want me to get his opinion on it?"

Hunter looks at me over the rim of the coffee mug.

"No. That can be our little secret."

"That's what I thought. Have a good day." I hang up and turn to Hunter. "Why are you sniffing my eggs?"

"Is it appropriate for a woman to ask a man that?"

I roll my eyes at his immature humor and pick up the bowl. "I got interrupted. There's nothing in it yet."

"Well, add about six more for me and get cooking." He nods when I look at him and takes over the egg duty. "I hope Ben knows how to cook because the two of you will starve if it's left up to you."

"Hey, I was going to do it, but you're here. You do it better."

He sighs and holds his arms out. "What every man wants to hear. You do it better." He turns to me with the whisk in hand. "Say it again."

"Oh, brother." I grab my coffee mug and take a sip. "What's on the agenda today? I thought I was going to your place to work out."

"Yeah, we could do that."

I wait, but he doesn't say anything. "Or?"

"*Or,* there was another murder last night."

"Damn." I look at my watch and turn the news on. I leave it on mute and hope to catch the story again. "What happened?"

"It was a waitress at a bar that Porter hangs out at. From what I hear, they found blood on her, and it wasn't hers."

I sit down at the table and place my head in my hands. He was bleeding when he left us in the parking lot. "What time did it happen?"

"It was early for him, and there are a few other things that were inconsistent. What do you know?"

"Ben and I went out last night. Porter followed us to a

drugstore, and when Ben went in, I stayed in the car. He used the opportunity to talk to me alone, but didn't say anything, you know? It's like he wanted me to know he was following us.

"Then Ben came out, and they fought. They were both pretty banged up by the end of it. He was bleeding when he drove off."

"Damn." He goes back to the eggs on the stove. "So, Ben was able to rough him up a little?"

"Ben did a lot of damage until Porter got him to the ground."

"How badly did Ben get hurt?"

"His forearms took most of the hits, but until he could protect himself, he got a fat lip and swollen eye." I shake my head. "His face looked terrible, but he busted Porter's lip wide open."

"Just because there's blood and Porter was bleeding when you last saw him doesn't mean anything. We'll wait until they come back with the blood results before jumping to any conclusions."

"You want to investigate today, don't you?"

He sets the plates of eggs onto the table and looks at me. "Hearing what I just heard, not really. I know I've suspected him for a while, but I don't think I can be the one to put the nail in the coffin for a member of our team."

I nod and reach for his hand. I don't think I can do it, either.

Hunter and I decide to run for a change to our workout routine. He needs to work on his endurance, and after the previous night's dinner, I need cardio. Weights and resistance training are important, but I'm glad we're switching gears.

As we pass by, I look at the bench where Porter had come up to me on a previous run. He always seems to be following me. I look around as we run.

"What are you looking for?"

"Porter."

He nods. "I've been looking for him, too." He slows to a walk, and I turn around to look at him. "Let's say we were going to investigate this latest murder. Where would you want to start?"

I walk back to him with my hands on my hips and breathe deeply. "We would need to start with the crime scene. Then move on and investigate the victim's last whereabouts along with the victim herself."

"There's no way we're getting close to any of that." He sighs and starts running again.

"You already know that." I catch up. "What's bugging you?"

"Why would he do it knowing blood evidence is irrefutable? He's smarter than that."

"Unless he thought it was closed and she reinjured him in the fight."

"That's a possibility. I'm not sure where the blood was found, but you think he'd clean it up. He'd have to know his lip or something was bleeding."

I tug on his arm to get him to stop running. "Now, you think he's innocent? Now, you want to clear him?"

"I don't know what to think. Someone who kills isn't really rational now, are they? Anything is possible."

"I agree with that. There are a million reasons why he would do it. Maybe he's tired of the game and wants to get caught. Maybe the fight with Ben triggered some need to kill, and he didn't have the patience to do it right. Maybe the fact I told him I never wanted to see him again sent him over the edge. I don't know!"

Hunter puts his arms around me. I wrap my arms around him. "Let's get some lunch."

I look up at him. "That's your answer? Food?"

"Right now, yes."

I put my forehead on his chest. "Okay."

CHAPTER 26

Brynn

I ROLL OVER AND SNUGGLE up to Ben. It's been a few days since the latest murder, and I've been on edge waiting for the blood results. My house is immaculate for it, but I'm tired of smelling like cleaning solution. I'm also tired of working out. I'd rather stay in bed today.

I look up as Ben opens his eyes. His face is healing, and the swelling is going down, but the bruising still looks awful. I stretch up to him and kiss him.

He smiles and kisses me back. "I like waking up this way."

"Me, too." I place my head on his chest. "I don't want to leave this bed today."

"Okay."

I look up at him. "Okay? You're not going to fight me on it?"

"No, I'll stay in here with you."

I snuggle closer and rub my hand over his torso. "I was hoping you'd say that."

"I want to hear about your parents."

I prop myself up on my elbow and look at him. "Why?"

"Well, I won't get the opportunity to meet them, but I'd still like to get to know them."

I move the pillows and sit up against the headboard. He rolls to his side and puts his arm over my legs. I don't usually talk about my parents. It's a hard subject to discuss. I miss them both terribly, and it's painful. I think about them often, but even that's difficult at times.

"I think my dad would've liked your protectiveness. I think he would've liked the fact you paid for cameras around my place."

"Yeah? At least someone would've appreciated it." He chuckles and sits up against the headboard next to me.

"I appreciate it. It just isn't necessary." I pull the covers further up my lap and grab a pillow to hug. "My mom would've liked the protectiveness, too, but she would've loved how handsome you are." I touch his face.

He takes my hand and kisses my palm. "Tell me about them, not what they'd love about me."

"My mom was a real beauty. I could sit and watch her for hours when she got ready. Not that it ever took her hours, but if that's all she wanted to do, I would've happily watched her.

"My dad wasn't around much while my mom was still alive. He was there, but he was working. I knew he loved me. Mom knew he loved us." I look at Ben. "I don't mean to make it sound as if he abandoned us."

"You aren't. I understand busy workloads."

I nod. "They were so much in love. You could see it when they were together. They were always touching, kissing, and the way they spoke to one another . . ." I shake my head as I think of memories I'd stored away long ago. I look to the ceiling when the tears threaten to spill.

Ben wraps his arms around me and pulls me close. "They sound like wonderful parents."

"They were the best." I wipe my tears away. "I didn't get much time with my mom, but my dad was my best friend."

"I'm sure they both would've been. What do you remember about what happened to your mom?"

"I don't remember much. I was just six. There was a lot of yelling, and I wasn't used to it. I was scared, so I hid in the closet. I took a stuffed animal with me, and we sat there until someone found us."

"You sound upset about that."

"I should've gone for help."

"Did you know your mother needed it?"

I shake my head. "I should've known. No one yelled in my house. I should've known something wasn't right."

"You did. You hid because of it." He holds me tighter. "If you hadn't have hidden, I wouldn't have you right now. They never found who did it?"

"No. It's been a cold case for as long as I can remember. I keep checking up on it, but no one is investigating it. What little evidence they have is probably rotting away in a box somewhere, and that's even if they still have it.

"My dad had more pull to have it investigated throughout the years, but I've not been as lucky. When he died, any investigating died with him."

"He never suspected anyone?"

"Yes, of course, he did, but he couldn't connect anyone to who he thought ordered it."

"Wait, I thought this was a random thing."

I sit up and look at him. "No, it definitely wasn't random."

"Then why are you still alive?"

"I don't think the killer could kill kids. It takes a special kind of asshole to do that, and since I hadn't seen him, he technically didn't have a witness."

He leans back against the headboard. "Wow."

"I have this fear that he'll come back for me." I look at Ben. "You know, to finish the job. Hunter thinks the training my dad gave me made me paranoid, but I'm not a kid anymore. He could easily kill me just as he killed my mother."

"I don't like hearing that. Wouldn't he have done it by now? How long's it been? Twenty years?"

"Yes, but if he went to prison for something else, he may not be able to do it." I get up and head to the bathroom. "Or maybe he's dead. Either way, I'm ready if he ever comes back."

Our day in bed only lasted until we got hungry and realized there was no food in my kitchen. I had meant to go to the store the day before, but I was caught up in working out with Hunter and cleaning my house.

"I really don't like shopping on Saturday mornings." I place the bunch of bananas into the cart.

"It's busier, that's for sure."

"It's the kids." I look at another kid who's screaming while the mom picks out tomatoes. "They need kid-free grocery stores."

"You don't like kids?" Ben places a pineapple into the cart while I look at the grapes.

"I like well-mannered kids." I turn and smile.

"All kids have bouts of fits and tantrums. What are you going to do when yours do that?"

"I haven't thought about it." I move over to the potatoes and try to change the subject. "Do you like sweet potatoes?"

"Do you not want children?"

I look at him and sigh. "I've never really given it much thought. This whole settle down thing really hasn't been on my radar. While other girls were worried about prom and who they were going to date for the year, I was learning about how many bullets fit in different magazines, how to throw a knife, and that figuring out your quickest exit when entering any room was the first priority in any survival situation. If you can't get out, you're dead. I think that was due to my hiding in the closet."

Ben walks behind me a little slower than when we first started shopping. It's a sure sign that he's thinking something over, and it's a matter of time before he says it. I'm just wondering if he'll wait until we get back home or if we're going to have this discussion in the middle of the supermarket.

We only talk about groceries and different things we need to pick up the rest of our shopping trip. I'm grateful because this isn't a conversation we should have in the frozen section. It really isn't a conversation I want to have at home, either, but it's probably time we do.

He carries most of the bags in on the first trip while I carry the fragile things like eggs and bread. I start to put things away when he goes back out for the remaining items. I also use the time to prepare for the talk we're about to have.

To my surprise, he helps put the groceries away without a word. It must've really upset him to hear I'd never given any thought to settling down. I couldn't even tell him if I want to settle down now. I don't see myself that way. I enjoy his time, and I'd be sad if it came to an end, but I don't want to promise him something I'm not ready to promise.

"What if I paid private investigators to look into your mother's death?"

I stop with the refrigerator door open. "What?"

"I think you need closure. I don't think you can move forward with your life until this is resolved. You're still that little kid hiding in the closet. I want to help you get out of that closet."

"Now, you're a shrink?" I start to throw things into the refrigerator. I don't like his assessment that I need help.

"No, I'm a man who's in love with you, and I want to spend the rest of my life with you. I want to have kids and be like your parents were. I want our kids to say that they had the best parents who loved each other more than life and were constantly touching or kissing."

I close the freezer door with my back to him. He comes up and wraps his arms around me. I understand what he's saying, and the thought of being the kind of parent my parents were to a child sparks something in me, but I can't let go and fully feel it yet. Maybe he's right. Maybe I am still hiding in the closet.

CHAPTER 27

Brynn

'VE AGREED TO LET BEN look into investigators, but I told him I wanted to check them out before he hired someone. I wasn't going to let him waste money on someone who would just rack up large bills and never produce results. He agreed.

We're sitting on the sofa watching mindless television, and I have to admit that it's nice. I've done this with Hunter, but usually on opposite sides of the sofa or with a tub of popcorn between us. I do like the snuggling with Ben.

Breaking news interrupts the program we're watching, and I throw my hands up. "They had to cut in on that part!" I sit up when I see Porter's photo on the screen.

"Tonight a local FBI Agent, Scott Porter, has been arrested for the murder of Dani Pilger. Our sources say more charges are possible with other murders."

I reach for my phone just as it rings. It's Hunter. "I'm watching!" I get up and go to the bedroom with Ben behind me.

"What are you doing?"

I hold my hand up when Hunter starts talking. "I'm going down there. I doubt we'll be able to find anything out, but I'm going down there."

"I'm getting ready. Pick me up." I toss the phone onto the bed and grab clothes out of my closet.

"May I speak now?"

"Yes, I'm sorry. I couldn't hear both of you."

"Where are you going?"

I take my shirt off. "Down to the bureau." I grab my other shirt.

"Why? They have their guy. What's left to do?"

I finish pulling it over my head and look at him. "You're kidding. I need to see what's going on."

"Do you really think they're going to tell you?"

"Probably not, but he's part of my team. I need to be there." I strip the pants I'm wearing and grab the slacks off the bed. "I'm sorry you don't understand. I wish there were magic words to help you, but one of my teammates has been arrested for a murder he may or may not have committed, and I need to be there."

"You're going to the jail?"

"I think we'll go to the bureau and see what evidence they have."

He follows me to the bathroom and stands in the doorway while I brush my hair. "You think they're going to lay it all out for you?"

I take a deep breath and look at him in the mirror. "I have to try. Hunter and I have to try. It's like saying someone you know is in the hospital. You *have* to be there, even if there's nothing you can do."

He nods and looks toward the front door as Hunter knocks. "What the fuck? Was he in the car when he called you?" He shakes his head. "I'll go let him in."

I grab his hand and tug before he leaves the doorway. I pull him close and kiss him. "Thank you for understanding."

Hunter and I walk inside, and everyone stops and looks at us. We expected this reaction, and it looks like SAC Matthews was waiting for us. He tilts his head toward his office, and we follow. Lopez is already there.

"I was going to call you all tomorrow, but the news broke sooner than we wanted it to."

"What the fuck?" Lopez is pissed and not afraid to show it.

"I know, I should've called. We all know I can't discuss the evidence that we've found, but it's no longer circumstantial. We have solid evidence that puts Porter with this victim."

Hunter speaks up. "Blood."

SAC Matthews doesn't deny it. "Where did you hear that?"

Hunter looks at him. We all know he won't tell.

"Look, there's nothing I can do at this point. I didn't want to believe it myself, but everything keeps pointing to him. He isn't exactly making things easy on himself, either. We all know how difficult he can be."

"So, when do we get another case then?" Lopez knows we won't get anything else out of him.

"Soon, but not yet. You need to clear your heads of this. It's a lot to take in. Trust me, I understand." He stands and walks to the door, effectively telling us the conversation is over. "One last thing, he's to have no visits from any of you."

"Why?"

He looks at me. "Because I want no one else on this team to be looked at as an accomplice. I won't lose another one of you. Is that clear?"

The three of us look at each other and nod. Walking out isn't as quick paced as walking in was. It seems none of us really want to leave. I look at my desk as I walk by and wish I could just sit down and forget the past few weeks ever happened.

Lopez hasn't been around much. I look at him on our way out. "How have you been?"

"At first, it was great. I got to spend time with my wife and kids. Now, I'm just going nuts. I don't know how my wife does it. I can't sit there all day. Honestly, I think it's driving her nuts, too. I'm doing the shit she usually does, and now she's bored."

"You should come work out with Brynn and me."

"Yeah?" Lopez looks to us, and we nod. "That actually sounds normal. I'll be there tomorrow. I'm sure my wife will appreciate the time apart, too."

"See you tomorrow." Hunter shakes his hand and turns to me. "Take you home?"

"I suppose."

He raises his eyebrow. "Something on your mind?"

"No, I'm just antsy. It's been a rough day."

He leans against the car and looks at me. "Because of Porter?"

I cross my arms and look at the pavement. "I talked about my parents this morning." I look at Hunter's surprised expression. "He asked."

"What did you tell him?"

"He just wanted to know what my parents were like." I look around. "Can we get in the car?"

"This is serious." He jogs around to his side while I get in the passenger side.

"I don't want to talk here."

He starts the car and nods. "No problem."

It will be difficult to discuss this if Hunter's really in love with me. I only have Jamie's drunk word on that, but I have no reason to not believe her. I look out the window.

"Don't shut down on me now."

"I'm not. It's just hard to talk about."

"Your parents?"

"No." I look at him. "Ben and I had the kid discussion at the grocery store of all places."

"What kid discussion?"

"Whether we want them or not." I put my head back on the headrest. "The store was filled with whiny brats crying for different reasons. It was hard to take after discussing my parents and thinking about my mom's murder."

"I can see that."

"Well, I voiced my frustration to Ben, and it started the

discussion on whether or not I want kids."

"What did you say?"

"I told him I never thought about it." I sigh and cover my face with my hands. "He's been dropping hints and starting conversations about settling down and now kids." I look at Hunter. "Don't you think that's too fast?"

"I think he's at an age where it's starting to matter to him, and you're not there yet." He glances my way. "He's a lucky man to have you in his life, and he realizes that. There's no reason for him to want to let you go. You're strong, independent, confident, and you're not dating him for his money. Why wouldn't that be the perfect catch for him?"

"He wants to hire a private investigator to find my mom's killer."

"That's the best idea I've heard yet."

I look at him. "You think they'll actually find something?"

"It couldn't hurt to let them try. We haven't been able to find anything, have we? When's the last time anyone cracked open that case? They may have better luck than us, and they may come up empty-handed just like the others who investigated before them. You'll never know unless you try."

"I feel bad having him spend that kind of money. I know it won't be cheap."

"He can afford it. Can you afford to go the rest of your life looking over your shoulder and wondering if your mother's killer is coming back for you?"

"That's kind of what he said, too. He thinks I'm still hiding in the closet."

Hunter reaches over, puts his hand on my knee, and squeezes. "He may be right, Brynn."

I put my hand on his and look out the window. "I know."

Hunter pulls up to my place. I unbuckle and twist in the seat to hug him. I know he won't get out since Ben's still here, but I need to hug my best friend. "Thank you."

He wraps his arms around me. "I'm always here for you. You know that."

I nod and kiss his cheek before getting out. I walk up and look for my keys on my way, but Ben opens the door before I get there. "Hey, did you find anything out?"

"No. We aren't allowed to see him, either."

Ben shuts and locks the door as I walk to the living room. "Why would you want to?"

"To see what he knows. SAC Matthews thinks we could be viewed as accomplices and wants us to stay away. I have to agree with him."

"So do I. I'm glad to hear you agree, too." He sits next to me and hands me a glass of wine. "They've probably already been looking into the rest of the team, and that's probably why you three have been removed from duty. Your boss doesn't want it on your record, so he found a different way to remove you."

"He didn't find a different way. I was sent all of that shit."

"Don't remind me."

CHAPTER 28

Brynn

I'VE AGREED TO MEET WITH the investigator Ben's hired for my mother's murder. His name is Paul Morris. I told him if I get any weird vibes, we're finding a different investigator. So far, I'm impressed with the office. It's professional, but not over the top with decoration and fluff.

There's an actual receptionist, and it looks like two other employees. Ben's running a little late, but he assures me he'll be here on time.

The door opens, and the investigator comes out. He appears to be in his late fifties with graying brown hair. It looks as if he still works out as the shirt he's wearing clings to his torso and arms. He smiles as he comes my way with his arm extended. "You must be Brynn Bennett. May I call you Brynn?"

I stand and shake his hand. "Yes, Brynn is fine."

"It's nice to meet you, Brynn. Please call me Paul."

As he turns to lead me into his office, Ben walks inside. "Paul, I'm sorry I'm late." He walks up to me and kisses my cheek. "Hi."

"You're not late at all. We're just about to head into the office."

I follow Paul into his office with Ben right behind me and take a seat. I'm growing more nervous as time goes on, and there's really nothing to be nervous about.

"Would either of you two like anything to drink?"

"No, Paul. I think we're good." Ben takes my hand. "I think we're anxious to get started."

"All right, then." He smiles at both of us. "Let's get started, shall we?"

I watch as he pulls a file out of his desk drawer and opens it. It's filled with blank forms, and I close my eyes. I hate paperwork. Ben squeezes my hand, and I open my eyes again.

"Okay, Brynn, Ben and I have worked together in the past for some clients of his, but I'd like to tell you a little bit about how we operate here.

"You've met my personal assistant, Claire. She sits at the front desk and holds the fort down for me out there." He leans forward a little. "To tell you the truth, she holds most of the fort down for the entire office, but don't tell her I admit that." He winks and sits back in his chair.

I look to Ben and arch an eyebrow. I'm starting to get weird vibes. He looks back to Paul and nods his direction to get me to pay attention.

"The other two gentlemen you probably saw in the next room are my go-to-guys. If someone or something can be found in the cyber world, they will find it. When something needs to be investigated out in the field, that's where I come in. I also handle most of the client interaction.

"As far as my credentials go, I was in the military before joining the police force in Austin. My beautiful wife of twenty-five years got a job offer that she couldn't refuse. I took the opportunity to start my own business, and here we are today. Do you have any questions?"

"Yes. Do you really think you have a chance in hell in finding my mother's killer?"

"No." Ben sits up, but Paul puts his hand up to silence him. "I offer no guarantees of finding the killer or bringing him or her to justice. I only promise to do my best to get you answers."

Once we cut through the cute bullshit he was trying to project, I actually like him. "How are you going to do that?"

"I've already set up appointments with a couple of the agents who were on the case. As you probably know, they were seasoned agents who've since retired. One of them has passed. They still think of this case and want to help close it. Your father was a well-respected man."

Ben takes my hand and moves it to his lap. "What do you say?"

I nod. "Let's do it."

I walk down the stairs to Hunter's basement. I didn't bother to change because I don't plan on working out today. Lopez is spotting him on the bench press, and it sounds as if there are more than two men down here. I smile just watching them.

I miss working with them and the feeling of seeing my family every day, but since being off, I've found myself thinking of other things. I joined the FBI to help people and put murderers away, but it isn't as fulfilling as I'd hoped it would be.

"One more! One more! You can do it!" Lopez is encouraging Hunter to keep going, but Hunter's arms are shaking. He gets the bar to the top, and Lopez helps him to place it onto the rack. "That's what I'm talking about!"

I clap as Lopez does his victory dance as if he's the one who made that lift. How they support one another is amazing. Maybe they should be partners. I shake my head at that thought.

"What?" Hunter's breathing hard. "You didn't think I had it in me?"

"Not at all, stud. I know you can do anything you set your mind to."

Lopez looks between us and raises his eyebrow. "Well, I need to get home. The wife likes it when I'm hot and sweaty, and the kids will still be in school for another hour."

"Ack! TMI there, Lopez." I act disgusted, but it makes me smile.

Hunter beats his fist on his chest as Lopez does the same, and they each give the peace sign before Lopez runs upstairs. I narrow my eyes. "What?" Hunter wipes his face with a towel. "We've had fun without you today."

"It looks like it."

He looks at my outfit. "That's going to be uncomfortable to work out in."

"That's because I'm not working out." I head upstairs.

He follows. "Is something wrong?"

"No. I just don't feel like it."

I sit on the sofa, and Hunter sits next to me. "How did it go with the investigator?"

"I actually think I like him. He tried to be cute at first. I don't know if it was because I was a girl or if it was because he knew I'd be upset, but once I cut through the bullshit, I actually kind of liked him."

"That's good." He looks at me. "Isn't it?"

"Yeah, that's great. He said he was part of the Austin PD before he followed his wife for her career. Could you do that?"

"Follow my wife?"

"No, quit law enforcement."

"Not a chance." He tilts his head. "I guess he hasn't really quit, but I wouldn't be able to sit around and wait for a real case. The amount of bullshit and go spy on this crap would drive me insane. I'll stick with the bureau where I get real cases."

I put my head back on the sofa and smile when he slides next to me and does the same. "You smell."

"I smell like a manly man who just worked out." He tilts his head my way. "You're going to have to deal with it because I can't lift my arms right now to take a shower."

I sit up and laugh. "Poor baby." I stand and move to the chair. "You don't smell as bad over here." I should go home, but sitting in his living room, no matter how badly he smells, is the only place I want to be right now.

I'm sitting on my sofa, looking at my laptop, and doing a lot of frustrated huffing. Ben's at the table finishing up some work on his computer, but I can see him out of the corner of my eye looking my way each time I let out a frustrated sigh.

He sets his pen down on the last breath I force out. "What's with you over there?"

"I'm sorry. I have nothing to do. Porter's case is still on my mind, we haven't heard from the investigator, and my on-line searches are pissing me off."

"You're going to have to let Porter's case go." He closes his laptop and comes over to me. "The investigator has only had your case for two days. Give him a little break."

"You're right."

He looks at my laptop screen. "What are you searching?"

"Self-defense classes."

"Do you need self-defense?"

"No, I'm just seeing what's out there. I think more lives could be saved if we start teaching women the tools they need to prevent these crimes instead of solving them after they're assaulted or dead."

"That's true." He sighs as his phone rings. "I knew this call was coming. Damn."

He gets up and takes his phone to the other room before answering. I understand he needs privacy when talking to cli-ents, but it reminds me of when he didn't trust me when I did the same.

I shut my laptop and go to the kitchen. Maybe I should start dinner. I open a couple of cupboards and the freezer. I'm standing in front of the open refrigerator when Ben walks back in.

"Trying to cool off?"

"What do you feel like eating?"

He slides his arms around my waist and kisses my neck. "What I want isn't in there."

I smile and hug his arms. "Later, okay?" I look back into the refrigerator.

"Are you sure everything is okay?"

I shut the door and turn in his arms. "Yes." I kiss him. "I just have a lot on my mind. Hunger is one of them."

I step aside and go back to the cupboards. We could have pasta, or we could order out."

"Whatever you feel like having is fine with me."

"I'm sorry I'm not a better cook. I think if my mom had been alive to teach me, I would've been a great cook. However, I've taken after my dad on that front."

He chuckles and looks into the freezer. "We'll find something."

I shut the cupboard door and turn to him. "You know, you've asked me a lot about my parents. So much that I'm bringing them up without even thinking about it. Why don't you tell me about yours?"

"Not much to tell." He won't stop looking in the freezer.

"I'd like to hear about them."

"I never met my mother."

I wrap my arms around him and press myself into his back. "What about your dad?"

"My dad taught me everything I know."

"He was an attorney?"

He shuts the freezer and turns in my arms. "No, but he knew his business. I just applied it to everything I did in life. It got me to where I am today." He kisses me. "And I'm exactly where I want to be."

"Starving in my kitchen?"

He leans down and kisses me, backing me up against the counter. "There's one thing I'm hungry for."

My phone rings, and we both groan. "Hold that thought."

I don't recognize the number and hesitate before answering. "Hello."

"Miss me?" Porter's voice causes the hair on my arms to stand.

"Who gave you a phone?"

Ben walks over with his eyes narrowed. "Who is it?"

I put my hand on his chest when he tries to take the phone.

Porter tsks. "You don't sound as happy to hear from me as I thought you would."

"How did you get out?"

"There are apparently some very generous people who posted my bond. If you find out who it was, I'd like to thank them." He ends the call.

I call Hunter while Ben is still staring me down. "Was that who I think it was?"

I nod and wait for Hunter to answer. "What's up?"

"Porter's out."

I hear his beer bottle hit the table as he sets it down hard. "No shit? How did he get that kind of money?"

"I don't know. I don't think he knows. He said if I find out who it was, he wants to thank them."

"He's fucking with you again. He knows exactly who it

was. That little fucker is just playing a game with you, and you're letting him."

"I'm not letting him."

"Who ended the call?" He scoffs when I don't answer. "That's what I thought. Don't take his calls anymore, and if you do, hang up on him!"

I didn't call to get a lecture. "Just be careful."

He sighs before I hear the suction from drinking from the beer bottle. "You be careful, too."

"Ben's here."

"I figured. Call me tomorrow."

I look at the floor. I hate that he's alone. I hate that I'm not with him. "Okay."

CHAPTER 29

Brynn

ETWEEN HUNTER AND BEN, I don't have two seconds to myself anymore. Ever since Porter's phone call letting me know he's out, those two have been with me around-the- clock. I'm trying to be patient, but a girl needs to have some time to herself.

I stand and Hunter looks at me. "This is really getting old."

"I know you. You're getting frustrated, and you're going to bolt."

I start to walk to the bedroom. "I wish you two would trust me. I'm taking a nap."

"I do trust you!" he yells when I shut the bedroom door. "It's Porter who I don't trust."

I don't even feel like taking a nap. I came in for the peace and quiet. Hunter's getting his protein fix by crunching nuts in my ear, and it's driving me crazy. There are a couple of sets of nuts I'd like to crunch.

I lie down and look at the ceiling. I'm a prisoner in my own home. The killer's made no move to contact me again, but Porter's filled the both of them with fear. I think Hunter knows something that he isn't telling me because this is a little extreme for him. He knows I can handle myself.

I roll over and lie on Ben's side of the bed. Maybe I should take a nap. Maybe it will help improve my mood. Anything has to help improve my mood.

Mr. Sparky doesn't sit as good as he used to. He's getting old. My mom says I have to stop taking him everywhere or he's going to fall apart, but I love him. I want him to be with me.

I finally get him to sit up and have tea with me, and the loud noise from the living room scares me. I grab Mr. Sparky, and his arm rips. "Oh, no." I hold him close. "Mommy will fix you." I start to walk out to find my mom, and I hear them yelling.

"Where is he?"

"He isn't here. He was called away."

"You're hiding him!"

"No! He was called away. Just go!" My mom sounds scared.

"I'll stay here all night if I have to!"

There are more loud noises, and I shut my door and get into my closet. I can't hear the noises as loud in here. I can still hear the yelling, but I don't know what they're saying. I hug my bear to my chest.

"We'll be okay, Mr. Sparky. Mommy will come for us soon."

I grip the shirt I feel under my fingers and continue to cry when I wake up. It takes a minute for me to realize I'm no longer in my closet, and it isn't Mr. Sparky who I'm clutching. I start to back away.

Hunter holds me tighter and doesn't let me leave. "It was just a dream. You're safe here."

I wrap my arms around him and hold on as if my life depends on it. I feel if I were to let go, I'd fall into an empty pit, forever forgotten. I never want to feel like that again. Hunter's become my anchor, and I can't let him go.

"This is what happens when I go to work?" Ben doesn't raise his voice, but I can tell in the tone he isn't pleased.

Hunter slides off the bed, and I know I need to let go of him, but it's really difficult. "She had a bad dream. That's all. I'm not surprised with all this talk about her mom and the two of us keeping a constant watch over her. We're causing her more anxiety instead of helping to protect her."

"Well, you can definitely be relieved of your *duty* to watch over her. I'll handle it from here."

"She's my best friend and my partner. It isn't a *duty* to watch over her. It's an honor."

I stand and wipe my eyes. "Ben, does this look like anything to be jealous of? There's nothing going on except me being comforted by a friend."

"You could've been comforted in the other room."

"Yes, except that I took a nap in here while Hunter stayed out there. Nothing is happening." I walk past him to go into the living room. It's too cozy with the three of us in my bedroom.

"I'm heading out." Hunter walks to the door and turns to Ben with his hand on the doorknob. "Nothing happened, man. If I were in your shoes, I'd be a little uneasy about what I just walked in on, too. You have my word; nothing happened." He turns to me. "I hope you feel better tonight."

I wait for the door to close before I turn to Ben. "Nothing happened, so don't even start with me."

"If you walked in on a woman lying on me, you'd be more than a little *uneasy* about the situation. Try to deny it!"

"You're right." I walk up and slide my hands inside his jacket and around his waist. "I'm sorry. I can't stand being cooped up in here anymore. I need space, and I need time to myself."

He holds my face and rubs his thumbs under my eyes. "Why were you crying?"

I look down. "I had a dream I was in the closet. It was so real."

He pulls me close and holds me. "We'll get to the bottom of this. I promise."

The phone is ringing, and I can't wake up fast enough to answer it. It's been a rough night. I was afraid to go to sleep again and dream about my mother's murder.

The phone starts ringing again. I slap the nightstand until I find it. "Hello."

"Brynn, I need you to come in." The serious tone of SAC Matthews causes me to sit straight up.

"What's happened?"

"Just be here in twenty." He hangs up.

"Fuck." I try to call Hunter, but he doesn't answer. "Fuck, fuck, fuck."

I get up and throw clothes all over trying to change. I don't even care if it matches. I need to get down there now. Just as I pull my shirt over my head, my phone rings again. It's Hunter. "I tried to call you."

"Matthews must have called you first. I was on the phone with him when you beeped in. I'll come get you."

"I'm already dressed. I'll just meet you there."

Ben's been quiet throughout all of this, but when I toss the phone onto the bed, he gets up. "Where are you going?"

"SAC Matthews has called us in. I'm not sure what's going on, but I'll call you later."

"I want to go with you."

"He won't let you in, and you work tomorrow. Just stay here and get some sleep. I'll wake you when I get home and tell you what's going on."

"I wish you'd let me go with you."

I stop as I'm about to walk out and walk back to my bedroom doorway that he's standing in. "I'm hoping that he's putting us back on a case. These are the kinds of calls we're used to getting."

He nods and accepts my kiss. "If you are going out on a case, please call me so I know everything is okay."

"I will."

I pull in next to Hunter's SUV and shake my head. If I didn't have to argue with Ben, I'd have beaten him here. I run inside and skip the elevator. I'm too impatient to hear what's happened. When I reach the top, I'm glad for the workouts Hunter put me through.

Hunter and Lopez are standing in SAC Matthews' office, but he isn't here yet. "Do either of you know what's going on? Do you think we have a new case?"

Lopez shakes his head. "I don't know. It seems a little weird to throw us on a case without warning."

"You'll get a new case in a week." SAC Matthews comes inside and shuts the door. "Have a seat."

He sits behind his desk and turns the ringer of his cell phone off. We know it's serious when he doesn't want to be disturbed. We look at each other and sit down. I don't have a good feeling about this.

"There were some complaints in Porter's complex that he'd moved back in."

I close my eyes. There's more trouble with Porter.

"The property manager had been instructed to give him notice that he was being asked to leave."

Lopez scoffs. "Can they do that?"

"They were trying. When the manager knocked on the door, it opened."

"And like a dumbass, they entered." Hunter sighs as if the conversation is boring him.

"Well, that dumbass found Porter dead."

We all sit up.

"That got your attention, didn't it?" SAC Matthews rubs the back of his neck. "Scott Porter was pronounced dead this evening. He was found strangled by a device it's believed he used on his victims. We're still processing the crime scene, but it's our belief that Porter did this to himself."

Hunter can't believe it. "Why would he do that?"

"The evidence against him was strong. You were right about the blood. Blood was found on the last victim, and it was his. He can't explain that.

"He was also put in isolation while he was incarcerated, but the brief interactions he had with the other inmates were not pleasant for him. I can't imagine he wanted to spend the rest of his life living like that. He deserved to for what he did to those women, but it wouldn't have been a great life."

I look at Lopez. His head is down, and I can see tears in his eyes. I reach out and hold his hand. He was Porter's partner.

"He called me, and I hung up on him."

"Don't do it, Lopez." SAC Matthews stands and walks over to him, slapping him on the shoulder. "You have nothing to feel guilty about. He's not worth it. This is why you're each getting one more week. Take your time to grieve, to process the ending of this case in your minds, and get back here stronger than ever. We need this team back."

I'm numb. I can't believe this is happening. I know Porter was an asshole who enjoyed messing with people, but I never wanted to believe he would actually kill young women.

"You said he was found in a device." Hunter's still processing what we've been told. "What do you mean by that?"

"I probably shouldn't have said that." He walks back over to his desk and sits. "This doesn't leave this room. There was a device attached to his headboard. It was hidden, but he would slide it up when he wanted to use it.

"The rope was threaded through it, and when fastened, the more you struggled, the tighter it got. I believe this is why the injuries were minimal to the victims. There wasn't a struggle. After they were dead, he'd hit the release to free them and slide it back into place for the next victim."

"That bastard just sat back and watched." Hunter stands and starts pacing. "While they were dying and gasping for air, that cold-hearted motherfucker just sat back and watched."

"It looks to be the case. The bruising on the back of the neck is consistent with this device, as well."

"No wonder he didn't have any marks on himself. Motherfucker!"

I stand and put my hand on his arm. "He can't hurt anyone anymore."

"If he were alive, I'd kill him. And to think he almost had me believing . . . I've got to go."

"Hunter." I start to go after him, but SAC Matthews calls after me.

"Brynn, let him go. We all need to process this. I've had a couple of hours, but I didn't want you to find out on the news again."

I nod, but look back out the door. I want to follow Hunter. I look down as my phone buzzes. I need to go home to Ben.

I take the long way home, not sure of what to think about tonight's information. We all suspected it. We all accused him.

And yet, when we're faced with the truth, it's so unbelievable.

I walk in the door and toss my keys onto the table. Ben comes up to me and the moment he touches me, I lose it. He scoops me up and carries me to the sofa.

"What happened?"

I wrap my arms around him and hang on tight. It's several minutes before I can talk, but he doesn't rush me. He just holds me and lets me cry.

When I'm more composed, I loosen my grip around his neck. "I'm sorry." I start to sit up, and he wipes my tears with his thumbs.

"Do you want to talk about it?"

"Porter killed himself."

He drops his jaw, and his mouth hangs open just like ours probably did when we were told. "Seriously?" He blinks a few times and wraps his arms around me. "What happened?"

"I don't really know yet. We were just told that he was found strangled, and they think he did it to get out of the prison time he would be serving."

"Wow." He shakes his head as if he's clearing it. "I suppose it wouldn't be an ideal place for an FBI agent to spend his time, but wow."

"I know."

"What happens next?"

"SAC Matthews is giving us another week to wrap our minds around it and grieve the loss of our teammate, but we're back to work after that."

"You don't sound too excited about that."

"I'm happy to get back to work. I just have a lot to process right now."

"I understand."

I snuggle into him. "Have you heard from the investigator yet?"

"No, but I'll call him tomorrow."

I don't let him finish before the sobbing starts. I can't control it. It's sunk in that Porter is dead. A member of my team is gone, and I couldn't protect him. It didn't matter if he took his own life. I helped push him to despair by not listening to him and cutting him out of my life. It's as much my fault as it is his own.

Ben picks me up and carries me to bed. I let him hold me, comfort me, and tell me everything will be okay even though I don't deserve any of it.

CHAPTER 30

Brynn

THINGS ARE SLOWLY GETTING BACK to normal. Hunter took a few days off to go fishing with his brother. Lopez and his wife took the kids on a vacation since we won't know when we'll get time off again. Ben and I are still dating and splitting our time between our houses.

Everything seems to be getting back to normal except for me. I can run without fear again or constantly looking over my shoulder for Porter to come out of the shadows, but that's the only thing that feels normal.

My hope is that I will feel like me again once we get a new case, but the thought of going through this again makes me sick. I don't want to chase down bad guys and hope we catch a break as we assess and investigate more victims. I want to work with living people and try to keep them alive instead of chasing after the assholes who murdered them.

I keep thinking back to my mother and the fact that my father trained me so hard after her death. I don't believe it was to get me to join the FBI anymore. Although, I'm sure he would've loved to have seen me in action.

I think he was trying to train me to protect myself and keep myself alive when he couldn't. He felt such guilt when my mother died. It never went away. He felt he should've taught her to protect herself, but he still could protect me. And he did.

I want to do that for women. I want to be to them what my father was to me. Unfortunately, it means giving up Hunter. I don't know if I can do that. If I stay on the job, it will only be to be with him, which is a pretty selfish reason when I can be doing so much good in a different position.

I round the corner and smile when I see Hunter standing next to his baby. His Cadillac CTS. I run faster and smile bigger. "You got it back!"

"I did. They still couldn't find any evidence of who did it, but they aren't really investigating anymore, so they towed it to my body guy while I was away."

"It's beautiful."

He rubs the top of it. "I think so." He looks at my sweaty body. "I wish I could tell you that you stink like you tell me when I work out, but you have some fancy smelling deodorant."

I laugh and walk up to my door. I pull the key out of my bra and smile when Hunter looks shocked. I shrug, unlock the door, and walk inside, holding the door open behind me.

"Things have changed since I left. I thought I was only gone for three days."

"Nothing's changed. I just figured that my father went to a lot of trouble to keep me safe, and I shouldn't throw that away."

"That's good. I don't want you to throw that away, either." He follows me to the living room. "So, what else is new?"

I shrug. "Nothing."

He takes two fingers and shoves my shoulder. "I don't buy it. How's Ben?"

"He's working."

"I didn't ask where he was. I asked how he was. What's he think about Porter?"

"He couldn't be happier, I don't think."

"I know the feeling."

I shove him. "Come on. He may not have deserved it, but let's show a little respect."

"You're right." He groans and puts his hands behind his head. "It's just still hard to believe, even though I suspected it. We worked with him. How many times were you alone with him?" He puts his arms down and shakes his head. "I hate to think about it."

"Yeah." I look at Hunter. "Are you going to his funeral?"

"Honestly, I don't know. I came back because of the funeral, but is it sending the wrong message if we go? He killed women, and we suspected him of it."

"I know. Lopez won't be back for it."

"We should just stay here and drink beer tomorrow. We'll have our own little memorial for him."

I nod. "Sounds good to me."

"What about the investigation into your mother's murder?"

"Nothing new there, either. I think it's a lost cause."

"It hasn't been that long. Give him some time. I'm sure there's a lot of shit to sift through."

"Yeah."

"We go back to work in a few days."

I lean my head back on the sofa. "Don't remind me."

"What? Come on! I can't wait to get back. I'd go back today if I could."

I roll my head to look at him. "Yes, but I enjoy being a bum."

He nods. "I do enjoy my day beer."

I laugh. "Your day beer?"

"Yeah, that's what I call it."

How am I going to give this up? I'd miss him too much to leave my job. I watch as his shirt rides up when he stands and stretches. It shows off his toned abs and spattering of hair that disappears into his waistband. I resist the urge to reach up and follow that trail.

"We've only got a few days to get your bum ass in shape again. Let's go!" He pulls me off the sofa as I groan. This part I wouldn't miss.

Since I go back to work tomorrow, I decide to make dinner for Ben tonight. I'm not sure we'll be given a big case so soon after coming back, but if we do, I'll have less time to spend with him. I'm nervous about going back, so my appetite isn't the greatest.

"Have you heard from Paul?" It's been long enough that

the investigator Ben hired should be able to give some sort of report to what they're doing, but I haven't heard anything.

"I put a call into the office today, but he hasn't returned my calls. The receptionist said he'd been in the field all day. That's good news. It means he's working on it. If he's got something, he won't let distractions get in his way."

I nod, fully understanding ignoring calls during an investigation. "Do you think he'll find something?"

Ben reaches across the table and takes my hand. "Whether he solves this case or not, I know it will give you closure. If not for finding your mother's killer, then proving your mother's killer isn't going to come back for you. If he's out there, Paul will find him."

"I'm glad you have confidence in him."

"He's done great work on things for me in the past."

"But they aren't finding murderers for twenty-year-old murders."

"He's the best." He squeezes my hand and lets go to finish his dinner."

"Will you text me the second you hear from him? No matter what case I'm on, I'll call as soon as I can."

"Of course."

I pick up my wine glass and drink what's left. I want to pour another glass, but I'm afraid of getting a call in the middle of the night for the next case. SAC Matthews likes getting us up in the middle of the night.

"Dinner was great." Ben sits back and pats his belly.

"Okay, now you're going overboard." I stand and start to clear the table.

"No, it was. I really enjoyed it."

"Well, I thought since it's my last free night for probably the rest of my life, I should try to cook something really nice." I look at the bowl of pasta. "Well, at least something edible from me."

"It was fabulous." He stands and starts to help me clear the table. "So, I wanted to talk to you about going back to work."

"Yeah? What about it?"

"Since my place is closer to our jobs, I thought we could stay there Sunday through Thursday and at your place on the weekends."

We're spending most nights together now, but we still aren't spending every night. We go our separate ways at least two nights a week. What he's proposing is more or less moving in together.

"I can understand you'd want to stay closer to your office, but I'm not comfortable with that situation. I'll stay over some nights, but we don't spend every night with each other now. That isn't going to change just because I'm going back to work. In fact, it may be less because I go back to work."

"I don't understand. I thought since things had calmed down and settled with Porter and that Shadow case you would be ready to move forward with our relationship. You've seemed so relaxed the past few days."

I scrape the plates into the garbage and start to load the dishwasher. I don't want to have this conversation again. "Ben, we're dating, not living together. I'm not ready for that."

"Will you ever be?"

"Asking me every few days isn't going to help speed it up. It's actually going to slow it down."

"I'm not getting any younger, so if you're not serious about us, I'd kind of like to know."

"Here's a news flash. No one is getting any younger." I turn and look at him. "We've only been dating for a few months. We barely know each other. I enjoy spending time with you, but I'm not going to rush into a commitment I'm not ready for."

"You won't even give me a hint that you'd consider a relationship."

"I've been honest with you from the start. I'm not looking for anything serious. In fact, you're the first serious boyfriend I've ever had. I've had friends and lovers, but I've never had anyone I called my boyfriend before. I'm further with you than I've been with anyone, but I can't promise anything more than that."

I slam the dishwasher door and walk to the living room, leaving him standing in the kitchen. I pick up a magazine I'd meant to toss into the recycle bin earlier, but now I'm glad I have it to keep me busy.

Ben walks over and leans over the sofa to kiss the top of my head. "I think we both need to think about some things. I'll call you tomorrow."

"Okay."

I stop looking at the magazine when the door shuts. I'm frustrated with myself. He's the perfect man in more ways than one, but I don't care that he's walked out. I should be more upset than I am, but I'm not sure if I'm not upset because I'm scared to move forward with him or if I just don't care.

I scream my frustration and throw the magazine across the room.

CHAPTER 31

Brynn

THE ROUTINE WE HAD BEFORE was easy enough to fall into. The first day back Hunter started picking me up again. He was a little hurt when I told him that night I wanted to start driving myself again. It's just easier when I don't know if I'm going to Ben's or home after work.

I haven't been to Ben's yet, but I'm sure I'll head back over there before the week's out, and I don't want to have to go home to get my car first. I'd rather just head over. Hunter understood, but I don't think he was too happy.

I'm sitting at my desk looking at the paperwork for the cases we've been given. I was right to think we wouldn't be given anything major when we first got back. It's understandable, but I'm bored out of my mind. Hunter's feeling it, too. He's itching to get a new case that will call us back out into the field. Lopez is just happy to be working. If Hunter and I had kids, I'm sure we'd be happy to get back to work, too.

I sit up when I think about Hunter and me having kids. I look over at him while he looks over the mountain of paperwork he's going through and smile. I think our kids could be cute. I clear my throat.

"I'm getting a refill. Do you want one?" I stand and wait for Hunter's response. I'm so bored that I'm thinking of fictional children with a man who isn't my boyfriend.

He looks in his coffee cup and shakes his head. "I'm good. Thanks."

"Lopez, Williams, and Bennett! Get in here!" SAC Matthews bellows as he used to when we were called to work a case. Hunter and Lopez trip over themselves to get to his office. I smile, but take my time walking.

"Nice of you to join us, Bennett." He rips off a piece of paper and hands it to Hunter. "A stabbing awaits you. The body was found in the trunk of the car, abandoned in a parking lot." He looks at the three of us before letting us go. "Don't disappoint me."

"We won't, sir." Hunter heads out as if it's Christmas morning and he just got what he asked Santa for. I follow and keep up this time.

When we reach the cars, Lopez looks at his car and back to us. "I know I'm getting assigned a new partner soon, but I kind of miss my old one."

It's the first time any of us have acknowledged Porter since we've been back. Hunter nods. "I think no matter how much of an asshole he was, we all kind of do. Maybe they'll give you a smoking hot babe like they gave me."

I look up to the sky and shake my head as I get into Hunter's car. I pity any woman who has to join this crew. Maybe I should hope for a woman to even it out.

Hunter gets in and looks at me. "You got in my car."

"Yeah? Am I not supposed to?"

"You didn't want me to drive you anymore. I'm happy you're in my car, but I'm surprised is all." He starts the car and backs up. While we follow Lopez to the scene, he takes the time to talk to me. "You're quiet lately. Is everything okay with you?"

"Yeah." I look out the window. "There are just a lot of changes."

He puts his hand on my knee. "More than Porter?"

I place my hand on top of his and squeeze. "Maybe. Let's just focus on the case, okay?"

We're quiet the rest of the drive. He wants me to talk to him, and if I knew what was bugging me, I would. It's hard to put into words when I don't know how to explain it myself.

We get to the parking lot where the car was discovered, and the trunk is up. The medical examiner hasn't arrived on the scene yet, so nothing's been disturbed.

We get out and approach the car. I recognize some of the local PD and expect a frosty reception, but they go on about things as if Porter never happened.

"We have a Caucasian male with what appears to be multiple stab wounds all over his side and back from what we can see. He looks to be late fifties, but it's difficult to tell without a clearer view of his face.

"A woman who works here dropped her keys and smelled a foul odor coming from the trunk when she bent over to pick them up. The car's been here for two days." He looks up to the sun. "It's been hot. That isn't a good combination."

"Why are the plates missing?" I look at the front of the car. "Both plates are gone."

"We snapped a photo of the VIN in the windshield. I haven't heard what they found out with that yet, but Kramer was calling that in."

We approach the trunk and look inside. I narrow my eyes. The man is curled up in a fetal position, but not as if he had been protecting himself. It looks more to be a stuffed job after he was killed. I tilt my head and look at him again.

"Oh, my fucking God."

Kramer walks up and starts to talk, but I cut him off. "It's—"

"Paul Morris." I cover my mouth and back up. "This cannot be happening." I look at Hunter.

"The investigator?"

My breathing starts to quicken, and my heartbeat races. If he found the killer that means the killer found him. Hunter takes me over to his car as he barks orders at the police watching. "No one is to touch this crime scene. Is that clear? No one!"

"Hunter . . ." I start to shake.

"He has more than just your case. It doesn't mean this is your guy. Do you hear me? It doesn't mean shit." He ushers me inside the car and calls SAC Matthews.

"I have to call Ben." I grab my phone, but I'm too shaky to dial it right. "I have to call Ben!"

Hunter helps me with the phone and hands it back when it starts to ring. He walks a few feet away to talk to Matthews while I wait for Ben to answer. I almost cry with relief when he picks up.

"Hey, I was just thinking about you."

"Ben, Paul's dead."

"What?"

"Paul's dead. Someone killed him!"

"Where are you? I'll come pick you up."

"I can't leave yet, but they're going to want to question everyone who hired him. I needed to make sure you were okay. He didn't tell you anything, did he?"

"No, he never got back to me."

I'm relieved and disappointed at the same time. I want to know who the killer is if Paul was able to find him, but I also want Ben to stay safe. If it was my mother's killer and Paul told him who had hired him, Ben could still be in trouble.

"Where are you? Ben, I need you to be safe."

"I'm at the office."

"Go to the bureau. I'll head back there soon. Just please meet me."

"I'll go there now."

"Thank you." My shaking has slowed, and my breathing is returning to normal now that I know Ben is safe. I'm still looking around trying to see if the killer may be watching us. If the car had been there for two days, I doubt he's hung around that long. Hunter's right; it could've been any case Paul was working on.

Ben's sitting at my desk when we get back to the bureau. I hug him tightly when I get to him. "I'm so happy you're okay."

"Bennett, in my office." SAC Matthews sticks his head out and calls for me.

I look at Ben. "I may be a little while."

"I'll wait. I'll always wait for you."

I walk into the office, closing the door behind me. "Yes?"

"Have a seat. Things seem to find you, huh?" He isn't gruff with his tone, but I still don't like the question. No one wants trouble to find them.

"I suppose it does."

"You hired this guy to investigate your mother's murder? Did you think he'd have a better shot than the FBI?"

"Ben hired him. He thinks I need the closure."

He nods and leans back in his chair. "He's probably right about that. You know I can't let you on this case, right?"

I shift in my seat. I think he expects a fight, but I'm probably going to shock him with my answer. "I've been thinking about taking a leave of absence."

He sits forward and places his forearms on the desk. "Have you? For how long?"

"I'm not sure how long I'll be gone, but it's been on my mind for a while." I look down. I feel as if he'll be disappointed in me.

"I think that's a good idea. We'll miss you around here, but if you need time I want you to take it."

"Let me tell Hunter?"

"Oh, that bear is yours."

"I've been thinking that he and Lopez make a pretty great team."

He looks me over. "You have been giving this some

thought. Should I even ask if you're coming back?"

"I can't answer what I don't know." I look behind me at the room I spent most of my time in for the last year and take a deep breath. "I'm not so sure I'm meant to do this." I look back to him. "I'd like to see about helping women before they become victims instead of helping when it's too late to really help."

"I think that would be a perfect fit for you. Take your time to figure out if that's what you really want, but I'll support you no matter what you choose."

I follow Ben to his house when we're finished with the questioning. I don't feel like being alone after seeing Paul's dead body. We're not sure it was the same person who killed my mother, but we're not sure it isn't.

It's awkward at first. We normally would kiss when we see each other for the first time, but it's been a few days since we've seen each other, so it's difficult to find that rhythm again.

"Do you want a glass of wine?" Ben locks the door behind us and secures his alarm.

"Wine would be great. Thank you." I follow him and sit on one of the stools he has at the bar as I rub my hands together.

He notices and nods in my direction. "Are you cold?"

"No, but my hands won't stop trembling. It's ridiculous, really."

"It isn't at all. Regardless of who did that to Paul, the possibility of who it could be is frightening. I don't blame you for being a little skittish."

I nod and take the glass. I should've started with a shot to get my nerves settled before talking to him. "I haven't told Hunter yet, but I just took a leave of absence from the agency."

"Really?" He puts his hand on the small of my back and leads me to the sofa. "What brought that on?"

I take a deep breath. "I want to make some changes. I want to help victims before they become victims, at least before they become murder victims."

"That's a nice idea, but how do you plan to do that?"

"I want to teach them how to protect themselves, like my dad taught me."

"And this is something you can make a living at?"

"I hope so. It'll be rough at first, but I have savings that will get me through."

"Where do we fit in all of this?"

"I'm not asking you to go away." I hold his hand. "I'm asking you to give me time. I need to get me settled before I work on any us."

He smiles and squeezes my hand. "That, I can understand. That, I can wait for." He lifts my fingers and kisses them. I only hope it goes as well when I tell Hunter.

I take a deep breath and knock on Hunter's door. This is going to be the most difficult conversation I'll ever have with someone. I force a smile when he opens the door.

"Hey, what are you doing here so early?" He steps back and lets me in.

"I need to talk to you." I follow him to the kitchen.

"I'll give you as much info as I can, but I still don't have any answers on Paul."

I accept the mug of coffee he hands me. "No, I'm not here about Paul."

"Well, what's up?" He leans against his counter just as he's leaned against mine almost every day for the past year. How am I going to give that up?

I clear my throat and look down. "I made a decision yesterday, and it isn't easy to talk to you about it."

"You can't talk to me?" He puts his mug onto the counter behind him and crosses his arms. "I'm not going to like this decision, am I?"

"I need your support no matter what your opinion is." I look at him. "I don't think I can do this without my best friend supporting me."

He rubs the back of his neck. "Will you just tell me what it is? Are you moving in with Ben? Are you marrying him? What is it?"

"It has nothing to do with Ben. I'm taking a leave of absence from the bureau." I pause and wait for his reaction.

"You don't have to do that. I think this case is going to be reassigned since Paul was working on a case for you. We'll work the next case."

"No, Hunter. There won't be a next case for me."

He narrows his eyes and grips the edge of the counter behind him. "Why?"

"I need more than what we can do. I want to help those who have the potential to be murdered rather than catch the bad guys who murder them."

He opens his mouth a few times, but no sounds come out. He turns his back to me to take a drink of his coffee. I knew his reaction wouldn't be great, but I was hopeful that it would've been better than what it actually is.

I hope I can make him understand. "When I put myself through their experience, it changed me. I was terrified in those brief moments when Ben was choking me, even though I knew I would live through it. I need to help women. I need to do for them what my father had done for me. Will you please understand that?"

I jump when he throws his mug into the sink, causing coffee to splatter everywhere and the mug to shatter. I stand still, afraid to make a move. My fear is not that Hunter will hurt me. My fear is my leaving the job will hurt Hunter beyond what will allow for a continued friendship. I can't lose him.

He leans on the sink and hangs his head. "Is it because I kissed you?"

"No."

He turns around and looks at me. "Because I'll promise to never do it again. If you're afraid to be alone with me—"

"Stop." I walk up and hold his face. "If you remember, I kissed you back. I'm not afraid of you."

He holds my hands. "Then why? We have a great thing going. Please don't quit on me."

I slip my hands out of his. "I'm not quitting on you. I'm redirecting my focus. I want to save women instead of catch their killers. Please understand."

We stand in his kitchen mere inches from each other, pleading for our side to win. Ultimately, I know I'll never go back to the bureau, so his side will never win. I still can lose big if he continues to take this personally and never speaks to me again. I can't return to dead bodies, but can I live without Hunter?

CHAPTER 32

Brynn

'M LOOKING THROUGH FITNESS EQUIPMENT sites and comparing prices to those in the magazines in my lap. It's funny that people don't go into this much planning and budgeting for their own lives, but putting a business together and thinking about what they need to get that started, and suddenly they become deal hunters.

There's a knock on my door, and I hang my head. I don't have time for visitors. This order needs to be placed today. I put my laptop onto the coffee table and bend the corners of the magazines to keep my place.

Looking through the window on the door, I see Hunter standing on the other side. Seeing him makes me smile. I open the door and let him in. "Hey, what's up?"

"Not much. Lopez had some family appointments, so I

thought I'd hop over and see how my favorite former partner was doing."

He walks over to the sofa and looks at the laptop. "Looks like I'm just in time. This is my area of expertise."

"Everything so far has been your area of expertise." I grab a couple of waters on my way back to the living room. "However, I really could use your opinion on what models to get. They all seem to have different options."

"I think you need to focus more on space issues. You don't even really need all that shit."

"I don't?" I look at him, completely taken off guard. I thought, if anyone, he would be the one to tell me I needed to buy more than what I budgeted for.

"No. You just need to work on resistance training and getting them strong. Sure, you could get this expensive shit, but for what you want to train them for, you don't need it."

"That saves me a ton of money, but I'm still nervous about not having any equipment."

He shakes his head and takes the laptop. "I didn't say no equipment." He searches for heavy bags and pull-up bars. "Teach them to box, to not be afraid to hit someone, and have them gain strength so when they do hit someone, they do damage. You don't need that other shit you were looking at to do that."

"That makes sense." I slouch on the sofa and sigh. "But now I'm wondering if I know what the fuck I'm doing."

"Hey, you'll be great. You're just too worried about trying to be great. I'm proud of you for taking this step."

"You are?"

"Of course, I am. Okay, I admit I was a little hurt at first, but we're still friends. It's all working out okay. I think you want this so badly that you're trying too hard. Just be the badass girl I know you to be, and you'll do great things."

I snuggle next to him. "I've missed you."

He lays on a dramatic sigh. "Fine. I'll help you pick out your equipment."

I laugh, but don't stop him as he looks through the site and the magazines. I really can use the help. It's overwhelming.

"So, how's Ben been?" He laughs at his own joke that only he thinks is funny.

"You know he hates it when you ask him that way, right?"

"Of course." He smiles at me before he gets serious. "Really, how are things?"

"Things are things, I guess." I sit up and take a drink of water.

Hunter looks at me and narrows his eyes. "I thought you two were happy?"

"We are." I look down. "Mostly."

"What—"

I cut him off as I get off the sofa and pace the room. "I don't know, Hunter. I told him I'd try, but I don't think I should have to *try* to want to be with someone. I should just want to be with him.

"I shouldn't feel this way. I know he'll never break my heart, so why am I having such a hard time deciding what to do? He's a great guy, and I should be happy with him."

"But?"

"I don't know. Maybe I'm not meant to be happy."

"You've never needed a man to feel happy." He rubs his chin. "Do you want me to be honest with you?"

"Yes! Please, tell me what I'm not seeing! I want to be happy with him."

"You can't be happy with him. You can be content, which is what you're feeling." He stands. "This is what I've learned from my experience with Jamie. You can settle down with anyone you get along with. You can convince yourself that you love them because you do have a good time. Hell, it's even better when you are compatible sexually.

"However." He takes a step toward me. "There's that one person who'll never make you feel as if you settled for anything. That one person who makes you wake up every day and strive to be the best person you can be."

He's casual when he walks toward me, but for some reason, I'm not feeling very casual at the moment. Every hair on my body is standing at attention, and there's tension in the air. I feel more like the prey he's tracking instead of the friend he's trying to console.

"You think you should feel happy because you don't think he'll ever hurt you. Really, what you're feeling is bored because you know he can't. The only person who can ever hurt you is the person who holds your heart, and it isn't him."

I back up with each step he takes toward me until I'm pinned against the wall. "You don't need to feel *happy*. You just need to feel."

He lowers his mouth to mine and whispers, "What do you feel now?"

He doesn't let me respond and presses his lips to mine. I'm consumed with feeling and not sure where to turn to first. He takes my hesitation as rejection and backs away. I look at his eyes, his lips, and back to his eyes again before I grab him and pull him in for another kiss. There's no hesitation from either of us at this point.

I know I should stop, and this will change everything in my life again, but I can't stop kissing him. He's right; I need to feel, and I feel so much when I'm with him.

He lifts me and presses me against the wall. I wrap my legs around him, pulling him closer. I gasp as he starts rocking his hips into me and kissing my neck. I look behind him and see the photo of Ben and me, and I close my eyes. I try to ignore the tug at my conscience, but I can't. I'm still in a relationship with Ben and cheating on him with Hunter.

He cups my breast. "I want you, Brynn."

I hold his face and make him look at me. "I want you, too. There's something I need to do first."

He closes his eyes and puts his forehead to mine. "You're killing me."

"It's killing me, too." He unwraps my legs from around his waist and starts to back up, but I hang on to him. "Don't be mad. I don't want to start this between us this way. I need to come clean with Ben. Please understand."

"I understand more than you know. It's why I didn't tell you the real reason I broke it off with Jamie. I figured it would be too soon, and people would talk. I didn't want them to think you were the one who broke us up."

He takes my hands and kisses them before letting me go and walking to the door. "Just remember when he's trying to say anything he can to hang onto you, that I'm waiting for you. I know Jamie told you, but you need to hear it from me. I'm in love with you, Brynn. When you realize you're in love with me, I'll be waiting. Come get me."

He shuts the door, and my heart drops. He's right; I am in love with him. I look at the photo with Ben again and see that while his smile is genuine and carefree, there's an absent look in my eyes. I may be smiling on the outside, but on the inside, I'm in love with another man.

"Hunter!" I run for the door and open it to see Hunter standing there waiting for me. I grab his shirt and pull him back inside my house.

He kicks the door shut and kisses me as he walks us back to my bedroom. "I'm not leaving this time."

"I won't ask you to." I pull my shirt over my head, toss it across the room, and kiss him.

Buttons scatter across the floor as he rips his shirt off. My hands go to his belt and unfasten it before moving on to his pants. I feel butterflies in my stomach as he places his fingers in my waistband to pull me closer. Both of our pants fall to the floor at the same time. We're tripping as we tug our feet out of our pants, but we never stop kissing.

I reach behind me to unfasten my bra, but he has his hands already there, making quick work of it. It falls to the floor as he crushes me to the bed.

We're still kissing. It's as if we're breathing air into each other. I suck on his tongue, and it causes him to smile. "This won't be a soft, loving, take-my-time kind of sex. I'm going to fuck you."

Adrenaline rushes through my body as he speaks each word. *I'm going to fuck you.* I slide my hand into his boxers and squeeze his hard cock. "I'm waiting."

His lips crush mine as he puts my hands above my head. I rock my hips into him, letting him know I'm growing impatient for his promise.

He sits up, breathing hard, and puts his head in his hands. "You're going to kill me before I even get inside you. I need a condom."

I get up, finish undressing, and pull the covers back on the bed while he grabs a condom. Before I can stand, he's behind me, holding my hips. My heart starts pounding. I back up a little, giving him permission and he takes it.

He fills me on the first thrust, and I fall forward, placing my hands onto the bed. He grips my hips harder and starts pounding into me. I fist the sheets. "Oh, God."

I feel his hands as he slides them around my hips and up to my breasts. He pulls me to stand with him. I move one hand behind his head and place my other arm over his that's around my waist.

We're in sync; every thrust, movement, caress, and touch seems to be without effort. We each know what the other needs the exact moment we need it.

He backs up, slipping out of me, and turns me around. "I want to look in your eyes when we come."

He backs me up to the bed and lays me down, getting on top of me. He kisses me this time when he thrusts into me. I move my hips with him, and the buildup is quick. I gasp when the first tremor comes forward.

"Don't stop. Please, don't stop."

He lifts his body up onto his elbows and moves his hips faster, looking down at me. I hold his face and lift my head to kiss him. Laying my head back down onto the pillow, I arch my back when my first orgasm hits.

"Fuck, yes!"

Hunter places his forehead in the crook of my neck. "Damn." He lifts his head and looks at me. "I almost lost it there for a minute."

He gets back on his elbows and thrusts harder. I wrap my legs around him and try to keep up, but he's a machine. I'll never complain about his workout routine again.

I look up at his face and see the signs of pleasure with his closed eyes, raised eyebrows, and opened mouth. I squeeze my walls around him, and he opens his eyes.

"You want to play that way?" His wicked smile makes me smile, but I soon have that look I was just admiring on him when he rubs my clit. "Open your eyes. I want to look at you when you come again."

I open my eyes and hold his face as he picks up the pace with his hips and his thumb. The squeezing is no longer voluntary as I grip him inside me. I need to get him deeper, and I need to feel all of him.

I bite my lip and try my best to not arch my back so I can still see his eyes as my orgasm hits me. I grip his shoulders while his hips and fingers are relentless. He's drawing out this orgasm as long as he can. I can't hold back anymore and scream while arching my back.

He thrusts a few more times and holds himself inside as far as he can. His back goes rigid, and the groan that escapes him is primal and full of lust. His body relaxes as he lies on top of me, panting. "I love you so much, Brynn."

I run my fingers through his hair and pull his face to mine. "I'm in love with you, too."

His entire face lights up, and it appears the weight of the world has fallen off his shoulders. It only lasts a moment before he's serious again. "What about Ben?"

"I love you, Hunter, but I do need to tell Ben tonight."

"Do you want me to go with you?"

"I think I need to do it alone. It's going to hurt him enough. He doesn't need the man I'm leaving him for to be there when I tell him."

He nods.

CHAPTER 33

Brynn

I PULL UP TO BEN'S and take a deep breath. No matter how many times I try to calm myself down, it doesn't help. The nerves are high knowing I'm going to break his heart. I don't feel the same way about him that he feels about me, and it isn't fair to either of us to continue this charade as long as we have.

I knock and wait for him to open the door. It's my problem that I need to handle, but I do wish Hunter had come with me. This is going to be awkward at best. I've ended relationships before, but those guys never cared for me the way Ben seems to.

He opens the door and smiles. When he bends down to kiss me, I turn my head. "Did I do something wrong?"

"No, but we do need to talk."

Concern and confusion flash across his face as he backs

up to let me inside. "Okay. What do you want to talk about?"

I know what I need to say, but I don't know how to say it. "This isn't working out."

"I see." He walks to the living room. "I figured this day was coming."

"Then why keep seeing me?"

"I didn't want to give up hope that you'd look at me the way you look at Hunter one day."

I look away, embarrassed that it was obvious. "I don't know what to say."

"How about answering a few questions for me?"

"I can try."

"Did you ever care for me?"

"I still care for you. I'm just not in love with you."

He sighs and takes a drink. I could use one, but I don't ask. I need to drive home as soon as this conversation is over. "It wasn't always like that with you and Hunter. What was the turning point?"

"I'm not sure. It wasn't as if one day I woke up and said to myself that I loved him. I think I fought it, actually."

"Why?"

"Afraid of being hurt, I guess."

"Yeah, I can understand that. Being hurt sucks."

I look at the floor. "I'm sorry."

"Why did you even agree to date me?"

"You were a great-looking guy. You had a solid job, and you seemed nice. What woman wouldn't date you? I just wasn't looking for love when you found me."

"You couldn't have been because you already found it."

I can't deny that. "I can't say I'm sorry enough for letting this go on as long as I did. I really thought I could be happy with you."

"How long has it been going on with Hunter?"

"I just made the decision today."

He scoffs. "Obviously, since you're here, but that isn't what I asked. I asked how long your affair had been going on."

I cross my arms and look directly at him. "I wasn't cheating on you."

"You're telling me that you've never slept with him."

I look down again. "Just today."

"At least you came clean about that." He walks over to the bar to pour himself another drink. "There are other ways to cheat, you know?"

"We had kissed or started to kiss a few times, but I always stopped it."

"Until today." He picks up the remote and presses *Play*. Hunter and I are pressed against my wall, kissing. I watch as Hunter backs up when I tell him I need to break it off with Ben. I watch as I look to Ben's photo and run after Hunter. He pauses it when I open the door.

Ben's standing within inches of me while I watch the television. I'm furious that he's had a copy of the feed run to his house.

"I thought you said I was the only one who would have access to that."

He bends down to my face and yells, "I lied!"

It's so loud and angry, causing me to take a few steps backward. He has every right to be angry, but I don't have to stay and take it. I turn toward the door.

"I'm not finished with my questions yet."

I stop and turn to him. "I'm finished answering them. It looks as if you have all the answers anyway!" I point to the screen. "You don't need me to rub it in." I turn to walk away, but his last question stops me in my tracks.

"Did you choose to wear your mom's perfume because it was your mom's, or do you even remember that's what she wore?"

I turn and look at him, trying to keep my composure. "What do you know about my mother's perfume?"

He inhales deeply and lets out a shaky breath. "I know it used to make me sick every time I smelled it on another person until I smelled it on you."

I run to the door and hear his glass hit the floor and shatter as he runs behind me. His door is completely locked, and I'm only halfway through unlocking the locks when he grabs me and turns me around.

"There's no reason to run. I'll always catch up to you. I always do."

I try to stomp on his foot, but he's wearing steel-toed boots. I raise my knee, but it meets a protective cup instead of his balls. He grips my arms harder and shakes me.

"Your father isn't the only one who taught his prodigy well." He turns me, shoves my chest against the wall, and starts to frisk me for my gun. I didn't bring it. "We had such a good thing going. You completed me. You were everything I wasn't. Our lives could've been beautiful together, but you ruined it!"

"Ben, we can talk about this."

His laugh is not that of a sane man. "You'll kill me the first chance you get. There is no more talking."

He turns me toward the stairs and shoves me. "Move!"

I'm trying to wrap my mind around what's happening, but I can't. It doesn't make sense. I turn and sit on the stairs. "I'm not moving until you tell me what the fuck is going on."

He shakes his head but bends down and speaks slowly. "I killed your mother."

I clench my jaw as I look into the face of the man who killed my mother. Could I believe it? I talked about her enough that he could be trying to mess with me to get back at me for choosing Hunter, but why would someone lie about that?

I continue to look him in the eye. "I'm going to need more than just your say so."

"I went there looking for your father. I didn't believe your mother when she said he wasn't home. He was supposed to be."

"I've told you all of that already."

"I think I would've believed her had I not seen the dinner she made. Who would make such a dinner for just a little girl? Your dad had to be home." He shrugs. "I enjoyed the pot roast, even if your father couldn't. It was nice of your mom to make that for me. It was quite the celebratory dinner for my first kill."

I start to throw punches and slap whatever I can make contact with. I want to throw up, but I'm more focused on killing him instead. I'm able to do some damage—his nose and lip are bleeding—but he gets control of my wrists and twists my arms behind my back.

"Get your ass upstairs!"

I walk because he's forcing me, but I'm looking around trying to find an escape. Even if I was able to get out of his grip, I see nothing that will help me.

He shoves me into his bedroom and lets go of my arms. I turn around as soon as I can and face him, putting my hands up in front of me.

"You want to fight me?" He looks me up and down and chuckles. "You think your little adventure into the self-defense world would've saved lives. I say it would've just made things more challenging." He takes a step closer. "I love a good challenge."

I don't move. I just wait my turn. It's all about patience, and he's a man with none left. As long as I keep my wits about me, I have the upper hand.

"Why did you kill my mother?"

"My father ordered it. Your father put him away. It was the best day of my life."

I swallow hard.

"I thought I was nothing like my father. He tried to teach me things as I grew up, but I wanted nothing of that lifestyle. I was wrong."

He walks over to his bed and pulls the covers down. "You see, I'd avoided killing people until that day. My father told me that if I didn't do that job, then he'd have someone do it in front of me and then kill me next. I had just turned eighteen. I had my entire life ahead of me.

"I thought I could do one job for him. Just one and then I'd be free." He tilts his head and raises his eyebrows. "I was free, but in a much different way." He narrows his eyes and looks at me. "But I was also haunted. I didn't expect the kid."

"I didn't see you. How did you see me?"

"I looked in the windows before I knocked on the door.

I needed to know where everyone was. Only, I couldn't find your father."

I'm starting to lose my breath, as it's all sinking in. "He wasn't home."

"We've covered that already!" He runs his hands through his hair. "You infuriate me. Sometimes I think it would've been better if I had just stayed away from you, but I couldn't stay away. I'd waited for the last twenty years to get close to you."

"So, you have been following me just as I thought."

"I was instructed to try to find an opening to kill you and your dad. I needed to finish the job." He shakes his head. "Your father was even more watchful after the death of your mother. I think he stressed over it so much that it caused the heart attack." He shrugs one shoulder. "After that, it was more fun watching him suffer. He sent my father to prison, but it was your father living through a life sentence with his guilt.

"And then I started seeing a beautiful young woman instead of that little kid who hid in the closet. I couldn't get over how much you seemed to change overnight."

I have to keep him talking, but I don't know what else to say. I look at his bed for the first time since coming into the room, and I can feel the blood drain from my face. "It's all you."

He looks at the device on the headboard with the rope attached to it and smiles. "It is all me. I can't tell you what a relief it is to finally tell you and show you."

"I don't want to hear it."

"You don't really have a choice now, do you?"

My phone starts ringing, and he sighs. He walks over and

takes it out of my pocket. "It's your boss. He's going to have to find a new partner for Hunter. However, I should thank him for starting that investigation against Porter."

He turns and throws the phone against the wall, shattering it. "Porter was a pain in my ass, though. He was catching on quicker than he should've been."

"How?" All those times he followed us. I shook my head. He wasn't trying to harass me. He was trying to protect me.

"I think he saw me with a couple of the girls. I didn't know he was an FBI agent, or I would've killed him long before I started dating you."

"You're the one who bailed him out."

"Yes. I had to kill him. I couldn't leave it up to the justice system. They may have found him to be not guilty. He needed to take the blame for those victims."

"Do you not have any feelings or remorse for anyone you've killed?" It's a stupid question because if he did, they wouldn't be dead.

"No. There are a couple I wish didn't have to die so soon, but they always have to die." He reaches out and touches my face. "I'm going to miss you the most."

I turn my head and bite his hand as I grab his wrist and twist it behind him. I enjoy hearing him in pain, but I need to do more to get out of here.

I kick the back of his knee and force him to the floor, but he grabs the back of my leg and pulls me with him. I can't hurt him below the belt with that protective cup, but I use everything else I have available to me.

I press my thumbs into his eyes until he backs off a little where I can try to scoot out from under him. He brings his fist down and hits me in the stomach, knocking the wind out of me. I roll over, coughing, and trying to crawl away.

I'm dragged back by my ankle. I roll over to my back and try to kick his chest. He splits my legs and gets between them. It hits me that I've had sex with this man. I roll to my side and vomit.

"You didn't complain when I was balls deep, baby."

I wipe my mouth with the back of my hand and look at him. "It's hard to complain about something you can't feel, needle dick."

He hits me. I spit blood and look at him again. "I would've loved you for the rest of your life!"

"I hate you. I've always hated you. And I will hate you for the rest of yours. Tell me. Why did you switch to stabbing when you killed Paul? I'm sure it was tempting to bring your little invention back out."

"I'm a jack-of-all-trades, sweetheart. My father always said to never kill the same way twice. Don't give them a trail. When you caught the first Shadow murder, I had to kill that way again. I wanted you to chase me."

I look into his eyes, trying to find some semblance of the man I thought I knew. "How many people have you killed?"

"Does it matter?"

I shake my head. "You won't live long enough to name them anyway."

"I've always loved your confidence."

"I've loved nothing about you."

"I'm not sure why you feel you have to hurt me. I've only treated you well."

"Well? You call killing my mother, watching my father

die, and calling me a slut treating me well? You're a fucking lunatic!"

He's getting too comfortable as he lies on top of me. I need to get him to let me up. "Why kill people at all? You could be such a great guy."

"Why save them? They aren't your problem." He brushes the hair out of my face. "I know you feel guilty for your mom's death, but if you had come out, I would've killed you, too."

"Why not just kill me after my dad died? You could've done it so many different times."

He strokes my face. "I fell in love with you."

"And you show me that by killing innocent women to get my attention?"

"They were pawns. Sometimes you have to kill the pawns to get to the queen."

I reach up and hold his face. I wait until he lowers his face to mine and twist my body to get on top. Putting my hands together, I sit up and slam his chest a few times and punch him in the face.

I hear his jaw crack when I hit him, but it isn't enough to stop him from fighting back. I stand and run toward the door, but he pulls me back by my hair. It's the last thing I remember.

CHAPTER 34

BEN

LOOK AT HER BODY on the floor. I couldn't take the threats, the insults, or the cruel words from the woman I've been in love with anymore. I only hit her a few times, but she blacked out. I look at her again. Unless she's faking.

I pick her up and hurry to put her into the device before she wakes up. I loosen it a little. I don't want it to choke her before she's aware of what's going on. The night she asked me to choke her during sex gave me a preview of what tonight will be like. I reach down and remove the cup I'm wearing, so I can rub my cock through my pants. I could get off just looking at her wearing my ropes.

It wasn't supposed to end like this, even though I always knew it would. I was hopeful when she agreed to date me, but she was just looking for someone to warm her bed at night. Ultimately, she's just like all the others and has to go.

There's no reason to keep her, but I want to. I sit next to her on the bed and brush the hair out of her face. "Why couldn't you love me? We could've been so happy together."

It's time to end my pain. I lean over and grab the smelling salts to wake her. It only takes a couple of passes for her to come to. She sits up, and her eyes grow wide when she hears the click. She knows she's locked into her death now. This is the first murder since her mother that I feel guilty for.

"Ben, can you live without me?"

I shrug. "I guess we'll find out. You've given me no option."

I stand and move to the foot of the bed. I have a feeling it's going to be a long night, but I'll watch her until she makes the mistake of trying to fight for her life like everyone before her.

I grab a chair and pull it to the bed. "Don't be frightened. You'll be with your parents soon."

Her eyes close as one tear falls. I reach out to brush it away, and she jerks her head but stops when the noose tightens a little.

"Be careful. Sudden movements make it nervous."

"Ben, think about this."

"Oh, I've thought about this moment my entire life." I tilt my head. "I've never told you that I like the name you gave me."

"Name?"

"Yes. Shadow. Whenever you talked about the case and called me that, it made me happy."

"I didn't come up with it."

"Well, that's disappointing."

"We don't name killers. The news named you. Our names

wouldn't be fit for television."

"You're trying to take this away from me. It isn't going to work."

"They did get it right, though. The way you linger in the shadows and stalk your victims was spot-on, even if they didn't know the facts of the case."

I smile and have a pang of regret for killing her. Maybe I can just keep her tied up somewhere.

"Of course, the names asshole, douche bag, and psychotic motherfucker have a nice ring to them, too."

I lose my smile and kick the bed, causing the ropes to tighten ever so slightly with the movement. The terror that flashes through her eyes gets me hard and reminds me why I'm doing this.

I move my hand to my belt and unfasten it. I can't keep my excitement down. I have to relieve some of the pressure. "There was a time when you enjoyed seeing me stroke my cock." I take it out and move my hand in long, slow strokes.

"I don't enjoy it while lying in this thing."

"You wouldn't enjoy it anyway. If I were Hunter, it'd be a different story." I stop stroking myself and look at her. "Say, do you think he'll get back with Jamie when you're dead?"

I sit back, smile, and start stroking my cock again. That one hurt her. It feels good to hurt her. I move my hand faster.

"You're sick. You wonder why I can't love a man like you? It's because you're a miserable excuse for a human be-ing. You're a pathetic piece of shit who deserves to rot in hell."

"Enough!" I stick my dick back into my pants and stand to pace the floor. "I've done nothing but treat you like a queen! You will not disrespect me further."

"Why did you hire Paul if you knew he'd find you?"

"I didn't know he'd find me. The plan was always to kill him. I had to get you scared to come back to me."

"So, he didn't learn who you were?"

"No, he did. I knew that fucker was amazing. I should've chosen someone else because I'll miss his work." I grab the chair and sit down again, propping my feet up onto the bed. "He talked to some old men who worked the case, and they told him about my old man. He connected the dots from there. It is kind of unsettling to be hired by the son of the man who set the hit on your mother. When he approached me and asked me if I wanted him to continue the search, I knew then he was wearing a recording device.

"I couldn't have that. I killed him where we met that night, but drove him to the parking lot later. I knew there weren't any cameras there because a client of mine had fallen in that parking lot, and we subpoenaed the video. They didn't have any.

"I would've disposed of the body better than just leaving it in the parking lot, but it wasn't a planned interaction. I had to be quick, and I had to get by without a car. It's difficult to be in two places at once."

"How did you get Porter's blood on Dani?"

"He was a hothead. Given the opportunity to fight me, I knew he would. I had his blood all over me."

"Weren't you afraid of getting your blood mixed in there?"

"Of course, but since we fought each other, I had a pretty good reason to have my blood there, too. They weren't looking at me, though."

I look at my watch and sit back. My attention is drawn to the hallway, and my heart rate accelerates. "Did you hear that?"

"I've only heard you."

I go to the door and listen, but I don't hear anything. As much as I don't want to say good-bye to her, it's time to end this and move on. I walk over to her and touch her face. "I'll miss you."

"Ben, don't."

She grips my arms as I grab her shirt. I yank her up and start the tightening of the ropes. At first, she does her best to not fight, but instinct kicks in and she fights against it, trying to get it to loosen. As she moves her fingers to try to grab the rope to pull it away from her, I move my hand into my pants and pull out my hardening cock.

I back up as I stroke to the vision of the angel dying in my bed. I try to let go of the little girl I spied on in the window twenty years ago and free my mind of the love I once had for her.

Brynn has no more air as she tries to take breaths. It's completely cut off her throat. This is when my orgasm comes to life—when their life is leaving their body. I grip my cock harder and imagine it to be the rope around her neck. Just a few more strokes, and we'll both be finished.

I turn to the sound of the bedroom door being kicked open and see Hunter walking in with his gun drawn. He lowers it, and I think he thinks Brynn is staying with me, but he pulls the trigger and shoots my hand holding my dick. I fall to the floor in pain as I hear a double tap of the gun.

Falling forward and landing with my head on the foot of the bed, I watch as he scrambles to free Brynn's lifeless body.

"Where's the release?" He's screaming, but I won't answer. "Where's the fucking release?"

"You can't protect her this time. She'll always be mine."

I close my eyes.

EPILOGUE

Hunter

IT'S CRAZY HOW MUCH CAN happen in a year or how much your life can change in the blink of an eye. The things you thought you wanted before are no longer relevant when you lose what you fought so hard to keep. I can dwell on the past and hate the decisions I made, but that's not what Brynn would want me to do.

My biggest regret of all was not listening to Porter in my basement that day. I listened and thought he was crazy. He told me he thought Ben was the killer. His first clue was the business card Ben threw at him after one of their scuffles at Brynn's house. That's why he was in the building across from the shopping center the day Brynn and I went there.

Ben had two offices, and he'd thrown the wrong card at him. He couldn't prove he'd met some of those women at the shopping center, but Ben's office overlooked the women's stores. He had the perfect view to pick his victims of choice.

He also couldn't prove anything just by witnessing Ben talking to some of the victims at the bars. Porter never saw him talking to them on the night they died, nor did he see Ben leave with any of them. He'd seen him leave with plenty of women who did survive the next day, which made him just as big of a douche as Porter, but didn't prove him to be the killer.

The only thing he'd missed was the name change Ben had done. Being the attorney he was, he changed his name, dropping his father's last name and having the records sealed. I'm not sure how many favors he had to call in to get that done, but there was no public record of his original name anywhere. I'm not sure what name they carved onto his tombstone, but as long as he's six feet under and dickless, that's all that matters to me.

I look at the space we've finally completed for the women's resource center Brynn wanted to have, and I have to say I'm proud of it. If someone told me last year that I'd quit the FBI and start this adventure, I would've told them they were out of their minds. Your priorities change when the love of your life is dying in front of you. You realize she's right, and the focus needs to be on helping women survive the attacks instead of finding the killers who murdered them.

I take a deep breath and swallow the lump in my throat. No matter how long I live, that will always be the hardest day of my life.

It's killing me to wait for her call. I should've gone with her. The longer she's there, the more worried I become. She can change her mind and choose him. I grab my keys.

I have to drive by to see if she's still there. Crazy and obsessive? Maybe, but I'm in love with her, and I can't handle the thought of her being alone with him. Part of it is jealousy; I can admit that. The other part is paranoia after Porter told me he suspected Ben to be the Shadow.

I shake my head. Porter was just trying to get the heat off him. I can't say I blame him. Most people do when caught. He did make some vital points and almost had me believing it, but the moment Brynn told me that Ben had cameras installed, I couldn't believe it anymore. Why would he want to record himself doing that shit to her?

I drive past, and her car is still in his driveway. I want to knock on the door or text her, but I don't. I have to give her the time to do what she needs to. I have to trust her. She said she loves me and never said she loved him. That has to mean something.

I jump as my phone rings on the seat next to me. I'm glad I drove past before she came outside. She'd kill me if she saw me. Or maybe she did. Fuck.

I pick up the phone. "I'm sorry. I just had to know what was going on."

"Williams, where's Bennett?" SAC Matthews is on the phone.

"She's with Ben."

"I was afraid of that."

"What's going on?"

"I can't get her on the phone."

I slam on the brakes and turn the car around.

"He's the Shadow. I'm sending a team there now."

"What the fuck do you mean?"

"The private investigator left some information behind in case he was murdered. We just found it."

"Goddammit! Brynn's breaking up with him!"

"There's more. He's the one who killed her mother."

"Are you fucking kidding me?" My head is spinning. This can't be real.

"The team will be there soon."

"I'm already here! Fuck the team!"

"Hunter, don't do anything—" I hang up on him.

I grab my gun and walk up to the door. It's locked. Fuck! I walk to the back, but it's locked, too. I stand back and look up and see a window open. I put my gun away and look around for a ladder. I look back up to the window.

He probably doesn't own a ladder. Motherfucker probably hires everything out. Fuck it. I'll get up there myself. I jump up to the lowest branch of the tree in the backyard and climb up. The further up and out I go, the thinner the branches get. I jump, praying I climbed far enough and land with a thud right outside the window.

I wait a few moments to see if there's any movement inside. That was louder than I wanted it to be. Hearing nothing, I take my gun and inch my way toward the window.

There's no sound. I'd at least expect to hear arguing, but there's nothing. Silence makes me nervous. I take the screen out and slide through, listening before moving further.

They're in the bedroom. My heart drops. I can't be too late. I can't be. I listen at the door.

"I'll miss you."

Brynn sounds stressed, but at least she's alive. *"Ben, don't."*

I hear the scuffle on the bed and ready my gun before I kick the door open. I'm taking aback by the sick image of Ben stroking his cock. I lower the gun and shoot once, ensuring that even if he does make it out of here alive, he'll never fuck with another woman.

I raise the gun and double tap into his chest to make sure he's at the least wounded enough to give me time to get Brynn out, but I won't be sad if he dies.

My heart stops when I see Brynn struggling and then stopping. I rush to her and look at the device. *"Where's the release?"* I know he won't tell me, but I have to try. I know there's a release somewhere, and that's how he got his victims freed after he killed them, but I can't find it.

"Where's the fucking release?"

"You can't protect her this time. She'll always be mine."

"The fuck she will."

SAC Matthews' team runs in just as I find the release and pull her out of the ropes. I breathe into her.

Again.

Once more.

"Don't give up, Brynn!" Again.

She coughs, and I cling tightly to her. The team Matthews sent is trying to revive Ben, but it's no use. They should let him rot in hell.

I pick up Brynn and carry her downstairs, ignoring an investigator's warning to leave her alone. I'll never leave her alone again. I will always protect her.

I sit on the sofa and cradle her in my arms. She's clinging to me just as much. "You're safe now, Brynn. I knew you were a fighter. I knew you wouldn't give up on me."

"He killed my mom." Her sobs wrack her body.

"I know, baby. I know. I promise we'll get through this together."

I smile as I feel hands slide around my waist. "What's the matter? Are the paint fumes getting to you?"

I turn and wrap my arms around Brynn. "No, I'm just so proud of you for putting this together."

She slips her hands into my back pockets. "*We* put this together. I'm proud of us." She kisses me.

I kiss a trail down to her neck and work my way from one side to the other. "I love you."

"Mmm. I love you, too." She holds my face. "But you've got to get past that day. Things happen for a reason. If that was what I had to go through to get you to be my partner in this, I would go through it a hundred more times. I got used to having you with me all day. I don't want to give that up."

"I don't want to give that up, either." I rub her belly. "I don't think you would've had to try very hard to convince me, though. I need this world to be safer for her." I kneel down and kiss my daughter. "I can't wait to meet you."

Brynn runs her fingers through my hair. "I can't wait to meet her, either. It means I can have wine again."

I stand and smile. "I believe wine is what got us into this in the first place."

"Hey, you were sober enough to stop me long enough to get the condom."

I walk her backward toward the office. "When your hands are on me, there's no stopping. I must have you."

"Oh, yeah? Is that why we're going to the office? You have to have me now?"

"I always have to have you." I kiss her, but don't let it go too far. "But right now, I want to give you something."

She reaches for my belt. "I was hoping you'd say that."

I laugh and thread my fingers with hers, looking at our wedding rings. "No, really. Just sit here and give me a minute."

I head over to the desk and take out the gift I've been hiding. "It's a little difficult shopping for someone who's with me every day."

"Any time you want to buy me something, I won't stop you."

I hand her the gift. "You'll have to share this one with our daughter."

She tilts her head and looks at the gift. "I can share."

She's taking too long trying to be nice about how she un-wraps the present. I think she's doing it to bug me, but I can wait it out. The lid of the box is finally off, and I hold my breath as she pulls the tissue paper back.

Her hand trembles as she touches the engraving on the back of the hand mirror. *Shea.* It was her mother's name, and what we instantly wanted to name our daughter as soon as we found out she was a girl.

"I want to hold it, but I'm afraid of dropping it."

I kneel down in front of her and take it out for her. "I thought you'd like to continue your tradition. I know how

311

much you enjoy the memories of you and your mother sitting together when she got ready."

She puts it back into the box and sets it onto the desk behind me. Wrapping her arms around me, she hugs me tightly—as tightly as her baby belly will allow. "I don't know what I did to deserve such a wonderful husband. Thank you."

I kiss her neck and hold her tightly. I'm the one who doesn't deserve to have her in my life, but I will protect her and my family from what lurks in the shadows until I take my final breath.

ACKNOWLEDGEMENTS

LAURA EMORY

I would like to show my deepest love for my wonderful husband and my boys. They put up with so much from me, and I am so thankful for their love and support! They are my whole world.

I'd also love to recognize all my family and friends who have been there for me and have always had my back. My closest friends (TCH)- In no particular order- Natalie, Tara, Jessie, Jaime, and Neta. My awesome friends and betas- Katye, Heather B, and Heather S. My talented author friends who have read and given wonderful advice and helped me get this book to where it is.

I would love to give a super special shout out to my collaborator and rock star writing buddy Brandy. She is so talented and wonderful. She put up with me working on deadlines and had my back the whole time. It was such a pleasure to work with her and to gain a wonderful friend during this whole process. Thanks, B.L.!

ACKNOWLEDGEMENTS

B.L. MOONEY

I couldn't do this without the support of my family and friends. They listen as I go on and on about plot twists, cover ideas, which story is next, new stories that pop into my head without warning, and why I felt the need to cut out half of my current work in progress to start fresh and make it better. I know I drive you all nuts, so thank you for sticking with me.

I want to thank Laura Emory for sharing this amazing story with me and asking me to collaborate with her. Not only did I fall in love with these characters as if they were with me all along, I gained a special friendship with Laura. It's an experience that will stay with me forever, and I'm very grateful she asked.

Beta readers are a very important part of this process, and I want to thank Chandra G., Sandi L., and Shely S. for their great feedback.

ACKNOWLEDGEMENTS

FROM BOTH

Paige Maroney Smith: Thank you for an amazing edit. This book—and the authors—are better for your insight and attention to details.

Okay Creations: This cover is brilliant and beautiful. Thank you, Sarah Hansen, for working your magic again.
http://www.okaycreations.com/

Perrywinkle Photography: Lauren Perry's eye for the perfect cover photo is second to none. Thank you for another amazing cover.
http://perrywinklephotography.com/

Special thanks to the gorgeous model, Lyman Winn, for helping to make this a stunning cover.

Champagne Formats: Our words now have a beautiful canvas for others to read from. Thank you, Stacey Blake, for helping us to make everything beautiful inside and out.
http://champagneformats.com/

We would like to add a special thank you to Trish, Roxie, and Chelcie for their valuable input and suggestions during the final phase of publishing. We enjoyed their enthusiasm while reading, colorful commentary, hilarious memes, and helpful suggestions.

Thank you to the readers who picked up this book and allowed us to entertain you. We hope enjoyed the ride as much as we did.

ABOUT THE AUTHOR

LAURA EMORY

Laura Emory was born and raised in sunny So. Cal! She moved to the beautiful state of Utah and met her husband and decided to trade beaches for mountains. She has a horrible potty mouth, an online shopping addiction, and a knack for cooking. Laura was a college athlete who found her creative outlet behind a camera and computer. Laura loves to travel and read and prefers to do both together. Don't let the minivan fool you; she can still rock tattoos and Vegas. She's also in a very serious relationship with Netflix.

Facebook: https://www.facebook.com/pages/Author-Laura-Emory/629949660470295

GoodReads: https://www.goodreads.com/author/show/13763165.Laura_Emory

Email: AuthorLauraEmory@gmail.com

ABOUT THE AUTHOR

B.L. MOONEY

B.L. Mooney started writing when the voices and storylines in her head ran out of room. They were getting too cramped and neither B.L. nor the characters could take it anymore, so she did the only thing she could do—she made room. She always knew she wanted to write, but vowed to make time for it later. Now that she's made time for writing, most everything else falls to the wayside. That seems to suit the characters that keep popping up in her head just fine.

B.L. lives in the Midwest, and her other talents include in-demand cookies, a very dry sense of humor, and stealth eavesdropping. Some mannerisms, attitudes, or twists come from random sentences picked up while passing by strangers. So speak up the next time you have something to gossip about. You never know; it may just end up on the pages of the next book you read.

Website: http://www.authorblmooney.com/
Facebook: https://www.facebook.com/AuthorBLMooney
Twitter: https://twitter.com/AuthorBLMooney
GoodReads: https://www.goodreads.com/author/
show/6999168.B_L_Mooney
Email: AuthorBLMooney@gmail.com